Different Times and Other Places

Polestars

Different Times and Other Places

POLESTARS 10

Juliet E. McKenna

NewCon Press
England

First edition, published in the UK October 2024
by NewCon Press
41 Wheatsheaf Road, Alconbury Weston, Cambs, PE28 4LF, UK

NCP343 (hardback)
NCP344 (softback)

10 9 8 7 6 5 4 3 2 1

ISBN: 978-1-914953-92-7 (hardback)
978-1-914953-93-4 (softback)

Cover Art by Enrique Meseguer; cover design by Ian Whates
Editing and typesetting by Ian Whates

Contents

Urban Renewal

'Disnae look bad.' The first man squared proud shoulders inside his fluorescent jacket.

'Aye.' His companion tipped back a white hard hat, squinting up at a vast hoarding. 'Near as good as the pictures.'

Sunlight sparkled on the painted Clyde as green leaves flourished on tall trees artfully planted around an open lawn where children played. Lovers strolled past apartment blocks elegant with tinted glass and unsullied stone.

For the present the recently laid turf was lumpy and lined with yellow. Spindly saplings merely offered twiggy optimism in their graceless sheaths of muddy plastic.

'It'll be better, come spring,' the builder insisted.

'Better than that old foundry,' the second agreed. 'Pint o' heavy?'

'Oh aye,' The first nodded.

They walked away.

The fey had slept for a long age. Better to dream of better days in the way of his deathless kind. When the river had lapped untilled land. When his brethren had danced the circles of sun, moon and stars.

Before the short-lived had come, fertile as the rabbits burrowing into the earthen mounds that the fey drew up to mark gates between this safe staid land and more tempting, more perilous realms. A curiosity, the short-lived, entertaining, especially when they were lured into the interstices of time and space. They proved wholly tied to their linear mortality, incurably reliant on physical senses so easily duped.

If they lacked the boundless perceptions of the fey, they had incalculable numbers. If they had no notion of shaping the land with mere will, they could hew stone, fell trees and bake bricks. Everything wild and free was tamed or killed or driven out. The fey fled or learned to live in the twilight.

The short-lived encumbered the land with herds and fields. They gathered to trade until their markets lasted year round. Their ships subdued the seas. They dug deeper than any rabbits, ripping rocks from mines and wringing out metals with fire and force. The waste from their smelting poisoned the earth. The river choked and died with the filth from their sprawling crowded warrens. Soot stained the very air. Those fey that stubbornly stayed retreated ever deeper underground, shifting into immaterial forms that couldn't be sullied by mortal folly.

In his dreams, the fey sensed a change and stirred. Waking he found the soured earth had been scoured away. A newly planted grove spread tender roots through fresh soil rich with the sleeping seeds of meadow flowers. The cleansed waters of the river nearby were flowing with life. Scarcely more than sea salt tainted the cold wind or the clear blue sky above.

Intrigued, he slid upwards to rise from his land's ancient embrace. Cautious, he realised the short-lived were still here. Why? He studied the advertising artist's vision, readily relating it to the unfulfilled reality around him. His kind always dealt in desire and illusion. His glittering eyes fastened on the children in the picture. He had always enjoyed stealing those. He could easily summon up a changeling.

Writers are made, not born. My interest in the unexpected intersection of the everyday world with the perilously mythical goes back to my childhood reading; not only but most notably Alan Garner's books The Weirdstone of Brisingamen, and Elidor.

The Roots of Aston Quercus

'Mora is late with her leaves again.' Gamella stood with her arms folded tight across her bosom.

Fraina longed to ask what exactly Gamella expected her to do about it. But of course, she knew the answer. Go and talk to her. But why was she always the one expected to go and talk to Mora? She knew the answer to that as well. Because hers was the closest oak tree to Mora's own, out here on the edge of the grove.

'Where is she?' Fraina stroked her own tree's rough bark and felt the deep thrum of his irritation. He didn't much like Gamella at the best of times and definitely didn't welcome her agitation when he was settling down for winter's sleep.

As usual the other dryad seemed oblivious to the oak tree's mood. 'Up aloft. Where else?'

Where else indeed? Fraina need not have asked that question either. After so many uncounted seasons living together in this grove, there was little that the dryads didn't know about each other. There were no quirks or foibles among their little group that didn't rub someone up the wrong way. Mostly annoying Gamella, if truth were told.

'I'll go and talk to her.' Fraina stepped inside her tree and rode the surge of life-giving water to his topmost twigs. She walked out onto the coppery leaves gently swaying in the wind to see Mora sitting in her own tree's crown staring up at the sky.

'May I join you?' Fraina called out.

'What?' Mora looked around, startled. 'Oh, yes, of course.'

Fraina stepped across the emptiness separating the two trees. Mora's tree welcomed her with a shiver of affection. There was no sign of him sinking into an autumnal doze, as was evident from his bright green leaves.

Mora grinned at her. 'I take it Gamella's been nagging you to come and nag me?'

Fraina reflected, not for the first time, that Mora had a fine instinct for tension and who was causing it, notable in a dryad who spent so little of her time associating with the others.

'He is the only tree still in summer foliage.' Fraina patted the nearest sprig and smiled as Mora's tree creaked amiably at her touch.

'We'll get round to changing that soon.' Mora was unconcerned.

As ever, Fraina was baffled that any dryad could have so little apparent interest in managing her tree in accord with the seasons and the weather. Fraina loved taking care of her oak and of every living thing that enjoyed his shelter, from the tiniest insects to the biggest birds.

'What do you suppose that is?' Mora was staring upwards at something flying so high that it was barely more than a bright speck. It was steadily drawing a white line of wholly unnatural straightness across the crisp blue sky.

'I've no idea.' Fraina wasn't much interested either. Now that the dragons were long gone with all the perils that trailed after them, she only came aloft to tend to her tree and its denizens.

'I think it's a human thing.' Mora was still gazing upwards, fascinated.

'Then it has nothing to do with us,' Fraina said flatly. 'It will all be wrought of iron.'

The other dryad stopped staring at the sky and looked at her instead. 'What's the matter?'

Fraina hesitated before answering. 'There was a dog.'

She had always liked dogs and horses too. They reminded her of her tree; loyal, trusting, uncomplicated in their enthusiasms and affections. But nowadays horses and dogs alike saw the fae so seldom now that their reactions were hard to predict.

Fraina held up a blistered hand. 'I was trying to soothe her but I didn't see the iron studs on her collar. It was my own silly fault.'

Dryads had long since learned there was no point in lamenting humankind's obsession with the iron which all the fae abominated.

But Mora wasn't listening, looking out across the grass instead. 'Who is that?'

A man was striding along the footpath that the dog walkers and horse riders used, cutting across the pastures surrounding the grove now hemmed in with the hedgerows which the humans had planted quite some while ago.

'What is he carrying?' Fraina was mystified. The man had an armful of yellow poles and a heavy black bag slung on his back.

'Let's find out.' Mora stood up and vanished to slide down through her tree's sapwood to the ground.

'But he's not alone!' Fraina called out, alarmed. Two more humans were coming over the crest of the hill, similarly burdened.

She leaped back to her own tree and slid downwards, apologising as she went for such unseemly haste. Her tree bathed her in his reassuring love before opening his bark to allow her to step out onto the grass.

'What is she doing?'

To Fraina's relief Gamella had gone off in search of someone else to harass. Adleria was watching Mora walking along the footpath.

Ordinarily humans couldn't see a dryad. Now that Mora chose to reveal herself, she had fashioned herself an outfit like the dog walkers at this season; sturdy shoes, blue trousers, a rustling coat over a fleecy shirt.

Fraina was surprised to see how adept she was at doing that. Of all the dryads in the grove, Mora spent more time than anyone in her ethereal form; a shifting image of naked femininity, roundly ripe of hip and breast, soft and welcoming.

'What are they doing?' Adleria persisted. She favoured a more constant form; long hair rippling to her shoulders and a high-waisted, round-necked gown. That was the dress she had worn when the young curate had fallen in love with her, pausing in the grove as he walked from the village church over the hill to the hamlet beyond the river, always wearing his long black coat, white linen bands and wide-brimmed shallow-crowned hat.

He had a passion for natural philosophy, so he had told her, noting down all the details of the trees and the flowers, the beetles

11

and birds in his leather-bound notebooks. Adleria had even gone to see him preach in the church. The humans asked so few questions in those days that mere mention of a mother visiting cousins in the next town was readily accepted.

But the young curate had grown old and died in the way of human men and the humans who came after him had put iron railings around the church. The last time that Fraina had walked that way, she'd seen the church roof had long since fallen in, only the stone walls still defying the winters.

'I don't know,' she belatedly answered Adleria.

They stood together and watched as Mora walked up to the first man. Fraina noted she was staying a prudent distance from the poles he carried, so those must be metal.

The man held the bundle upright and then pulled the poles apart, to set up a bright yellow tripod. Crouching to open his bag, he took out something with a single shining eye and fixed it firmly on the top. His companions were opening their own bags and taking out shallow black boxes that unfolded rather like the long-dead curate's book.

They couldn't hear what Mora was saying or what the man was telling her. His companions didn't pause in their activities and it wasn't long before Mora was heading back to the grove.

Fraina shifted from foot to foot, impatient. Now that the humans had seen her, Mora must stay in that form until she was out of their sight. She had to walk every step of the path rather than ride the gentle breezes which a dryad could summon with a flick of a finger.

'What is it? Who are they?' Vaseya stepped out of her own tree just as Mora reached the edge of the grove.

'They are surveyors,' Mora scowled. 'He says there's to be a road built through here.'

'A road?' Adleria asked cautiously. 'Is that so very bad?'

'It is,' Mora told her, forthright. 'This isn't a stone and gravel road like the ones your curate walked. They will scour away the grass and earth and lay stones and layers of tar before fencing the whole thing in with metal.'

'Why would they do that?' Adleria was alarmed.

'Because they won't be riding horses or having horses draw their carriages.' Vaseya looked grim. 'They will be riding in their automobiles, those things that I told you about, wrought from metal. That's what they need such roads for.'

She had fallen in love most recently of all the dryads, with a young man who came to the grove seeking healing and peace. He'd told Vaseya of a great war in a distant land, where men had drowned in mud if they hadn't been killed by devices which he called guns, hurling deadly showers of metal bullets. If the men escaped the guns, other evil contrivances had thrown still bigger missiles. Those burst into myriad lethal steel splinters to slice innocents into quivering shreds.

Gamella and a good many of the other dryads had decided there was no hope for humanity after that. They'd avoided the dog walkers and everyone else ever since.

'That won't be very nice.' Adleria's lip quivered. 'To have such a thing so close to our grove.'

'It's worse than that,' Mora said bluntly. 'The road won't run alongside our grove but straight through it. He says our trees will be felled.'

Fraina was still watching the vile humans as the dryads all listened aghast to Mora's news. As the entire grove shook with their trees' anger, she saw the box with the glass eye tumble off the top of the yellow tripod. One of the men with the folding black book or box things looked up at the sky, apprehensive.

'What are we to do?' Adleria cried.

'Where are we to go?' Vaseya wasn't inclined to panic but Fraina could see the terror in her eyes.

That frightened Fraina. Vaseya knew better than most what the humans had made of the world, from talking to her wounded soldier. There was metal everywhere now, in the most unexpected places. Getting her soldier out of his clothes to make love to her on the summer grass had been quite a trial, with all the buttons and zips that would so readily raise welts on her skin.

Adleria looked around, hunted. 'Where do you suppose the nearest forest is? Do you suppose –?' She gazed at the dead stump of the fallen oak by the river.

'Lusita was old and her tree older still.' Vaseya's voice shook. 'Besides, she was a hamadryad. Truly, she was,' she insisted.

'She never said.' Adleria scrubbed a tear from her cheek.

'Would you?' Fraina didn't expect an answer. Who among them would admit to such frailty? Dryads outlived their trees, tending a new sapling when their first beloved companion finally succumbed to the cycle of nature. Hamadryads were bound to the acorns of their mother's tree. When the tree they were given to died, so did they.

'Gamella says that Lusita had already left before her tree began to fail,' Adleria persisted. 'She says that one of us should have borne a daughter to take care of it.'

That had always been the custom, whenever a dryad had left in search of a new home. A tree used to such loving care could not be abandoned.

'Let me guess,' Mora said sarcastically. 'Gamella would have done her duty for the grove? What if she was wrong? Then we'd be stuck with her daughter fretting and whining because she didn't have a tree of her own.'

While the humans were content to leave the grove's mature trees well alone, they persisted in uprooting any saplings long before they were tall enough to benefit from a dryad's care. So they had all given up bearing children a long age ago. No one was prepared to send a daughter wandering when they had no idea if she could find a tree before she withered and died.

Nor could they rid themselves of the likes of Gamella, for the sake of the grove's harmony. In days gone by, if a community of dryads agreed that one of their number was too discontented, too disruptive, the offender would be asked to leave. She could wander through the trees that had cloaked the land until whatever tormented her was left far behind, or until she had learned some humility. Once the wanderer found peace with herself, there would always be a community of dryads to welcome a new sister.

Had Lusita gone in search of a forest untouched by humankind, only to perish, bereft and alone? Or was it better to believe that she had indeed been a hamadryad and had died in the loving embrace of her own failing tree? Either alternative was too distressing for Fraina to contemplate for long.

'I miss sex,' Adleria said wistfully.

'Me too.' Fraina nodded, glad of the change of subject.

It had been such a pleasant pastime, whether or not she had any intention of bearing a daughter for the grove or a son to send out into the human world.

Her own beloved, bringing his pigs here so long ago to eat the fallen acorns each autumn, he had been lucky to have a few copper pence in the purse tied inside his jerkin and the only iron he ever carried was the little knife on his belt, readily discarded. Fraina had no problem undoing the horn buttons on his shirt and the linen ties securing his hose as he pushed her homespun skirt up her silken thighs.

Sleeping out under the stars, such youths could easily be persuaded to share their blankets with a beautiful stranger. When they woke up all alone, they would either believe it had all been a wondrous dream, or just cherish their delightful secret in silence, lest they be mocked as a simpleton.

'Never mind that,' Vaseya snapped, exasperated. 'Where are we to go?'

'I have no intention of going anywhere,' Mora said tartly. 'There must be some way to stop them.'

'A troll?' Adleria said hopefully. 'Boggarts?'

'Don't be a fool.' Gamella stepped out of her tree on the far side of the grove. She looked at Adleria, scathing. 'When did you last see a troll? And what would anyone want with boggarts? Filthy little beasts. What are you talking about, anyway?' she demanded.

'The humans want to cut down our trees,' Adleria wailed.

'What?'

If this hadn't all been so serious, Fraina would have been meanly delighted to see the panic shattering Gamella's arrogance.

'Not all of them will agree to this,' Mora asserted.

'What difference will that make?' Gamella recovered in an instant and now sought a target for her fear and anger. 'What do you know about it anyway?'

'More than you.' Mora waved a hand and the grove was suddenly filled with voices.

Adleria screamed while Vaseya ran for her tree, pressing close to his bark. Other dryads appeared, standing half inside their trees, half out.

'What is that?' Gamella shrieked.

Mora waved her hand and the din ceased. The dryads stood in stunned silence while the grove rang with the harsh calls of alarmed blackbirds.

'That,' she said calmly, 'is radio. It's a human thing. They talk about all sorts of things using devices to send their words through the air to each other. If you listen, you can learn all manner of things about their lives.'

That must be what she did up aloft, Fraina realised, sitting in her tree's crown for days at a time.

'Their lives?' Gamella was even angrier after being taken so unawares. 'We care nothing for them!'

'We should,' Mora said bluntly. 'They are of this world and so are we and they have mastered it in ways which the fae never could. If we wish to live on according to our own needs and customs, we must understand theirs.'

Gamella shook her head in absolute denial. 'We do not –'

'What has this to do with the road?' Fraina couldn't recall ever interrupting Gamella before but all at once, she was wholeheartedly sick of the other dryad's bossiness.

'There are still humans who love the wild places and the trees,' Mora assured her. 'They won't want to see our grove cut down. We must find out who they are.'

'How?' Adleria quavered.

Mora smiled at her. 'We talk to the dog walkers and the horse riders. They'll be able to tell us.'

'Talk to them?' Prina stepped out of her tree. 'Reveal ourselves?'

As Fraina recalled, Prina hadn't shown herself to any human since she'd fallen in love with a young man with flowing black curls who'd hidden in the grove for fear of the enemies who he'd called Roundheads. While he'd been camping among the trees, he'd written Prina lengthy poems and sung her intricate songs which the dryads had all enjoyed.

'What do we say to them?' Adleria's voice strengthened though her tree was still shaking as though a high wind pummelled his branches.

Mora considered this. 'The first thing we must ask is whether there's an alternate route for the road.'

Gamella pounced. 'And if there isn't?'

Mora was more than ready for her. 'Then at very worst, we persuade the humans to insist a new grove of saplings is planted a short distance away so we won't be without a home.'

'But our trees...' Fraina laid her hand on her beloved oak's bark and felt him stir with agitation. Disquiet rustled through all the trees and she saw her own grief reflected on her sisters' faces.

All except Mora's. She looked ready for a fight, willing to take on a troll if such a beast might stray across her path.

'Come on.' Her eyes were bright with challenge. 'Or do you want to start coaxing your trees into a deep enough sleep that they won't feel the humans' axes?'

Fraina saw her sisters found that prospect as unthinkable as she did.

Though Gamella wasn't going to let Mora have the last word. 'We cannot –'

'Shut up, Gamella.' Nalfina stepped fully out of her tree. 'Show us how these humans dress nowadays, Mora, and how we can listen to these voices on the breeze.'

'They will ask us who we are,' Adleria said hesitantly, 'and where we are from. Humans always do that.'

She was right, Fraina knew. The days were long gone when a dryad's son could walk for a turn of the moon and then present himself in a village, looking for work and offering a tale of seeking his fortune with the blessing of his family in some distant county which these locals had barely heard tell of.

Once he had proved himself honest and hard-working, a village would soon welcome such a son as one of their own, to live a long and healthy life by the standards of his father's blood, if all too fleeting by a dryad's measure.

17

Mora grinned. 'Tell them you're from Hawbury and then ask where they're from. If they say they're from Hawbury too, ask whereabouts. Whatever their answer, say that you live on the other side of the town. It's not like it used to be when humans lived in the village by the church. There are so many of them now that they can't possibly all know each other.'

'She's right,' Vaseya nodded.

So that very afternoon, all the dryads dressed themselves in the same garb as Mora; the sturdy shoes, the blue trousers and a fleecy shirt with a rustling coat to ward off the rain. All except Vaseya but once she had shortened her hair and frosted it with grey, her tweeds proved perfectly acceptable, especially to the older men walking their dogs.

It felt most peculiar to Fraina, to be so far removed from the grass and the trees, with such clothing shielding her from the wind and the occasional spatter of rain from the grey clouds now scudding across the blue sky. These people were supposedly coming out here to enjoy the beauties of nature. But humans were very strange. The dryads had always known that.

Strange, but as it turned out, oddly passionate about preserving the oak grove.

'It's an absolute disgrace,' the horse rider told Fraina. 'There's no good reason why the bypass can't follow the old railway line on the other side of town. Except that the developers want to open up more land for housing.'

'Of course.' Fraina nodded sagely and hoped this nice woman in the green coat didn't see how little she understood. She really must start listening to these radio voices of Mora's.

'He's perfectly safe,' the woman remarked. 'If you want to pat him, go ahead. I can see you like horses.'

'I do.' Fraina smiled but couldn't see how to stroke the glorious chestnut's neck without getting too close to the iron rings and buckles of his harness. It was such a shame.

'We need to gather as much evidence as possible,' the woman continued briskly, 'to put before the planning enquiry. Any evidence of special scientific interest hereabouts and as much proof as possible of the history of this right of way.' She gestured with her short whip, indicating the path through the fields.

'History?' Fraina knew that's what the humans called everything that went before their own short lives.

'The more, the better.' The brisk woman gathered up her horse's reins. 'Well, we'd better get on. It's a bit chilly to keep the old boy standing here. Will we see you at the town hall meeting opposing these wretched plans?'

'I'm not sure.' Fraina smiled apologetically.

'Do try and make the demo,' the woman urged as she rode off.

Fraina watched her go, still sad that she couldn't have petted the horse. Then she hurried back to the grove. 'Adleria?'

'Yes?' Even in these uncouth clothes, Adleria looked winsomely beautiful as she stepped out of her tree.

'Your curate, what was his name?'

'The Reverend Quintus Norris,' Adleria said promptly.

'Did he ever mention anything –' Fraina paused to recall the horsewoman's words correctly, '– of special scientific interest in our grove?'

Adleria thought for a moment. 'He was very taken with our slipper orchids and the fritillaries.'

'So was my soldier, and he wrote about them too.' Vaseya appeared beside them. 'I've been talking to a gentleman who's going to look for his diaries in the library at the university. Apparently that's just the sort of evidence they need, to persuade the planning authorities to send the road another way.'

Fraina looked at her in awe.

Vaseya grinned. 'No, I don't know what all that means either. But you know how devoted the humans are to writing everything down.'

Fraina nodded. They had all done it; Adleria's curate, Vaseya's soldier, Prina's poet. Perhaps it was because their lives were so fleeting. If they didn't leave such records, who would know that they have ever lived?

Adleria had grasped the essential point. 'So if we can show them where those plants still bloom, that should make a real difference?'

Vaseya nodded. 'And the butterflies and just about anything else.'

19

'Quintus used to study at the university.' Adleria smiled mistily before looking bright-eyed at Vaseya. 'Could your new friend look for his notebooks there?'

'I'll suggest it.' Vaseya nodded.

'And they want to know how long the footpath has been here,' Fraina remembered. 'Oh, by the way, does anyone know what a demo is? Because there's going to be one, apparently.'

'We had better ask Mora,' Adleria said uncertainly. 'Here she comes.'

'With a human.' Vaseya froze like a deer scenting trouble on the breeze.

'We should hide.' Fraina was abruptly convinced of it. 'Let Mora handle him.'

Adleria's chuckle was surprisingly earthy. 'She seems to be doing that well enough.'

The others vanished and Fraina stepped inside her own tree. Feeling his unease, she did her best to soothe him as Mora and her companion reached the grove.

The two of them sat down, their backs against Mora's tree. The young man was very good looking, Fraina observed. As handsome as any lover a dryad had ever brought to the grove.

Adleria slipped into Fraina's tree, pressing close beside her. 'Do you suppose they –'

'He certainly wants to.' Vaseya joined them too.

'By all means, step in.' Fraina's half-hearted rebuke died on her lips as the young man wrapped his arms around Mora and kissed her long and deeply.

'There seems to be much less metal in clothes these days,' Vaseya observed.

But Mora still pulled abruptly away.

'I'm sorry, I'm sorry,' the young man said hastily. 'I just –'

'It's okay.' Mora's smile reassured him with the allure that came as naturally to dryads as the leaves came to their trees. 'But what have you got in your pocket?'

'What?' The young man hastily searched his coat. 'Sorry, my pen knife.' He held out a folded blade. 'Did it –?'

'Never mind.' Mora waved a hand. 'Just keep it away from me. I don't approve of metal.'

'You don't approve?' The young man was bewildered.

'Metal, oil, mining. It all damages the earth.' Mora smiled, still more seductive.

'You're really hardcore.' The young man seemed impressed. 'Vegan?'

'What do you think?' Mora grinned.

'Vegan?' Vaseya looked at Fraina and Adleria, baffled.

'Hardcore?' Adleria was completely at a loss.

'I've no idea what he means.' Fraina wondered if Mora understood these strange words. Her smile was sweetly confident, as though she and the young man shared a secret. Of course that could just be Mora bluffing. She did seem very good at that.

'You say your group's called The Friends of Aston Quercus –' the young man hesitated.

'Aston Quercus Medieval Village.' Mora pointed over the hill towards the ruined church. 'It's a very important site and really should be scheduled as a monument.'

'What is she talking about?' Adleria was still more bemused.

'History,' Fraina guessed promptly. 'The humans want to know everything that's gone on in this place.'

Vaseya looked askance at her. 'We can hardly tell them what we know.'

'Quintus's notebooks should help,' Adleria said hopefully.

'Perhaps they can find out something from the church's graveyard. We must suggest that to the dog walkers and horse riders.' Though as Fraina recalled, the engraving on the few remaining stones was worn almost to oblivion. Still, these humans must have kept records.

Aston Quercus had been the name of the village where her loving swineherd had lived. Though all that remained of his cottage was one of the lumps and bumps rising in the field beyond the church, the long-dead hearths marked by flourishing clumps of nettles.

Adleria nudged her elbow. 'She's kissing him again.'

21

'We won't let them cut down these trees,' the young man said breathlessly as he pulled reluctantly away some while later. 'Even if we can't get them to change the plans, we can set up a camp here, break their chainsaws with nails driven into the wood –'

'No!' The dryads' collective gasp of horror sent Fraina's tree into a frenzy of rustling leaves.

While the young man looked up, startled, Mora looked straight across at the three of them and scowled.

'Wow, I thought a branch was about to come down.' The young man tried to cover his embarrassment with a laugh.

Mora looked upwards. 'Not today.'

'You really know about this place, don't you?' The young man was intrigued.

'So will you get all your friends involved?' Mora shifted closer, pressing against him. 'Here and in London? Can you get the story on the radio and in the papers? It really needs to go national.'

'We'll see it go viral.' The young man promised her fervently. 'Look, can I ring you? Email?'

Mora shook her head. 'I don't have a phone or a computer.'

'Totally off the grid?' The young man marvelled. 'Right. But when will I see you again?'

Mora leaned forward to kiss him. 'At the demo. I could do an interview there?'

'Okay. And after?' he asked hopefully.

'Maybe.' Mora's smile promised untold delights.

'What are they talking about?' Vaseya wondered.

'I really have no idea,' Adleria said helplessly.

'Mora seems to know what she's doing,' Fraina observed.

She never did find out exactly what a demo was. Mora did invite her, saying it was a gathering to oppose the planned road but Fraina really couldn't bring herself to mingle with so many humans at once.

So she sat in the crown of her tree and searched the radio voices just as Mora had taught her. Finally she lit upon Mora's own voice, eloquent and impassioned. The dryad talked about the ancient woodlands so brutally stripped from the lands and how vital it was to save these last precious remnants.

Hearing Mora's voice, all the trees shook their branches in fervent agreement. Their golden autumn leaves fell in thick showers. Looking down, Fraina saw all the other dryads in the grove looking up with desperate hope.

Mora's young man came to the grove regularly after that. Her tree swiftly coloured his leaves with autumn's hues and shed them to make a soft bed in the sheltered hollow of his roots. Even though the weather was growing colder, the young man and Mora would make love swathed in long woollen coats, their ardour burning all the hotter for such constraints upon it.

One afternoon, while the two of them were occupied, Fraina slipped out of her tree and carefully borrowed the mass of folded sheets of paper which the young man had brought with him. Of course he couldn't see her but she had to make it look as though his paper was blowing away, not being carried by some unseen sprite.

She hurried to the far side of the grove and spread the sheets on the fading grass. Whatever was in here must be important. Mora was rewarding her young man with sensual enchantments that few living humans had ever enjoyed.

'What's that?' Adleria appeared beside her.

'A newspaper.' Fraina was proud of knowing that now. 'It's a human thing.'

'Oh, poor thing.' Adleria stroked the white expanse sprinkled all over with blackness. 'It was once a tree.'

'I know.' Fraina had just about got used to the lingering echoes of the paper's mistreatment, pounded and crushed between great iron rollers. This was a far cry from the paper which the curate and the poet had used. 'But see, it can tell us so many things.'

As she ran her fingertips across the words, the paper eagerly gave up their meaning.

'The Hawbury Bypass Campaign has successfully persuaded the County Council to adopt the western, railway route rather than risk the considerable environmental damage that the Aston Quercus option would entail. The proposals for the establishment of the Aston Quercus Country Park have also won council endorsement and will be presented at a series of public consultations before the end of the year.'

'But what does that mean?' Vaseya had joined them.

'It means that we're safe.' Fraina looked up at the oak trees and smiled.

Mora was late with her leaves again, when the spring arrived. No one said anything, not even Gamella.

I was invited to write a story for an anthology called The Modern Fae's Guide to Surviving Humanity. I didn't have any hint of an idea until 48 hours before the deadline. Then a local oak tree that's always out of sync with its neighbours, and a local news story about objections to a planned road, caught my eye. For me, as for so many writers, the truest answer to 'where do you get your ideas from?' is 'absolutely anywhere and often unexpectedly'.

Insight

She entered the classroom, put her handbag on the desk and opened it, taking out her glasses case. 'Good morning, everyone. Settle down please.'

11JW did as she asked, with greater or lesser alacrity.

Swapping her everyday glasses for the ones in the case, Maeve reached for the textbook and opened it. 'Keats, please. St Agnes Eve.'

'New specs, Miss?' Amy looked up from the front row.

Maeve smiled. 'They're verification lenses.'

Sitting next to Amy, Emma laughed. 'You mean varifocals, Miss.'

'Do I?' Maeve smiled again before looking up to survey the class. 'Well, now, I hope everyone has read the poem and made some notes after last time. Who wants to start today's discussion?'

'Oh, Miss, it was so romantic. Like Twilight.' Becky propped her chin on her hand, eyes dreamy.

'Romantic?' In the row behind Becky, Josh laughed lewdly. 'It's about some bloke sneaking in to a girl's bedroom to give her one.'

As the other boys sniggered, though, Maeve saw the silver thread of yearning stretch from the centre of Josh's chest to hover, stopping just short of caressing Natalie's exuberant, black curls.

'Do you think that sort of coarseness will improve your chances with a girl, Josh?' she asked mildly.

As the boys subsided, abashed, Maeve nodded, satisfied. 'Though you do have a point, Josh, and we'll consider that when we reach that part of the poem. Becky's also raised an interesting question. Where do we draw the line between romantic pursuit and stalking? Why do some remarkably old-fashioned ideas persist in modern literature?'

That prompted a lively debate between the Twihards and the rest. Maeve let it run for a few minutes, noting which pupils could now usefully be directed towards reading Jane Eyre and Northanger Abbey.

'So –' she raised her voice to reclaim the class's attention '– let's get back to Keats. Oliver, you haven't had anything to say so far. Did you do your homework?'

'Yes, Miss,' he said defensively. 'Just didn't like it.'

He was lying, obviously. Maeve could see the telltale crackles of black suffusing his aura.

'Appreciating literature is just as much about understanding why we don't like a piece of work,' she said sternly. 'I will expect you to set out your reasons with relevant quotes in your essay. Vicky, bring your phone to me.'

'What?' Vicky looked up, aghast. 'Miss?'

'Your phone, Vicky.' Maeve held out her open hand.

Blushing furiously, Vicky heaved herself out of her seat and slouched to the front of the class. She handed over the phone with an exaggerated sigh.

Maeve noted the furtive shuffling of the others who had imagined they could keep their phones unseen in their laps beneath the tabletops. Doubtless they could, when they were dealing with other teachers who couldn't see right through the tables.

'Thank you. Collect it from the office at the end of the day.' She smiled at the rest of the class. 'Now, let's start with the poem's first stanza.'

The rest of the lesson proceeded according to plan and by the time the bell rang, Maeve was well satisfied with the class's contributions.

'Thank you, everyone. I will expect your essays first thing on Friday.' She closed her text book with a sharp slap as the teenagers began leaving their seats and hauling their bags up from the floor.

'Sarah, one moment.' Maeve raised her hand to command the girl's attention. 'You've got a free now, I believe? Could you take this note to Miss Williams in the library for me, please?'

'Yes, Miss, of course.' Sarah tried to hide her relief.

Maeve handed the envelope to the girl, walking to the classroom door with her. 'What are you three waiting for?' She looked sternly at Jade, Tasha and Jenna who were loitering in the corridor. 'Get to your next lesson!'

Maeve stood in the doorway, her expression expectant, until the vicious trio retreated. The acid green tendrils of their spite which had been coiling around Sarah all through the class shrivelled as they departed. They were bullies but they weren't stupid. They wouldn't risk cornering this week's chosen victim when she was running an errand for a teacher.

'I'll go and start work on my essay, Miss.' Sarah turned in the other direction, heading for sanctuary in the library.

As 9TW surged noisily through the double doors at the end of the corridor, Maeve smiled, satisfied.

She knew that Jade, Tasha and Jenna called her an old witch behind her back. What the girls didn't know, of course, was they were perfectly correct. Though not an old witch. Maeve was merely a middle-aged one, and perfectly capable of taking the necessary measures when her third eye's vision started to feel the passing years' effects.

Juliet E. McKenna

Autocorrect turned a friend's message about her new varifocals into the inspiration for this quick story. Once again, my fascination with apparently ordinary people being far more than they seem goes back to my early reading. In this case? I think there are echoes of E.Nesbit's books, and the Carbonel series by Barbara Sleigh.

The Green Man's Guest

Trees die, like every living thing. Left to their own devices, they'll gradually succumb to old age after decades or even centuries. If they're not so lucky, a storm or a nearby tree toppled by strong winds can bring them crashing down. These days, if they're really unlucky, some spreading blight can make felling them essential.

However it happens, whoever's in charge of that back garden or public park or private woodland faces the same question. How do we get the stump out? What do we do about the hole? Even a smallish tree has a sizeable root ball.

Or... how about doing something else? I don't know who came up with the idea of turning tree stumps into sculptures instead of grubbing them out, but as soon as I came across it, I wanted to give it a try. I did a load of research online and watched a lot of videos. I bought some specialist power tools and taught myself to use them on scrap timber from various projects. I've been taking care of the estate's woods at Blithehurst Manor for the past few years, so I reckoned I'd get my chance sooner or later.

Last autumn, a sudden squall snapped a venerable sweet chestnut in half. It already had dead wood in its crown, and the gardeners and I agreed there was no saving the tree. So I turned the stump into a life-sized statue of Sir Graelent de Beauchene, who had been given the manor and its lands by William the Conqueror. One of his descendants had planted that chestnut tree when the family were building the Tudor house to replace Sir Graelent's original, damp and draughty medieval stone home down by the river. The Beauchene family still own the estate, but these days the house and gardens are run as a tourist attraction.

I should have remembered that doing a good job guarantees you'll be asked to do it again. My boss, Eleanor Beauchene, had photos of Sir Graelent on her phone when she went to a country landowner's conference. A few months later, she got a call. The owners of this arboretum in West Sussex wanted to know the going rate for me carving them a tree sculpture. One of their cedars of Lebanon had been risk-assessed as far too likely to start dropping branches on visitors' heads.

I wasn't complaining. Driving down from Staffordshire this late spring morning, I was keen to get to grips with this interesting challenge. Now I walked slowly around the sizeable remnant of the cedar, pressing the button on my tape measure to rewind the flexible metal. The arboretum's tree surgeon had done a good job making the condemned tree safe and still leaving me plenty of wood to work with. Ideally, I wanted at least a couple of meters of sound timber which was a minimum of thirty or forty centimetres across. I'd have far more here, even after the tree's bark and outer layers had been stripped off to get to the heartwood.

So now I needed some ideas to suggest to Alexander, who was in charge of the arboretum. He was paying for my time and skill, but he didn't seem to have a clue what sort of sculpture he wanted. I started taking photos with my phone from every possible angle. Then I stood and looked at the stump again, hoping for inspiration.

'Good afternoon,' a cheerful voice said behind me. 'Who are you?'

I turned around to see a little girl smiling up at me. She wore denim dungarees over a pale yellow sweater and I guessed she was somewhere around ten years old. Her long black hair was tied up in bunches high on her head, and her eyes were dark brown. I thought she was most probably Japanese, though I reminded myself not to make assumptions that might cause unintended offence.

'Hello.' I looked around for whatever tour party or family group she must be part of. The arboretum was full of visitors on this fine and sunny Saturday afternoon.

'Why are you interested in this tree?' She spoke slowly and carefully, though she had barely any accent.

She was looking past me towards the cedar stump. I realised seeing me measuring and taking photographs must have made her curious. Back at Blithehurst I'm not usually a visitor's first choice when they want to practise their English by talking to someone on the staff. I'm six foot four and, according to my mate Aled, my usual expression can be described as 'off-putting'.

'This tree had to be cut down because it wasn't safe. I'm going to carve the wood that's left into a statue.' I waited to see if she understood me. I wasn't sure what I could do if she didn't. I don't speak a word of Japanese.

'That is a good idea,' she said, approving. 'My name is Moriko. What is your name?'

'Dan.' I looked around again for whoever she should be with. At Blithehurst, I'd take a lost kid to the cafe, where Lynne would dry tears and offer reassurance along with chocolate biscuits. One of her teenage staff would alert everyone working in the house and the grounds. Someone would soon spot an exasperated or frantic parent. Here, there was only Alexander, sitting in the ticket office. That was right over on the far side of the site with the loos in what had once been a big country house's gate lodge. 'Did you come here with your mum and dad?'

The little girl frowned and took a lot longer to reply than I expected. 'I am here with my grandfather.'

'Right.' Shit. Her parents must be a sensitive subject. I'd better not ask again. The last thing I needed was passing visitors seeing I'd made a little girl cry. 'Can you see him? Your grandfather?'

She surprised me with another bright smile. 'He will come and find me. What will your statue be?'

'I don't know. I haven't decided.' I took a few steps to look at the cedar from another angle. Now I was far enough away from the little girl so passers-by wouldn't think I was about to grab her and carry her off. I was still close enough to stop anyone else trying. I looked around for anyone who could possibly be her grandfather. The sooner I could hand her over to an adult she knew, the happier I would be.

I was looking in the wrong direction. When I glanced back, to be sure where Moriko was, an older man stood beside her. How old? Old enough to be her grandfather. Beyond that, I couldn't say. His hair was dark without a hint of grey, but his face was deeply lined and weathered. His trousers and collared shirt were more suited to an office rather than a day out in the English countryside, but his casual jacket and the camera around his neck were typical tourist gear.

Moriko was holding his hand and talking to him, fast and eager. He listened and nodded, and his shrewd, dark eyes were studying me. I must have been close to a foot taller than him, and my shoulders were twice as wide. I saw that didn't bother him in the slightest.

'Good afternoon.' I used my best customer service training course manners.

He said something to Moriko. For a small man, his voice was surprisingly deep and resonant. His tone made me think he was used to people paying attention.

'Grandfather says your statue should be an owl,' she said, excited.

'That's a good idea.' It was, but I couldn't commit to anything before I'd spoken to Alexander.

I saw the old man watching for my reaction. Something about the intensity in his eyes made me think he spoke more English than he was going to admit. Or at least, he understood English when he heard it.

He gazed back at me. I was the first one to blink. I thought he smiled, but if he did, that was gone so fast that I could have imagined it. He looked down at Moriko, definitely smiling as he spoke to her.

She looked at me, her little face serious. 'Grandfather wishes you good luck with your work.'

That was unexpected. I appreciated it all the same. 'Thank you. I mean, please say thank you to your grandfather from me.'

As Moriko spoke, the old man grunted with satisfaction, deep in his chest. He looked at me and nodded slowly. I did the same. I think I was supposed to bow, but I had no idea how to do that right, and I wasn't going to risk getting it wrong.

At least he didn't look offended. He grunted a second time and turned to walk away. Moriko skipped along beside him, holding his hand and talking excitedly. They didn't head for the lodge and the gates. They went over to the far side of the arboretum... and walked into a mature conifer.

To be clear, when I say 'walked into', I don't mean they smacked into it like some cartoon animal. The two of them passed into the trunk as easily as I would walk through a curtain. That was one hell of a surprise. Again, to be clear, I don't mean I was surprised that they could do that. I've seen my mother passing in and out of her oak trees since I was a kid myself. She's a dryad after all.

But it had never once occurred to me that eighteenth and nineteenth century plant hunters and explorers could have brought other tree spirits to places like this, when they came back to England with the saplings and seeds they had gathered all over the world.

I wondered how old their tree might be. It was an impressive specimen, easily thirty metres tall and with a trunk over two metres in diameter. It had reddish fibrous bark and fine, feathery foliage on well-spaced branches.

I took out my phone and checked the time. Nearly four o'clock. When I'd arrived, Alexander had said that's when he stopped selling entry tickets. At half past, he had told me, he'd do a circuit of the paths on his bicycle, reminding any lingering visitors that the gates would be locked promptly at five pm. While I was waiting for him to do that, I decided, I could get a drink from the snack wagon in the car park. I'd noticed their menu board said they would be open until five.

Before I took the path to the gates, I went over to the tree where Moriko and her grandfather lived. Since this was an arboretum, a helpfully informative plaque on a little white post told me the tree's different names. Japanese Red Cedar. Cryptomeria Japonica. Sugi. The last line was a Japanese character which, obviously, I couldn't read.

I looked more closely at the nearest branch. A botanical genius who didn't know nearly as much as he should, might have called this species of tree a cedar when he first came across one, but this was no relative of that cedar of Lebanon I would be carving. I didn't need to see its different Latin name to know that.

I took a photo of the plaque with my phone. I waited to see if Moriko or her grandfather would reappear. They didn't, so I walked back to the car park. I got myself a cup of tea and a lemon drizzle muffin and sat in my Land Rover while I waited for Alexander to close up. I studied the photos on my phone and sketched a few rough ideas on a pad I'd brought with me.

Every so often, I looked up as an engine started and a car drove away. When my Landy and Alexander's Prius were the only vehicles left, I got out and walked over to the lodge where he was locking the front door. He was quite a bit younger than me.

He shoved his bunch of keys into a pocket of his battered waxed jacket. 'How did you get on?'

'Very well.' I didn't say anything about meeting Moriko or her grandfather, obviously. 'How do you feel about a sculpture of an owl?' That might have been the old tree spirit's suggestion, but the more I had studied my photos of the stump, the more I liked the idea.

Alexander brushed long wavy hair out of his eyes with a skinny hand. 'That's certainly a thought.'

'I'll do a few sketches this evening,' I offered. 'You can take your time to think it over. I won't be getting started until I've got the chainsaw work done tomorrow.'

'That sounds like a plan,' he agreed. 'Now, let me show you where you'll be staying, and you can get settled in before dinner.'

'Thanks.' I headed back to the Landy while he got into his Prius.

I only needed to do that to avoid getting the Land Rover locked inside the car park. Identical brick and flint houses in terraces of four lined both sides of the road that led up to the gates and the lodge. This village had been purpose-built for the servants who once worked on this estate, Alexander had explained. He and his older brothers and sisters still owned them, Eleanor had told me, along with most of the estate land that went with the arboretum. Only the stately home itself had been sold off in the 1960s, to be turned into a hotel.

Alexander pulled into the left-hand kerb, about halfway down the village street. As I stopped behind him, he got out of the Prius and made an open-your-window gesture. When I did that, he pointed to the entry between this terrace and the next.

'You can park around the back.'

'Right. Thanks.' I turned the wheel and drove slowly over the gravel to tuck the Land Rover behind the little house. That was fine with me. Since I'd come here to do at least a week's work, I had a lot of my tools in the back, even if the sticker on the door said the opposite. No one could see inside to call me a liar.

Alexander was unlocking the cottage's back door. I got my overnight bag out of the passenger footwell. He held up the keys so I could take them from him. 'Here you are.'

'Thanks.' I followed him into a kitchen fitted with modern units and a quarry tiled floor. 'This is nice.'

He nodded. 'You should have everything you need, but give me a shout if not. I'm only over the road. I'll pick you up for dinner at seven thirty?'

'Fine with me.'

'Right then. See you later.'

He closed the back door behind him. I took my laptop out of my overnight bag and set it up on the kitchen table. A folder with instruction booklets for the kitchen appliances had the Wi-Fi details printed on a label stuck to the front. I sat down and logged on. I honestly only meant to look up a couple of things, but I was still sitting there when my phone startled me with a text. Alexander was waiting outside to take me to dinner. I grabbed the keys off the table and my jacket off the chair and headed out.

I had learned a lot of interesting things. For a start, Japanese tree spirits are called kodama. They can appear as men or women, unlike dryads who are always female. They can also appear as animals or mysterious lights, and no dryad I've ever met can do that. Kodama live in remote mountainous forests and they are most often associated with sugi trees, especially the oldest, giant specimens. I wasn't remotely surprised that cutting down a tree where a kodama lives is an instant guarantee of bad luck. I've seen what a pissed off dryad can do.

Sugi trees themselves were absolutely fascinating. The oldest ones are protected and revered, and some could be up to seven thousand years old. Sugi are often planted around temples, but historically they were extensively cultivated for aromatic, rot-resistant and durable wood that could be used to make pretty much anything. That's not the half of it. Around eight hundred years ago, the Japanese developed a technique somewhere between pollarding and coppicing called daisugi. This keeps the great trees alive and producing a harvest of straight logs big enough for building houses every couple of decades. The photos online were astonishing. As far as I was concerned, there's no way any of that could have happened without the kodama lending a hand.

But none of that was remotely relevant to the job I had come here to do. To my relief, once I got into the Prius, Alexander was more interested in telling me about his family and their various businesses, than asking what I'd been doing.

He accelerated down the road, gesturing at the terraces on either side. 'We keep a couple of the cottages for the use of contractors like yourself, who need accommodation locally, and for anyone in the family who wants to come down from London for a weekend or a bit of a holiday. The rest are long term rentals.'

I realised I was supposed to make conversation. 'Not holiday lets?'

He shook his head. 'We've got a dozen forest lodges over on the other side of the golf course. What with last-minute bookings and cancellations, as well as never knowing how much mess will need cleaning up for weekly turnarounds, they're more than enough hassle.'

'Right.' I tried to think of something else to say. I pictured the map of the estate I'd looked at online. 'How far are they from your paintball place?'

'Far enough for us not to get complaints about the noise,' Alexander said with relief as he turned the steering wheel.

Since I was thinking about the estate, I realised we were heading up what had once been the main drive to the big house. 'Where are we going for dinner?'

'The hotel.' Alexander grinned. 'I get a discount. We've done a nice deal with the new owners so their guests can use our golf course, and some of their corporate team-building conferences go paintballing.'

The Prius crested a rise in the driveway. I saw an imposing Palladian building ahead. If he'd told me where we were going, I might have put on my good jeans. On the other hand, Alexander was still wearing the same faded brown cords and checked shirt.

'You don't wish your family still owned this place?'

'Not for a second,' he assured me. 'The best thing great-Grandad ever did was offload it before the upkeep and repairs bankrupted him.'

'Right.' I wondered how often the house had been sold, if new owners had taken it on recently.

We reached the car park and Alexander pulled into a space marked as reserved. That was useful as every other space looked taken. As we got out of the Prius, I saw a couple of Porsches and an Aston Martin. Not much sign of a cost of living crisis around here. I hoped the new owners were turning a profit to keep their staff in work.

'The restaurant's in what used to be the Orangery.' Alexander led the way along a path towards the side of the house. 'Great-great – I forget how many greats – Uncle William had that built in 1853 at the same time as he was setting up the Arboretum. He was supposed to be a clergyman carrying the gospel to far-flung corners of the Empire, but he only went into the church because that's what third sons were expected to do. He came home every year or so with a whole load of new specimens, and his will insisted the Arboretum had to be kept in the family. Fortunately the botany gene passed down the family tree to me. I loved coming here as a kid, and I was more than happy to take it on when I finished uni.'

'Right.' I wondered if any dryads living here in days gone by had got Great Uncle William interested in trees. If so, they were long gone now. I also wondered how they might have reacted when one of his specimens had arrived from Japan with a passenger.

'So how did you get on?' Alexander asked as we turned a corner of the path and saw the Orangery lit up ahead. 'Any suggestions for the sculpture?'

'The more I think about it, the more I like the idea of an owl. If you're going to let people come right up to it, a solid shape will be much less vulnerable to damage.'

'That's a very good point,' he agreed.

I'd also learned from the Internet that in Japanese culture, the owl supposedly brings good luck, wisdom, and success in business. Since annoying the old kodama would most likely guarantee the opposite, following up on his suggestion made sense to me.

We had a very good meal in the fancy restaurant, then Alexander drove us back to the village. This time I did take a look around the cottage, opening the fridge and the kitchen cupboards. He was right. I did have everything I needed. I plugged in the power packs for my various power tools to charge them overnight and went to bed.

I woke up bright and early and cooked myself a big breakfast. It might be Sunday but I wasn't having a lie-in. The Arboretum wouldn't open until midday. That had been specified when it first opened to the public, to make sure no one was tempted to skip church, according to Alexander. That meant I could get the chainsaw preparation work done this morning with no one else around. That meant a lot less hassle with risk assessments as well as saving a day's cost for the Heras safety fencing that was arriving tomorrow morning. Though, as far as I was concerned, the main purpose of that would be to stop members of the public helping themselves to my tools when my back was turned.

Alexander had given me a key to the car park. As I locked the gate behind me, I looked around for Moriko or her grandfather. Not that he would actually be her grandfather, I guessed, not by any human definition of their relationship. Calling him her elder was probably more accurate. I wondered how old she was, and how she had come to be here, sharing the old kodama's tree. I didn't expect to get any answers to those questions. Most likely I wouldn't ever find out. Dryads keep themselves to themselves, and I couldn't see any reason why kodama would be different.

I drove the Landy slowly along the wide gravel path and parked close to the cedar of Lebanon stump. I got my protective gear and my new shaping chainsaw out of the back. After a last look around and a final glance towards the sugi, I put on the PPE and started stripping off the cedar's bark and sapwood. I put the tree spirits out of my mind as I concentrated. Working with power tools and letting your mind wander is a bad idea.

It was sweaty work, even though it wasn't a particularly warm day. When I was about halfway done, I stopped the chainsaw and took a step back, ready to go and get a bottle of water. I pulled off my ear defenders and lifted my helmet's safety visor on. Feeling the breeze on my face helped ease the claustrophobic sensation of not being able to hear clearly. I turned around and nearly dropped the chainsaw on my foot. Moriko and her grandfather stood there. How long had they been watching?

'Good morning, Dan,' she said cheerfully.

'Good morning, Moriko.' I looked at the old kodama and nodded politely. 'Good morning.'

He nodded and grunted, but this time he definitely smiled, just for a few seconds. He looked as if he'd stepped out of a samurai movie, dressed in traditional Japanese clothing in muted shades of grey and green. He didn't have any swords, obviously, but he carried a stick in one hand. It was a couple of centimetres in diameter and maybe a metre and a quarter long.

I remembered something I'd read. The biggest threat in a dojo is the little old man with the broom. Okay, that wasn't a broom handle, but the old kodama was smiling again, as if he knew exactly what I was thinking. Could he read my mind? The Internet hadn't said anything about that.

'Excuse me, please.' I walked over to the Landy and opened the back door to find the bottle of water I'd chilled in the fridge overnight. Moriko and her grandfather came with me. She was wearing some sort of pale green kimono that was nowhere near as fancy or complicated as the ones I'd seen on TV.

She peered inside the Land Rover, openly curious. 'How will you carve the wood?'

I opened a wooden box to show her the various cutting and burr bits I'd bought to go with my new rotary carving tool. 'With these.'

The old kodama reached past me to pick up one of old chisels I'd put in the box as well, in case I needed to do something by hand. Studying the different initials burned into the wooden handle, he asked Moriko a question, before looking at me expecting an answer. She took a moment to find the right words. She must have learned her English from people visiting the arboretum and this was hardly a typical tourist conversation.

'Grandfather asks how many generations of craftsmen have taught you.'

I picked up another chisel and pointed to each set of initials in turn. 'This is me, Daniel Mackmain. J M, that's my dad. Bill Mackmain was his father and he was Gilbert's son.'

The old kodama grunted with what sounded like satisfaction. He said something else to Moriko that surprised her. She answered him back, objecting, but he insisted. She looked at me, unexpectedly shy.

'Please, Dan, my grandfather asks, who is your mother?'

'That's okay.' I'd been expecting this. The kodama must have realised I was a bit more than ordinarily human as soon as I'd set foot in the arboretum. That had to be why Moriko come to talk to me. I told them about the remnant of ancient woodland on the Oxfordshire-Warwickshire border where my mum tended her trees. I explained how she'd fallen in love with my dad, when the land became a nature reserve and he joined the volunteers who looked after it. A bit later, I was born. My mother's blood means I can see supernatural folk and creatures that ordinary people think are myths.

Moriko was delighted by my parents' story. Grandfather looked thoughtful. I heard church bells on the breeze and realised the time was getting on. I took a long drink and put the bottle of water back in the Landy. 'I had better get on.'

The two tree spirits stepped aside. They stood and watched as I put my PPE on again and started up the chainsaw. I don't like being watched when I'm working, but I focused on preparing the cedar, and soon forgot they were there.

When I was finished, I was very satisfied with my morning's work. Now I needed to put my tools and safety gear away, and clear up the stripped bark and sapwood, before Alexander unlocked the gates for today's visitors.

When I turned around, I saw the old kodama sitting cross-legged on the grass, busy with something in his lap. Moriko stood beside him with pieces of scrap cedar in one hand and one of my old chisels in the other. Grandfather saw me and stood up to offer me what he'd been working on. A square with sides as long as my hand framed an intricate design made from interlaced strips of wood.

'This is incredible.' I let him see I was impressed, as I took it and studied it closely.

He grunted with satisfaction. 'Kumiko.'

I recognised that word. I'd discovered it online last night, clicking from link to link about traditional Japanese woodworking. This an ancient craft where strips of wood are used to make anything from window shutters to storage boxes to table mats. The skill is in the way the strips hold each other securely in place without any need for nails or glue.

'Thank you, Dan.' Moriko handed me the chisel and disappeared.

The old kodama smiled and vanished as well.

Hang on a bloody minute. I looked at the tool I was holding. No dryad I knew, or any other spirit of wood or water, earth or air, could handle steel. Kodama were very different to the unseen folk I was used to encountering.

Eleanor put the kumiko piece down on her desk. 'This really is gorgeous, and so unusual.'

'I'm going to have a go at doing it.' I was sitting on the small sofa in her private study, upstairs in the Tudor house. I'd got back to Blithehurst late the night before. 'I've been seeing what I can find out about designs and techniques online.'

Kumiko didn't look easy. That was okay. Things worth doing are worth the effort.

'Well, the sculpture looks fantastic. Alexander is delighted, and he's already paid the invoice, so that's good news.' Eleanor had her laptop open. She clicked through the photographs I'd sent her. 'What sort of owl is it?'

'A Japanese scops owl. At least, that's what it's supposed to be.' I think the old kodama approved. I was sure he'd have let me know if he didn't.

'I like those tufts of feathers on its head. Like big bushy eyebrows.' Eleanor closed her laptop and looked at the earthenware pot I'd put on her desk. It held a small sapling with reddish bark and feathery, dull green foliage. 'And you didn't see Grandad kodama again till the end of the week?'

I nodded. 'He appeared when I was clearing up after finishing work on the sculpture.

She gestured at the seedling. 'What exactly does he want you to do with this?'

'He asked me to take it to my mum's wood, but I explained that the nature reserve volunteers are always on watch for anyone sneakily digging up plants, so they'd be bound to notice this turning up. It's not a native species so someone would have it out of there as soon as they could fetch a trowel.'

I really hoped Moriko had understood what I was saying. I didn't want her grandfather to think I was being deliberately unhelpful. 'So I suggested bringing it here instead.'

A good few Beauchenes came home from their travels with interesting plants over the centuries. Plenty of them are still flourishing in the carefully tended grounds. More importantly, Eleanor's the boss here. She could ask the gardeners to find this little sugi sapling a suitable home and no one would think twice about it. Well, no one human.

'You told him about Blithehurst's dryads.'

That wasn't a question. Greenwood blood from a couple of centuries back flows through the Beauchene family's veins. Eleanor has been able to see the manor's resident dryads all her life, even if her brothers and sister never could. At least she didn't have to deal with them on her own now. That wasn't the only reason I'd got this job, but it certainly didn't hurt.

'What are you going to tell them?' Her expression was somewhere between amused and apprehensive.

'Do I have to tell them anything?'

Eleanor gave me the scathing look that deserved. 'You seriously think Frai won't want to know what's going on as soon as she lays eyes on this?'

'I suppose,' I admitted.

Frai is the older of the two dryads at Blithehurst, and to call her a force of nature is an understatement. While I'd been working on that wooden sculpture of Sir Graelent, she had advised me as I carved every millimetre. At least, that's what it felt like. Frai had known Sir Graelent personally, and if she hadn't been satisfied the statue was a good likeness, I was pretty sure she would have blasted it into matchsticks somehow.

'What are you going to say to her?' Eleanor persisted. 'And why did the grandfather kodama want you to have a seedling from their tree?'

I shrugged. 'According to Moriko, he said that no one knows what the future might bring. He wants her to have some way to contact a friend if she ever needs help. Until I turned up, though, he had no idea how to find someone he could trust.' By trustworthy, he meant another tree spirit. I was under no illusions about that.

'She'll be able to come straight here to this tree?'

'That seems to be how it works.' I hadn't been able to get any more details. Just the idea of being without her grandfather had upset Moriko horribly. She had vanished in floods of tears. He disappeared a moment later. 'That's what I'll tell Frai. It's the truth after all.'

Dryads can always tell if someone is lying; though that wouldn't necessarily get me off the hook if Frai refused to accept the little tree. We'd have to appeal to her daughter. Asca is equally strong-willed, but not nearly so abrasive.

Eleanor stood up. 'Let's go and see what she says. We'd probably better let her decide where to plant it.'

'Right.' I picked up the little tree in its pot and followed her downstairs and out of the house.

We walked through the gardens, down towards the river and the medieval ruins overlooked by the manor. We reached the fork in the path, and I turned towards the wooded pasture where we'd hopefully find the dryads.

Frai and Asca appeared. Both dryads wore flowing draperies like something off a Greek vase, so that meant only Eleanor and I could see them.

'This way.' Frai strode towards the Wilderness Garden on the other side of the velvety green lawn. She didn't look back to see if we were following.

Asca was still standing there. I couldn't guess what she was thinking. I glanced at Eleanor. She shrugged. I shrugged back. We started walking towards the Wilderness Garden. There were a good few visitors around, but none of them were over that way.

'What is this?' Frai demanded as soon as we reached her.

I told her everything I had just told Eleanor. The old dryad's face gave nothing away as she listened to me. When I finished speaking, I waited for her response. She didn't say anything.

'How fascinating.' Asca stepped forward to take the little tree from me. 'Of course we will accept this gift. Leave it with me.'

She turned away, but not before I saw her secretive, satisfied smile. I didn't ask any questions. That smile was good enough for me.

The little sugi is flourishing in a sheltered spot where a magnificent Douglas fir once stood. That tree hadn't fallen victim to old age, accident or disease, but that's another story. A few years ago now, Eleanor, the dryads and I had to fight to save Blithehurst from a far more dangerous threat than any of those calamities.

Whenever I'm working in the manor grounds, I see how the sapling is getting on. I've seen Frai as well as Asca checking up on it too. None the manor gardeners have ever asked where the sugi came from, or who planted it there. Dryads can't read minds, but they can twist human perceptions to suit their own purposes when they choose to.

I wonder if kodama can do that sort of thing. I can't help wondering if I will see Moriko or her grandfather again. Obviously, I don't want anything bad to happen to them. Maybe I should drive down to Surrey sometime, when I've got a day or two off. I can tell Alexander I've come to see how the owl looks, now that the wood's had a few months to weather.

And I wonder what other gardens and botanical collections might be home to unsuspected visitors from overseas.

One story often provides inspiration for another. The passing reference to dryads' sons in The Roots of Aston Quercus prompted The Green Man's Heir, leading to the series of books that have followed. These days, I'm not the only one seeing the world through Dan Mackmain's eyes from time to time. We were visiting a National Trust garden when my husband Steve brought up the possibility of plant hunters bringing home more than they realised. The timing could not have been better, as Ian Whates had asked for at least one entirely new story for this collection.

Now You See Him,
Now You Don't

'I'm really no' sure about this, gentlemen.' Standing in the doorway, the speaker jangled a ring of keys.

'Come on, man, it has to be tonight. Now!' The man loomed menacingly over the rotund policeman, even though he was standing on the step below him.

'Now then, sir.' Unnerved, the policeman groped for his whistle chain among the silver buttons on his dark blue serge tunic.

The second man awaiting admittance put a restraining hand on the tall man's black sleeve. 'Officer, this villain is responsible for killing four young women of good family and irreproachable character.'

Where the constable's accent was that of a gruff lowlander of humble origins, both the other men spoke with the precision of education at Fettes and Oxford.

'Oh aye.' The policeman huffed through his ferociously bristling moustache and his breath clouded the cold night air. 'But gentlemen...' He shook his head uncertainly.

'Come and see for yourself. We'll do no damage.' The black-clad man plucked the ring of keys from the constable's unwary fingers and unlocked the door himself. 'Hurry!'

Ignoring the policeman's protests, he hurried away through the ground floor of the tall narrow building tucked into the grandeur of Edinburgh's Royal Mile.

'I'm sorry.' The second man smiled apologetically. 'But we really don't have time to waste.' He ran after the tall man, both of them heading for the stairs.

The constable muttered something under his breath and followed, after turning to close the door securely behind him.

'Hurry, James.' The tall man was taking the steps two or three at a time, the tails of his black evening dress lashing as he took the turns. Despite the autumn chill he wore no hat, gloves or overcoat.

'She's my sister, Arthur,' the second man snapped back. He wore a tweed covert coat, leather gloves and trousers more suited to a grouse moor than polite society. As he ran up the seemingly endless flights of stairs, he snatched off his brown bowler hat.

Reaching the building's pinnacle, Arthur searched the ring of keys for the one that would open the camera obscura itself. The starched white linen of his shirt front shone, diamond studs brilliant, as the full moon above sailed blithely through a cloudless sky.

'Hurry!' Now it was James who was impatient, lighting a shuttered oil lamp with an angry scrape of a match against his boot sole.

'You, in here.' As the puffing policeman climbed laboriously onto the roof, Arthur grabbed his shoulder to pull him into the closeted darkness of the camera obscura.

'Now, sir –' the constable protested.

'Have you ever been up here before?' Arthur found the levers to control the mechanism high above their heads.

'No,' the constable began. 'What –' He fell silent, open-mouthed, as a vision of the Castle Esplanade appeared on the wide white circular table in the centre of the room. 'Now will ye look at that,' he breathed in wonder.

'Stand by the door.' Hawk-like with his prominent nose and intense dark eyes, Arthur was studying the minute figures crossing the cobbled expanse in the image. 'No, don't open it, not more than a crack. We need darkness in here.'

'How does it work, sir?' The constable meekly complied. 'Is it mirrors?'

'The image is brought to the table by means of a prism in the apex of the roof.' Out on the roof, James obliged with an explanation, determinedly courteous. 'It's what the scientists call refraction, rather than reflection. The man we're following has no reflection. Possibly because of the silvering used to make mirrors –'

Arthur interrupted without apology. 'James, is Robert down there?'

James was standing by the rail guarding the edge of the roof. He lifted his lantern and snapped the shutter once, twice and a third time. Down in the darkness in front of the castle gate a light blinked twice in answer. 'Yes.' His voice cracked with relief. 'Can you see Isobel? Is there enough moonlight.'

'I told you. The moon's brighter tonight than it's been for eighteen years, brighter than it will be for another eighteen.' Arthur bent to study the tiny images more closely. 'Yes, I see her.'

His eyes followed a figure wearing a billowing evening cloak. The hood wasn't raised to avoid disturbing the young woman's high-piled hair so frivolously dressed with feathers. Clasped low on her breast, the cloak had slipped to one side to reveal a glimpse of white shoulder.

'Can you see him?' James's voice thickened with loathing.

'Not yet.' Arthur's reply was clipped.

'But ye say this man's a murderer,' the policeman protested breathlessly. 'Why has there been no hue and cry? I've heard nothing –'

'Because the medical profession calls it *chlorosis*.' Arthur's contempt resonated around the high ceiling. 'Green sickness; an affliction peculiar to virgins. Because doctors have no more wit than to wring their hands, watch their patients die and then send in their bills as swiftly as possible thereafter.'

'Can you see him?' demanded James from out on the roof.

'Wait.' Arthur's eyes had not moved from the round table carrying the image of the esplanade. 'Yes, there he is.'

'How close?' James rasped.

'Who is he?' The policeman took a step towards the table. 'Is it poison, then? How he kills them?'

'There.' Arthur pointed. As his sleeve cast a black shadow across the image, a tiny figure walked across his white cuff, lifted up from the table beneath.

'How does this thing work?' The constable looked upwards once again, quite bemused.

'How close is he to Isobel?' James's words cracked with anger.

'She's safe at present, James,' Arthur said tersely. 'Wait until I give the word. We won't get a second chance.'

'I won't lose a second sister,' James hissed.

The constable watched the figure Arthur had identified as the murderer. 'You're waiting for him to make some move? That'll give ye proof?' As his fingers strayed to the handcuffs at his belt, his gaze flickered to the solitary female walking steadily up the esplanade. 'The lassie's his sister, ye say? Couldn't ye find some trollop and pay her to lure the brute? They risk death and worse every night –'

'Whores are old before their time, foul and diseased.' Arthur was still watching intently. 'This monster wants pure blood and unsullied flesh.'

'Pure, ye say?' The constable stirred, his splendid moustache now bristling with disquiet. 'You've a man down there, though? This Robert? Will he save the lassie if needs be?'

'He won't be able to.' As Arthur shook his head slowly, his eyes never left the tiny figures on the table. 'Any more than you could arrest this murderous villain, my good fellow. As soon as he locks eyes with someone, man or woman, he can wipe their memory of him clean away.'

'That's what they call hypnotism?' The constable groped for understanding. 'Mesmerism?'

'Call it what you will, you'd be left standing there wondering what you'd been thinking of doing –' Arthur broke off as the image dulled and wavered before fading altogether. 'Damnation! What's happening? James?'

The only answer from the roof was a paroxysm of coughing.

The constable pushed open the door to reveal choking skeins of sooty smoke swirling around the lofty structure. 'Aye, the wind's changed. That's Auld Reekie for ye.' His voice quavered between tight-throated apprehension and a certain satisfaction that these educated gentlemen had foolishly overlooked Edinburgh's notorious pall of chimney smoke. 'Are ye all right, sir? And what about the lassie?'

James couldn't reply, doubled over with coughing, the back of one gloved hand pressed to his eyes.

'Shut the door, man!' Arthur bellowed, scowling ferociously.

Startled, the constable did as he was bid. As he did so, all was darkness, no hint of light or life on the camera obscura table.

'Oh God.' Arthur's voice rose on a note of uncertainty for the first time. 'Open the door! James!' he shouted, 'it's no good! Signal to Robert –'

The table shivered and the vision of the esplanade reappeared.

'There!' The constable stabbed an urgent finger at the image. 'Him in the tall hat, that's him, isn't it? And there's the lassie.'

'Good man.' Arthur fixed his burning gaze on their target. 'Stand ready to open the door. Tell James – no, wait, not till I give the word…'

'What's the lassie going tae do?' the constable asked dubiously. 'If it's some kind of assault –'

'Now!' yelled Arthur.

'Robert!' There was no hope of James's hoarse and desperate shout reaching their distant ally but the light flashing from the frantic shutter of his lantern spoke for him.

Down in the darkness by the castle gate, the second lamp reflected the frenzied signal.

The girl in the evening cloak whirled around, one forearm raised to shield her eyes. Her other hand brought a heavy glass and silver bottle out from the concealing folds of heavy silk.

The man in the tall hat had been reaching for her slender shoulders. He recoiled, throwing up his own hands. It was to no avail. The moonlight caught a glittering spray of liquid soaking him from head to toe. The man lurched away, weaving from side to side. He staggered a few paces and then fell to his knees, hands pressed to his face.

'Vitriol!' The constable choked, aghast. He threw open the door.

'No, wait.' Arthur abandoned the mechanism of the camera obscura and the image vanished.

'Please.' James spread beseeching hands and moved to intercept the policeman, tears borne of his coughing fit still glistening on his cheeks.

'Out o' the way!' The constable shoved him aside with a firm hand to the chest and ran for the stairs, his heavy boots resounding on the treads. James rushed after him, slower and still audibly wheezing.

Arthur followed, taking the time to lock the doors, both to the camera obscura and to the building itself as he emerged onto the Royal Mile.

Up on the Castle Esplanade, he heard a single breathless blast of a police whistle, suddenly cut short. That prompted him to pick up his pace, frowning darkly.

On the broad expanse, a knot of men were gathered around Isobel, several in uniform, the silver spikes and chain straps on their helmets shining in the moonlight. Even that brief alarm had summoned rapid assistance.

Arthur joined them and tapped the closest policeman on one shoulder. 'What's going on, officer?'

It was the hapless constable who'd accompanied them up to the camera obscura. 'You, you...' He struggled for words, bristling moustache eloquent with outrage and confusion.

'Some villain was about to attack my sister,' James explained to the newly assembled policemen, his face wholly open and innocent, apparently breathless in his urgency.

'I saw him.' Robert stepped forward, all honest concern in his frock coat and top hat. 'The villain ran off.' He shook his head regretfully.

'Ran off?' the constable expostulated wrathfully. 'Miss, just what have you got there?'

Isobel looked at him, limpid blue eyes wide. 'A *gazogène*.'

'A soda siphon, officer,' Arthur added helpfully.

'We were at dinner and it was such a curious thing.' Within the loose neck of her cloak, it was plain she was wearing a pale pink evening gown, the wide neck trimmed with scarlet satin roses. 'I was bringing it to show James –' Isobel shivered violently and not merely from the cold. There was nothing feigned about the shock racking her.

'I told you to wait for me,' Arthur scolded her nevertheless.

'Let me see that.' The constable growled as he pulled on his white gloves with suppressed violence. He took the silver and glass device from her unresisting hands and sniffed cautiously at it.

'I've only just arrived in town,' James explained with a rueful gesture at his clothing. 'The nearside horse went lame —'

'He ran off, ye say?' One of the other officers turned to scan the empty expanse of the esplanade. The others were already drifting away, glowering at the dark alleys leading away all around. 'Would you know him again, miss?'

'I — I don't believe so.' Isobel looked quite woebegone as she clutched at her silken cloak with demure lace-mittened hands, drawing the slippery cloth up under her chin.

'You, sir?' The policeman demanded of Robert.

He shook his head regretfully. 'I was too concerned with assisting Miss Murray to get a good look at the scoundrel.'

'Ay well, we'll see if we can find him all the same.' The helpful officer gave her a grimly encouraging nod.

As the other police all departed, intent on the hunt, the constable thrust the soda siphon at Arthur with a scowl. 'Water? He ran off because the lassie sprayed him with fizzy water.'

'Holy water, officer.' Arthur smiled with vicious satisfaction as he took the device. 'And no, he didn't run off.'

'Then where is he?' cried the constable, exasperated. 'How's this to stop these murders you speak of?'

'He won't be killing any more innocent girls.' Isobel stirred a slough of fine dust with one dainty satin-slippered toe. 'All that's left of him lies here under our feet.' A single tear slid down her porcelain cheek before she broke into violent sobs.

Robert folded her in a firm embrace.

'Now then.' The constable's moustache bristled with indignation at such an unseemly display.

'They are engaged to be married,' James said firmly.

'As I was, to the eldest Miss Murray,' Arthur said with cold composure. 'Before this monster sapped the life from her and we laid her in an early grave.'

'We knew he couldn't resist following me.' Isobel's voice was muffled against the lapels of Robert's coat. 'We knew I was the only one who could get close enough to douse him.'

'As long as she didn't look at him and risk meeting his gaze.' James gestured vaguely in the direction of the lofty camera obscura.

'He'd know any of the rest of us, and use his hypnosis to disable us. We had to watch him from a distance and use lamp signals to let Isobel know he was about to pounce.'

'But who was he?' The constable was beside himself with frustration.

'A better question would be *"what* was he?",' Arthur began.

James took pity on the hapless policeman. 'There's a novel you should read, my good fellow. It was published in London last May. That should answer all your questions.'

'Excuse me, but we should get Isobel home,' Robert said firmly.

'Oh aye,' the constable said, now quite bemused. 'This book, ye say?'

James turned to speak over his shoulder as the three men departed, Isobel safe between them. 'The chap who runs the Lyceum wrote it. It's called *Dracula.*'

The SF, Fantasy and Horror genres today have roots reaching back to Victorian popular fiction that knew no such boundaries. I read many of these books in my teens, enjoying the heroics of square-jawed, stalwart men. Later, I noted the lack of female characters in such tales. This was the first of several stories I wrote to address that omission, with women taking initiative in ways which would have been possible for them in that era. This led to the creation of that unusual firm of solicitors, Challoner, Murray & Balfour: Monster Hunters at Law.

The Hand That
Rocks the Cradle

Charlotte woke. The five chimes from St Barnabas' soot-blackened tower faded with her dreams of the summer countryside. The memory of meadows sweetly scented with flowers was replaced with the reek of slops from the alley which her grimy window overlooked. Despite this early hour, with the May sun barely risen above the rooftops, carts rattled, horses neighed and draymen shouted in the brewery yard on the far side.

Even in the dead of night, London was never silent. Charlotte obstinately screwed her eyes tight shut. She wished that she could find herself back in Eastridge Parva by means of some unforeseen miracle. Even as she did so, her conscience pricked her. What sort of behaviour was that for a governess? Such self-indulgence was shameful in a young woman offering moral and spiritual guidance to impressionable girls.

Besides, why did she deserve such a miracle? Charlotte knew what her father would have said. She had her health and her strength and her good character. She should thank The Good Lord for His blessings and do His bidding with dutiful humility, trusting that His divine mercy would pour down on those in genuine need.

She opened her eyes and blinked away tears springing half from grief and half from anger. She missed her father so sorely; his unfailing kindness, his patience with his own pupils and his modesty, whether parsing Virgil with a true scholar's aptitude or preaching with quiet authority from the St Michael and All Angels' pulpit.

The thought of Lord Palgrave's feckless third son Albert standing in her father's place prompted Charlotte's anger. Where was divine providence when that chinless wastrel held the keys to the church and the rectory? Henry VIII might have rewarded his ancestors' loyalty with the long-dissolved abbey's lands, but where was the justice in his father using his right to appoint the parish priest to give this otherwise useless young man the pretence of an occupation and income?

Where was divine mercy now that her mother and her three younger sisters and two hopeful brothers had been turned out of the only home they had ever known, dependent on distant relatives' cold charity?

Charlotte drew a deep breath and threw back the threadbare sheet and equally worn blanket. She had declared she had no need of such grudging benevolence. She would earn her own living like countless other respectable and blamelessly impoverished women. So if she wasn't to be forced into a humiliating return, begging for forgiveness, she had better make haste.

She sat on the edge of the sagging mattress, straining her ears for any sound of the slatternly maid-of-all-work's feet on the stairs. Nothing. Another morning when she must go without the hot water supposedly included in her rent. Well, at least a brisk wash in the cold water from her basin's ewer helped wake her up.

St Barnabas' clock struck the half hour as she made her way downstairs, dressed in her sober grey dress. She had long since given up hope of the buttered bread and coffee which Mrs Foster invariably promised but so rarely provided. No matter. Charlotte had saved a roll from her dinner the night before, now wrapped in a linen napkin inside her purse. It would be somewhat stale but she could break her fast on the walk to her first pupil. No one in London would give her a second glance and there was no one who knew her to tell her mother that her eldest daughter was so lost to propriety that she had been seen eating in public.

Charlotte halted in the ill-swept hallway to raise her brown cloak's hood over her bonnet. The morning would still be chilly and, besides, hiding her face saved her from errand boys' impertinences.

She paused and looked at the closed door at the foot of the stairs. She could hear Mrs Foster moving around in her own apartment in the basement but there was no sound at all from Miss Lewes who had this ground floor room. Belatedly Charlotte recalled that the door had been closed yesterday morning and the previous two mornings as well. But last week she had always passed a few words with Miss Lewes as she left the house. The kindly old lady was always awake before six after a lifetime spent educating recalcitrant children. The silence took on an ominous tone.

Charlotte walked to the top of the stairs leading down to the kitchen. 'Mrs Foster?' When a genteel call won her no reply, she shouted more loudly. 'Mrs Foster!'

'I was just coming up. The fire won't draw, you see –'

Charlotte wasn't interested in the shifty-eyed landlady's excuses. 'Is Miss Lewes away?'

Mrs Foster stared upwards, her toothless mouth gaping in momentary surprise. 'Gone away? She said nothing to me.'

She came stumping up the stairs, one hand fumbling in her grimy apron's pocket as her face darkened wrathfully. 'Done a flit? We'll see about that.'

'I didn't say she's gone away,' Charlotte protested, 'I only asked if she had.'

'She must have left Sunday. That's when I last seen her.' Mrs Foster sorted through her keys before thrusting one into the lock and twisting it furiously. 'Sly cat. Calls herself a lady –'

They both heard Miss Lewes's key fall from the lock to land with a sharp bang on the bare boards on the inside of the door. Mrs Foster sucked at her gums before reaching for the knob. She shoved the door open, only to baulk on the threshold.

A head taller, Charlotte could see past the landlady into the room. It was as meanly furnished as her own but at least Miss Lewes had mementos of her long life to brighten the walls and adorn the mantelshelf. Sunlight glinted on the frame of a daguerreotype showing the grand house where she had first served as a governess.

Miss Lewes would never look fondly on such memories again. Charlotte pressed a trembling hand to her mouth as she contemplated the figure slumped motionless in the chair by the window. There could be no question that the old lady was several days dead with the greenish pallor of her face only relieved by the bruise-like darkness of her lips and eyelids.

'Turned up her toes?' Mrs Foster screeched. 'Who's to be put to the trouble of dealing with this, might I ask?'

'Her family —' But even as Charlotte spoke, she recalled Miss Lewes speaking of her parents and only brother, all long dead of the Asiatic Cholera, and of her brother's widow and son, whom she had so faithfully supported with her own earnings after the bank where all their legacies were invested had failed through unwise speculation.

The widow had died three years ago of a broken heart after her son had fallen in the Crimea. The regiment's repayment of the hundreds of pounds spent purchasing his cavalry commission had gone to settle the profligate young man's debts. Charlotte looked around the room and wondered if Miss Lewes had ever begrudged such lifelong sacrifice of her own daily comfort and any prospect of a secure old age.

Walking stealthily, as though the dead woman was only sleeping and might wake, she crossed the room to look at the cup and saucer on the sill. The stain of a last drink of tea was dry as a bone. Charlotte looked around the room. There was no sign of any food.

There was a neat stack of letters on the small writing desk. She moved a little closer, trying to read the topmost without openly intruding.

Dear Miss Lewes,
Thank you for your letter concerning our advertisement in The Times.
Regretfully I must inform you that the position has been filled –

Charlotte didn't need to read any more. She had her own collection of such letters. Miss Lewes had seen her distress when she had made the mistake of opening one in the hall, in her first week in London.

She knew that Miss Lewes had been trying in vain to secure a position since Michaelmas last year, with skills and testimonials far superior to Charlotte's own. In her youth, before such subjects were deemed unsuitable for girls, the older woman had learned Latin and Greek alongside her lost brother, together with Mathematics and Natural Philosophy. She had been governess to three titled families until her charges had married, all to advantage naturally. Each time Miss Lewes' services had been dispensed with, her future of no concern to her erstwhile employers.

Charlotte looked at the dead woman again. 'She just gave up. She locked herself in and sat in that chair and closed her eyes until her trials ended.'

How truly desolate Miss Lewes must have been, for her hopelessness to outweigh whatever torments of hunger and thirst she must have suffered. Charlotte shuddered.

In the next moment, she stiffened as Mrs Foster bustled across to the mantelshelf and began examining the candlesticks and picture frames.

The landlady sniffed with contempt. 'Brummagem ware. Not a hallmark to be seen. Might fetch a few bob all together, I suppose.'

'What are you doing?' Charlotte's question was as curt a rebuke as any she might offer an impertinent pupil.

Mrs Forster turned to her, brazen. 'You want to see her buried by the parish? Thrown into a pauper's grave? If she's to go to her rest with some dignity someone will have to pay and it won't be me, my girl.'

Before Charlotte could find a response, the woman smiled, slyly. 'Shouldn't you be on your way? Don't want to lose your place, do you?'

St Barnabas's clock chimed the third quarter. A chill ran through Charlotte. 'I –'

Her feet were already carrying her to the front door and down the stained steps to the stinking street. She ran, hitching her skirts up above her ankles in shameless fashion, with no thought of trying to eat her bread. Even so, she knew it was well past the hour as she rounded the corner into Parmenter Street.

'Oh!' Charlotte barely escaped disaster as she came face to face with a chimney sweep's boy carrying a bundle of rods and brushes over one shoulder, his suit and face alike as black as pitch.

'I beg your pardon, miss.' The lad stepped aside with a bow and flourish of his free soot-stained hand, as elegant as any gentleman on a Sunday in the park.

'You are excused,' Charlotte said breathlessly.

She forced herself to slow to a ladylike walk, not least in case she was spotted from some upstairs window before she reached the Warringtons' house. Opening the gate in the black iron railings, she made haste down the basement steps, already scrubbed to gleaming whiteness this morning.

'Miss Cheriton.'

'Mr Leigh.' Charlotte was surprised into an unseemly squeak.

Why was the tall butler answering her ring on the kitchen door bell? He should be above stairs, directing the footmen about their duties while he stood ready to receive cards and callers at the house's pillared entrance.

'Mr Warrington has instructed me to give you this.' He handed Charlotte a letter sealed with wax dark as blood. 'Good day to you, Miss Cheriton.'

'I'm sorry I am late, but –' She stood, aghast, as the butler closed the door in her face.

She looked down at the letter. The seal was so fresh that smeared wax stained her glove. She would never get the mark out of the pale kidskin, Charlotte thought numbly, and she could not afford a new pair.

She unsealed and unfolded the letter. She read the few curt lines in Mr Warrington's sweeping script. At least, Charlotte discovered, she had not been dismissed for being late this morning.

Mr Warrington regretted that he had been so foolish to concede to his wife's importuning. There could be no possible need for his daughters to amuse themselves learning French and Italian and History. Their own mother could perfectly well instruct them in the genteel manners and artistic and musical accomplishments desirable in a wife.

As a loving father, he rejected the cruelty of cramming his cherished children's heads with unnecessary knowledge and corrupting their innocence with notions they could have no use for in their future lives.

Anger momentarily overwhelmed Charlotte's anguish. Did Mr Warrington mean to slight her so thoroughly? Did he realise how grievously he insulted her father?

The Reverend Cheriton had not scorned to educate his own daughters. Indeed, her own governess had lived under the family's roof, bed and board all found with a respectable salary besides. Miss Andrews had not been paid a miserly penny per pupil per hour for the onerous task of disciplining and instructing three vain and spiteful little girls while their mother made her leisurely breakfast and prepared herself for a day of selfish indolence.

Charlotte screwed the letter into a wrathful ball and hurled it at the closed door. Mr Warrington was no gentleman He was a coward if he couldn't even dismiss her from his service in person. As for his daughters, let him see how their marriages prospered once they burdened their husbands with debt for lack of the basic arithmetic to count their pin money.

She climbed the steps back to the pavement and strode purposefully away. As she reached the far end of the street, though, her furious pace slowed. It wasn't as if she had anywhere to go until mid-morning; to the Martin house where she was engaged to instruct their four daughters from ten till twelve, before the Barlows' two girls benefited from her tuition from half past the hour until half past three, leaving Charlotte barely enough time to reach the Armitage residence to commence lessons promptly at four until the three fractious children were swept away to their nursery at seven.

Apprehension weighed her down as she walked aimlessly onwards. How soon would she be able to find another family to employ her at the start of each day? Charlotte's pace slowed still further as she realised her unguarded feet were already taking her towards the elegant square where the Martins lived. She really didn't want to arrive early. Master Robert Martin and his brother George were both home from school and fancied themselves great flirts even though they were barely whiskered. Charlotte had already made the mistake of treating them as familiarly as her own brothers. She had suffered a most unjust reprimand from the Martin's housekeeper, accused of seeking to lure one or other of the young masters into an illicit entanglement.

Had the vinegar-faced woman told her mistress of such scandalous suspicions? Weary tears stung Charlotte's eyes. She would be unable to help her mother, sisters and brothers without the Warringtons' money. If the Martins dismissed her, she would be hard pressed to keep body and soul together.

'You're better off out of that house, miss. The master takes liberties with the parlour maids and old Leigh cheats the mistress by selling off the linens what he claims the laundry has spoiled.'

Startled to hear a voice so close behind her, Charlotte spun around. She gaped, astonished to see the chimney sweep's boy whom she had so nearly collided with in her earlier hurry.

'I been going into that house since I was a climbing boy,' he assured her. 'You hear no end of secrets when no one realises you're up a flue.'

Charlotte's surprise was overtaken by indignation. 'How dare you address me?'

'No need to cut up rough with me, miss,' he chided her mildly. 'I've done you no wrong.'

Charlotte drew a sharp breath but could not deny the truth of his words. 'No, indeed.' It was unjust to vent her fear and anger on this luckless youth.

'I might be able to do you a good turn, miss,' he ventured.

She had already turned her back on him. Now Charlotte stood stock still save for a tremor running through her.

Mr Barnett, her mother's remote cousin, had warned her of the countless perils lurking in London. Indeed, he had prophesied disgrace and disaster when Charlotte had announced her intention of making her own way in the metropolis, although, abruptly red-faced, he declined to explain precisely what catastrophes might befall unprotected young women.

'There's help for young ladies like yourself, miss.'

Charlotte turned to look warily at the sweep. 'The Governesses Benevolent Fund.'

She had heard rumour of such charity but making any application meant admitting the abject failure of all her hopes.

The sweep grinned, his teeth startlingly white against the soot blackening his face. 'Wouldn't you rather have help finding a good position? I know a governesses' registry office.'

Charlotte shook her head. 'They won't want me.'

She had visited several such offices when she had first arrived in London, only to be looked up and down disapprovingly by those whiskered gentlemen. Governesses must bring more maturity to a schoolroom, they had explained in quelling tones, in order to impose adequate authority.

'Never mind, they cannot hold your youth against you forever.' Miss Lewes had comforted her with typical kindness even though those same officious gentlemen had rejected her on account of her advanced years.

The chimney sweep was still grinning. 'You should meet these ladies before you're so sure of that.'

'Ladies?' Faint hope kindled in Charlotte's heart. Surely gentlewomen would have a better appreciation of her plight.

'Come along with me.' The sweep was already crossing the road, heading towards a narrow entry.

Charlotte followed, suddenly resolute. *Audaces Fortuna iuvat*, as her father would have said. Fortune favours the bold. Though as she belatedly recalled the Reverend Cheriton reading Mr Dryden's translation to the family in the parlour, she rather thought the heroic young gentleman proclaiming such sentiments in Virgil's Aeneid had come to an unfortunate end.

She thrust away unbidden recollection of the tales of deceit and stealthy murder which she had glimpsed in those illustrated papers read illicitly below stairs in the Warrington and Barlow households. It was broad daylight after all with plenty of respectable men and women about their business on the streets and lanes which the sweep led her through.

Granted, after turning the fifth or sixth corner, Charlotte realised she had lost her bearings. No matter. These scholarly ladies could doubtless direct her to a thoroughfare she would recognise. All Charlotte needed to do was keep an ear cocked for the sound of a church clock's bells in order to leave in good time to reach the Martin's house at her appointed hour.

'Here we are, miss.' Rounding a final corner, the youthful sweep pointed to the end house of the neat brick-built terrace.

Charlotte looked up the steps to see a modest brass plate on the wall beside the black-painted door.

The Alice Street Educational Registry.

It certainly looked a respectable house. The brass was polished, the paint was gleaming and the steps were scrubbed clean. The muslin curtains hanging at the windows were crisp and fresh.

'Go on, miss,' the sweep urged.

'One moment.' Charlotte reached into her purse, steeling herself to part with a thruppeny piece to reward the boy, but when she looked up, he was nowhere to be seen.

Indeed, she realised somewhat nervously, there was no one on this street at all. The pavements and road alike were deserted, unlike the thronged streets they had been walking through. There was no sign of life anywhere, until she looked up at the house and saw a muslin drape twitch.

Charlotte squared her shoulders and marched up the steps. She grasped the polished brass knocker in her gloved hand and rapped a brisk request for admittance.

Alea jacta est. The die is cast. She frowned as she recalled Julius Caesar had said that. Were there no Latin proverbs from stories with more promising outcomes?

'Good morning.' A small, stout lady dressed in rusty black opened the door to reveal a hallway tiled in black and white with a staircase immediately ahead and a door to the left standing ajar.

Even to call the stout lady plain would be stretching truth to breaking point. In all honesty, she was breathtakingly ugly with her face as round and wrinkled as a discarded apple, her complexion coarse and brown and her eyes as black as boot buttons. Her nose was as bulbous and round as a misshapen potato.

'I –' Charlotte realised she was staring, transfixed by the sight of the single front tooth protruding over the woman's lower lip. Blushing, she turned as though to indicate the chimney sweep even though she knew full well he wasn't there.

She got herself in hand and cleared her throat as she looked back at the ugly woman. 'Good morning. I understand this is an educational registry. I am a daily governess at present and am seeking a permanent position in a private household or perhaps in a school. I was directed here.' She chose not to say who had led her to this door.

The ugly woman in black looked at her unsmiling. Charlotte lifted her chin and looked back at her. After a moment, she raised her eyebrows in mild enquiry.

The black-gowned woman's lips twitched, though Charlotte was unable to decide whether that signified amusement or contempt.

The woman rapped sharply on the tiles with the stick she had been leaning on. Startled, Charlotte thought she was being dismissed. Then she realised the woman was opening the door wider, using her stick to beckon Charlotte inside.

'Our Principal will wish to interview you.' The black-gowned woman stumped towards the half-open door.

'Naturally.' Charlotte followed, bracing herself for an encounter with someone even more formidable as the ugly woman ushered her into the sitting room.

Entering the room, however, she was disarmed to see a small and slightly-built woman seated behind a substantial leather-topped desk. Charlotte could not have guessed at her age; her face was as unlined as a doll's and her shiny black hair showed no hint of grey.

'Please, be seated.' The woman leaned forward to indicate the empty chair on the other side of the desk.

Other than that, there was no furniture in the room beyond a hat stand in the corner, with a sensible black hat perched above a plain coat and an umbrella with an unexpectedly frivolous handle tucked into the base along with a large bag.

As Charlotte took the empty seat, the Principal folded her rather large hands on the desk before her. Charlotte wondered if she was near-sighted since she seemed to be peering intently at her. Perhaps, perhaps not. Regardless, the woman's bright blue eyes looked shrewd.

'I can provide references –' Charlotte began.

'Oh, we make it a rule never to give references,' the Principal said firmly.

'Never?' Charlotte gaped.

The Principal smiled. 'We find it unnecessary with our particular clientele. Tell me about yourself. Where have you come from? Why seek employment as a governess?'

'I was born and raised in Hampshire.' Unaccountably, Charlotte found herself telling this stranger all the trials and tribulations which had beset her since her father's untimely death. Blushing as she realised she was imparting unseemly confidences, she hurriedly explained her hope of finding work in London.

'My mother was a governess before her marriage and she continued to help my father teach the pupils whom he prepared for the Universities –'

'Do you believe that women should be admitted to the Universities?' The Principal cocked her head to one side, bird-like.

'I do.' Charlotte hesitated before continuing boldly. 'I see no reason why women shouldn't be educated alongside their brothers. I believe that women could be doctors or scientists to equal any man. That we could run shops and railways and factories and anything else we put our minds to.'

Charlotte didn't read the blood-curdling tales of murder and mayhem when she could abstract a newspaper from an employer's kitchen but the social and political writings of Mr Dickens and his fellow thinkers.

'I believe in reform of education and of the franchise and of the Poor Laws and the mines –' Her courage abruptly failed her and she bit her lip.

'Good,' the Principal said firmly. 'We have no time for old-fashioned attitudes here.'

Charlotte was startled. 'Your clientele accept such radical –?' She couldn't think how to frame her question without offering unintended insult.

'Our clientele accept us for who we are and for the particular services we can render them.' The Principal smiled mysteriously. 'Do you think that you can teach kindness and consideration for the rest of humanity to the over-indulged children of the blinkered and foolish?'

'I can try,' Charlotte ventured. Before she could find a way to ask how exactly she might do so, she heard the clangour of church bells a few streets away.

'Excuse me, I must –' she broke off, puzzled to hear the bells ringing a peal rather than sounding the hour.

'Did you wish to attend divine service today?' The Principal enquired. 'I believe you will have to wait for Evensong.'

'Today?' Charlotte stared at her.

'It is Sunday, after all.' The Principal raised her fine black brows.

Charlotte frowned. 'Sunday? No –'

'Of course it's Sunday. Didn't you see how empty the streets were?' That mysterious smile still curved the Principal's lips.

Charlotte shook her head. 'Forgive me –'

'You are excused.' The Principal rose to her feet and offered Charlotte her hand. 'Call again tomorrow if you wish to join our register. I hope you will. You are precisely the sort of young woman who will do very well with our help.'

'I –' Charlotte drew a deep breath and stood up. 'Thank you. Good day.'

The ugly woman in black opened the door. Had she been listening at the keyhole, Charlotte wondered as she went out into the hallway.

'Good day,' she said politely as the stout woman opened the door.

'Do call again.' The woman's smile rendered her more hideous than ever with that protruding tooth.

Charlotte forbore to say she had no intention of returning to this strange place where people didn't even know what day of the week it was. She smiled with meaningless politeness and hurried down the steps.

It was only when she reached the end of the street that Charlotte realised she had neglected to ask for directions to some more familiar district. She had no idea which way to go to reach the Martin house. She didn't even know what time it was. Those dratted church bells were ringing another peal.

Charlotte's heart began to beat more quickly, her mouth dry with apprehension as all her cares came flocking back. Looking desperately this way and that, she saw a top-hatted gentleman approaching at a leisurely pace. She hurried towards him, heedless of propriety.

'Sir, I beg your pardon, but could you direct me towards Parmenter Street?' Retracing her steps was surely the swiftest way of returning to some recognisable locale.

'Parmenter Street?' The gentleman politely doffed his hat. 'By all means. If you follow that road over there and then take the first left and the second right and carry straight on, you'll find it soon enough.'

'Thank you.' Charlotte broke off as the bells rang through the air again. 'Excuse me, is there some celebration to prompt those peals?'

'Celebration?' The top-hatted man looked puzzled. 'Not beyond celebrating the Sabbath and a day of rest from our labours.'

'Day of rest?'

Charlotte stared at the man for so long that he coloured uncomfortably.

'Good day to you.' He took a step.

'No, wait.' Casting decorum to the winds, Charlotte seized his arm. 'Please, I beg of you, what is the date?'

He stared at her, bemused. 'It's the fifth of the month.'

'The fifth?' Charlotte repeated faintly. 'Then it really is Sunday.'

'What other day would it be, to come after Saturday and before Monday?' The top-hatted man was growing distinctly uneasy.

'Then she's still alive.' Charlotte didn't attempt to explain. She didn't bother trying to fathom this mystery. All such considerations could wait. She took to her heels.

With her back to the Alice Street house, Charlotte hadn't seen the muslin curtain twitch aside to give the sitting room's occupant a clear view of her encounter.

'Who brought her here, Mary?' As the woman in rusty black entered, she grew taller and more slender. Her shapeless gown was transformed into an elegant golden-brown dress while her complexion and features were smoothed into gentle loveliness.

'Tom, the sweep.' The small woman with keen blue eyes continued to watch Charlotte running pell-mell down the road which the top-hatted man had indicated. She smiled as he looked up and doffed his hat before heading back the way he had come. 'Was there something you wanted, Matilda?'

The transformed woman came to stand at the window beside her. 'Ursula has written again. She says that while they are undoubtedly darling children, she is finding life as a Newfoundland dog increasingly tedious.'

'Tell her it won't be for much longer. Peter will arrive soon.' Mary crossed the room to the hat stand. She shrugged on the plain coat and secured her sensible black hat with a pin.

Matilda was still looking out of the window. 'Do you think we will see her again?'

'I believe so.' Mary smiled, leaning down to pick up the large bag and the umbrella with the parrot's head handle.

'Do you suppose she will bring the old woman with her?' Matilda drew the curtains aside.

'Let us hope so.' Mary took a moment to admire her reflection in the window. 'We can do a great deal as nurses and nannies but it's time we found suitable governesses to continue our work.'

'Indeed.' Matilda threw up the heavy sash to open the window wide and the briskly blowing east wind carried Mary away.

The magical nursemaids I encountered in classic children's fiction were all very well, but I did wonder what would happen as those children grew up. The boys might well be sent away to school, but the girls would be educated at home, if they were educated at all. Social history shows us this was merely one of the systemic disadvantages holding back Victorian women and girls. Writers at the time and in later decades highlighted these problems. Some of these authors used fantasy fiction and I have done the same.

The Echoes of a Shot

Standing at the edge of an airstrip in France, as the summer dusk deepened, Charlie was starting to wonder if he had made this trip in vain. There were barely a dozen reporters still waiting and he was the only one watching the westward skies. The rest were clustered together, sharing their cigarettes and buying glasses of white wine from an enterprising local bar owner. The beaming man had appeared some hours earlier with a horse-drawn cart carrying tables, chairs, a basket of bottles, and an ice chest. Whoever was in charge of this aviation hobbyists' airfield near Amiens had made no effort to send him away.

Squinting into the setting sun was giving him a headache, but Charlie didn't think drinking the local *vin ordinaire* would help with that. He wandered over to the solitary, single-storey building and peered through the open door. The radio operator sat hunched close to her Marconi set, intent on whatever was coming through her earphones.

As Charlie's shadow fell across the floor, she glanced over to see what was dimming the fading daylight. He raised his eyebrows, his expression hopeful. She smiled briefly but shook her head.

He couldn't understand how she could be so calm, but she was one of the small coterie of mechanics and assistants who had come ahead from New York by the weekly scheduled Zeppelin service. He supposed such uncertainty must be par for the course among these experimental aviators.

'Can you hear that?' A shout outside turned everyone's heads, as much for its unfamiliar American accent as for anything else.

Just as quickly, the speaker was hushed. Charlie hurried to the edge of the airstrip and strained his ears for any suggestion of engine noise. All he could hear was insouciant birdsong and the rustle of wind in the poplar trees. He scanned the skies and the breath caught in his throat as he saw a distant silhouette against the gold streaks of cloud.

'There!' Charlie pointed with a shaking hand. Turning, he saw his fellow journalists still smoking their cigarettes and sipping their wine as they watched the plane's approach. It seemed to be flying very low to Charlie, and the engine laboured.

He reminded himself that he knew nothing about airplanes. He'd only ever seen such a thing twice before and those had been kite-like contraptions of wire, wood, and canvas, flying in low circles over county shows. This machine was a very different beast, made entirely of metal with a powerful engine to drive the propeller at the front and a broad single wing extending across the top of a sleek body shaped somewhat like a fat cigar.

'You'd never get me up in one of those things,' one shirtsleeved hack remarked.

'Do you think she'll crash?' a woman in a blue linen dress asked with mild interest.

'Might make the front page if she does. It's not as if there's much else happening in London,' a third reporter observed. 'Otherwise it's bottom right, page three, if she's lucky.'

'She'd better get a move on,' the man in shirtsleeves said testily, 'if we're going to have any chance of filing copy tonight.'

Charlie walked away before he was tempted to punch someone. As far as he was concerned 28th of June 1939 should be a date to go down in the history books. He only prayed it would be for a story of triumph rather than tragedy.

He didn't return to the pack of press until the bright red airplane had swooped low, touched down, bounced upwards, touched down again, and rolled sedately along the landing strip to come to a halt at the end. The photographers who'd been waiting in their own little gaggle began filling the air with dazzling bursts of light and the metallic reek of flash powder.

The American mechanics and the aviatrix's other supporters ran forward with a set of steps almost before the propeller had stopped turning. The reporters followed more slowly and warily. Cigarettes and wine glasses had been swapped for notepads and pens.

Breathless with relief, Charlie watched as the pilot climbed stiffly out of the door in the side that presumably gave access to the airplane's wheelhouse. No, the cockpit is what these Americans called it. He glanced at the notes he had already made and wondered why none of them had been inclined to explain why.

The other reporters were shouting questions. How old was Miss Earhart? When had she started flying? Where had she started her journey? Charlie already had those answers, thanks to his conversations with the Americans. Forty-two. 1920. Harbour Grace, Newfoundland.

'Mrs. Putnam! Quentin Morgan, *Daily Mail*.' The man in shirtsleeves smirked at his fellow journalist who clearly had no idea that the lady flier was married. 'What's your plucky little airplane called?'

'I go by my own name, thanks all the same,' the slender, leather-jacketed woman said sardonically, 'and I'm flying a Modernaire AE, call sign 7083.'

She grinned, suddenly charming as she pulled off her flying helmet and ran a hand through her short curls. The hairstyle was as practical as her breeches and boots, and just as startling on a woman. 'The airplane's called The Spirit of St Christopher.'

Charlie wrote that down as eagerly as the rest of the assembled reporters, before sticking up his own hand. 'Charles Oliver, *Daily Herald*. How long did your journey take?'

Miss Earhart checked her watch. 'Twenty-seven hours and fifteen minutes.'

More questions came thick and fast. 'What did you eat and drink?' 'Surely you were unable to sleep?' 'How did you navigate?' The aviatrix responded to them all, her answers composed and concise.

As the queries finally died away, Miss Earhart raised her voice. 'I've been told for years that no one could ever fly non-stop across the Atlantic. This flight proves beyond all doubt that airplanes have the capacity to cross the world's oceans and continents. These machines should be far more than rich men's playthings and engineering curiosities. The potential of fixed-wing flight is tremendous and the time has come to explore it. The skies do not belong to Zeppelins alone, as of unquestioned right.'

She drew a breath and Charlie could see that she had more to say, despite her evident weariness. But the other journalists had seized their chance and hurried away towards their parked cars. The photographers had already gone and Charlie wondered what arrangements they had made to send their film for developing across the Channel. Without some decent pictures, the story would be lucky to make page five.

He found a clean glass and poured some wine. As he went over and offered it to Miss Earhart, he smiled apologetically. 'We all have deadlines, and soon. They need to find a telephone, if they're going to file their copy before the London papers go to press.'

'And you don't?' The lady flier looked exhausted and years older than her true age. 'Or are you just not going to bother? Who cares what mad Americans get up to anyway? The Yankees aren't interested in Europe, so who gives a damn about them?'

Charlie flipped back a few pages in his notebook to show her a page of neat shorthand outlines. 'I've written almost all of my story and your young wireless lady is going to use her equipment to send it to a friend of mine in London.'

Miss Earhart laughed. 'Well, aren't you an enterprising fellow?' She took the glass of wine and drained it, before looking at Charlie, suddenly severe. 'Were you listening to what I said? Are you interested in the potential of fixed wing aviation?'

'More than you can imagine,' he assured her. 'May I call on you tomorrow, to discuss the subject further?'

She looked at him for a long moment, clearly intrigued. Equally obvious, she was far too tired to pursue the matter this evening. 'Okay then. Make it first thing. I have a full schedule on this trip.'

She might have said something more, but one of the mechanics by the plane shouted an urgent summons and she strode away. As Charlie watched her go, his hand strayed to the breast of his suit, where the letter that nobody knew about was hidden in an inside pocket.

He found a room for the night in a modest *pension* and set out bright and early for the considerably more luxurious hotel where the Marconi girl had told him the American flying expedition would be based for the next week. As he entered, Charlie saw a handful of wide-eyed staff clustered by the dining room door. Voices and laughter were loud within. The Americans were still getting used to the Continental style of breakfasting on coffee and croissants and made no secret of their bemusement. Thankfully the hotel staff weren't offended, as far as Charlie could tell. Indeed, the French seemed far more entertained by the novelty of such unfamiliar guests.

As he headed for the concierge's desk, one of the mechanics came down the stairs. 'Hey, you were at the airstrip yesterday. Can I help you, buddy?'

His tone made it clear that it was a friendly greeting, so Charlie smiled. 'Miss Earhart said I should call on her today.'

'Okay,' the mechanic said, obliging. 'Room 214. Go on up.'

Charlie was somewhat taken aback by such informality, but the mechanic was already on his way to the dining room. The concierge was nowhere to be seen, so he couldn't ask for a message to be sent to the room. He considered taking a seat in the lobby to wait, but recalled what the aviatrix had said about having a lot to get done. His hand strayed to the hidden letter again. He dared not miss his chance.

Upstairs, he counted the brass numbers along the corridor and found the door to 214 ajar. He knocked politely all the same.

'Come on in!' The summons was somewhat muffled, but Miss Earhart's voice was unmistakable.

Charlie entered, only to stop dead, blushing scarlet with embarrassment. Miss Earhart was in her dressing gown, sitting at a table with a bowl of steaming water in front of her, holding a towel over her head. There was a strong smell of menthol and other aromatics.

'I'm so sorry.' He turned to leave.

'Don't go.' She sat up straight, settling the towel around her shoulders. 'I thought you were the girl with more hot water. Never mind, I reckon I'm done.'

She sniffed experimentally and blew her nose with a thoroughness that made Charlie pity whoever laundered her handkerchiefs.

'Sinus trouble,' she explained briefly, 'ever since I had that damned Chicago Horse Flu. I guess that's something you can thank President Taft and his Isolationists for. They say it never got over here.'

'There were a few thousand cases, but we certainly heard how dreadfully your country suffered,' Charlie assured her. 'Did it really come from horses?'

'Horses, or pigs, or chickens. So they say.' She shrugged. 'Make no odds to the millions who died. I may have sinus trouble, but at least I'm still here. So what did you want to talk to me about?'

Charlie took out his notebook. 'I'd like our readers to understand the future you see for your airplanes. When Zeppelins can carry so many more people in safety and comfort —'

Miss Earhart interrupted him with a laugh. 'Ever been in a zep facing a headwind? They can end up going nowhere. A fixed-wing airplane can fly in all sorts of weather.'

'If the weather's too bad for flying, we take the train,' Charlie pointed out.

'Do you, indeed?' She changed the subject abruptly. 'I asked around about your paper. They say it backs the working man and pushed for votes for women. It supports labour unions and the like. Do you? Or do you just take their paycheques?'

'I absolutely believe in the *Herald*'s message,' Charlie assured her, even as he wondered where this was going.

'Cards on the table then, and off the record.' She wiped her face with the corner of the towel, wholly serious. 'Your governments run your trains. We have railway barons. Robber barons, we call them, and they don't just control the trains, but steel and coal and petroleum, as well as copper, silver, and gold mining, along with real estate and every sort of finance. Ever heard of the Astors, the Carnegies, the Rockefellers?'

Charlie shook his head and she sighed. 'No reason you would have. They don't want Europeans taking an interest in US affairs, any more than they want ordinary Americans getting wind of your social democracy. God forbid we should see how you make it work, now that you've gotten rid of the real-life barons you used to have over here.'

Charlie raised his pen politely. 'I thought you had government by the people, for the people.'

'Maybe once upon a time.' Miss Earhart laughed bitterly. 'These days our politicians are bought and paid for, and the Isolationists don't just own the railroads. They own the newspapers and the telegraph wires and that means the only news the American man and woman in the street gets is the news they're given. The barons own the telephone exchanges, so they soon hear who's talking out of turn. Make a noise and you'll find a Pinkerton on your doorstep, saying you should pipe down if you know what's good for you. Or there'll be one telling the train conductor to put you off at the next stop, with a full refund for your ticket of course.'

'Goodness me.' Charlie wondered what a Pinkerton was. Nothing good, by the sound of it. 'But surely you have automobiles to go wherever you want?'

'Courtesy of Henry Ford? Ten dollars off, if you sign up for a free lifetime subscription to *The Dearborn Independent*. Have you ever seen a copy of that rag?'

'Once or twice. It did have some eccentric views.' Charlie chose his words carefully.

He was aware that some Americans had views on race that were as distasteful as the prejudice against Jews that was still all too common across Europe; though he had understood that the extreme eugenicists' cause in America had been fatally undermined by the far greater resistance to the Chicago Flu amongst the descendants of slaves.

'That's what you call British understatement, I take it.' Miss Earhart waved Henry Ford and his works away, contemptuous. 'The thing is, automobiles can still be pulled over, especially when the local cops are in rich men's pockets. Oh, the bookleggers give them a run for their money, but that's a dangerous game. More than that, ours is a big country. I don't think you realise just how big it is, over here. Travel from coast to coast by road when decent pavement stops at most city limits?' She shook her head.

'That's where your airplanes come in?' hazarded Charlie.

'Right.' She favoured him with that sudden, charming smile. 'No one owns the skies. An airplane can carry the real news from place to place and land on a gravel country road or a farmer's field if needs be.'

'But can't you do that already?' Charlie gestured vaguely in the direction of the airstrip.

'We can, but we need bigger airplanes.' Miss Earhart leaned forward, her expression intense. 'We need airplanes that can take ten passengers from New York to San Francisco, twenty passengers, maybe more. Then we can start getting people from place to place, to talk to each other. Women, and negroes, and Indians, and anyone else who those rich white men don't want having their say. Then maybe we can get back to government by the people, for the people.'

'So you've come to Europe –?' Charlie prompted.

'To find investors, because we won't ever get a dime out of the Rockefellers and their pals. We want to find engineers and mechanics who can invent and test prototypes without finding their workshops burning down in the night. Men and women we can work with, who can build on what we've already developed.'

She leaned back from the table. 'More than that, if air travel becomes commonplace in Europe, those Carnegies and Rockefellers won't have any good reason to deny it to the American people. They're no fools. They know their hold on power only lasts as long as no one really sees the iron hand inside the velvet glove. That's why they won't actually stop the likes of me studying engineering, however much they might try to discourage us from making use of what we learn.'

'I see.' Charlie nodded. He reached into his jacket's inner breast pocket. 'I think we can do that and more besides.'

He handed Miss Earhart the letter. He sat with his heart pounding as she slit the envelope and extracted the contents. He watched her eyes widen as she studied the diagrams and read the accompanying note.

She looked up. 'Is this for real?'

He nodded. 'Absolutely.'

A knock on the door interrupted them. It was the wireless operator. 'Miss Amelia? Your appointment?'

'I know.' She stuffed the papers back in the envelope and stood up, addressing Charlie. 'I'll need to see this for myself. Give me an address where I can telegraph you, when I've freed up some time in my calendar.'

Charlie wrote in his notebook and tore out the page. 'Here.'

As she took it, she looked at him, shrewdly assessing. 'What do you get out of this?'

He grinned. 'A front page exclusive. Hopefully more than one.'

Her appreciative laughter followed him out of the door as the wireless operator escorted him down the stairs.

Three days later, on the train from London to Bedford, Charlie sat quietly as Miss Earhart studied the engineering drawings for what must have been the fifth time. Then she went over them yet again. Finally, seeing the landmarks that indicated they had nearly arrived, he cleared his throat.

'We'll take a taxi from the station.'

'What?' She looked up and, realising the train was slowing, folded the drawings to stow them in her handbag. 'Oh, okay.'

As she took her gloves from her coat pocket, a shilling fell to the compartment floor. Charlie bent forward to retrieve it. As Miss Earhart took the coin from him, she studied Edward VIII's portrait. 'How come you British kept your king, when everyone else was getting rid of theirs? Come to that, why did the Germans and Russians and the rest decide they'd had enough of emperors?'

Charlie smiled. 'Have you ever heard of Archduke Franz Ferdinand of Austria, heir to the Austro-Hungarian Empire?'

'Can't say that I have,' said Miss Earhart, mystified.

'Don't worry,' Charlie assured her. 'Half the men and women on any London omnibus would say the same. The most memorable thing that ever happened to him was getting assassinated in Sarajevo in 1914.'

'Good Lord!' Miss Earhart was startled.

'The Serbs caught the killers and executed them and everyone was satisfied apart from Wilhelm of Germany and Nicholas of Russia. They were outraged. They started making accusations and threatening each other until there were rumours that one or other of them would declare outright war. That was going too far. No one with any sense was going to see blood shed for a quarrel between two cousins.'

Charlie sat with his elbows resting on his knees. 'It's not as if either of them were overly popular. Silly Billy had been making a fool of himself for years. Read his interview in *The Daily Telegraph* from 1908. That sparked the first round of calls for his abdication. As for the Czar, he'd dragged the Russians into that disastrous war with Japan. He only survived popular fury at those losses by granting parliamentary reforms in 1905.'

Miss Earhart shook her head, 'I had no idea.'

'No one saw what was coming. Austria and Hungary broke apart first, when the old Emperor Franz Joseph died and all the Slavs declared independence. They'd been demanding more say in their own governments for decades. The Czar went completely to pieces when his poor little boy died and he withdrew from public life, so that was the end of his dynasty. Then the Germans who'd been reading their Engels realised their Kaiser's demands for more and bigger battleships were bankrupting their country, so they gave him his marching orders.'

Charlie laughed as he remembered the cartoons. Bruce Bairnsfather in *The Morning Post* drawing Silly Billy with his spiked helmet and that ridiculous moustache, plodding off with a red spotted bundle on a stick over his shoulder.

'George V wasn't the sharpest knife in the drawer, but he was bright enough to see he was on very thin ice after what happened to his cousins in Germany and Russia. Then India declared independence and the rest of the Empire followed suit. We have your Chicago Flu to thank for that.'

'Really?' Miss Earhart was surprised.

'The Flu may not have crossed the Atlantic, but it swept across the Pacific with a vengeance. The death toll in India was appalling, but the government here couldn't do anything about it, least of all send troops to replace the British soldiers who died. They were up to their necks dealing with the Irish Insurrection. As soon as the Irish went their own way, the Suffragette Summer erupted, thanks to Asquith going back on his word to give women the vote yet again.'

Charlie shook off a sudden memory of walking across broken glass in the high street, six years old and not understanding why the shops were closed, as he clung to his mother's hand and the stink of smoke hung heavy in the air.

'Master Gandhi proclaimed that the British Empire had broken faith with India, by failing in its duty to its subjects. The Indian Congress declared independence and Asquith dared not make a fight of it. That loss strengthened calls for constitutional reform here, there, and everywhere else under British rule. Sailor George decided not to wait until he was pushed. He handed over the keys to Windsor Castle and Buckingham Palace and retreated to Sandringham, to live a quiet life with his stamp collection.'

He nodded at the coin in Miss Earhart's hand. 'That's where Edward the Unsteady lives now, gambling and drinking and enjoying the bachelor life, since he can't find the right woman to wed. If he doesn't have any children, the Duke of York will succeed to the throne, although that is purely ceremonial now. He lives up in Scotland, at Balmoral, with his wife and daughters.'

'I see,' Miss Earhart said politely.

Charlie realised that he'd more than satisfied her curiosity. He needed to remember not everyone shared his passion for history or he risked becoming a crashing bore.

As the train pulled into Bedford Station, he stood up. 'Let's get to Cardington.'

The village was only five miles or so from the town. Their destination was soon obvious, as the great steel hangars dominated the flat landscape, their cantilevered roofs 170 feet tall.

Miss Earhart turned to Charlie in the back seat of the cab.

'That's an airship shed.'

He nodded. 'And much more besides.'

Miss Earhart leaned forward, impatient. As soon as they reached the airship facility, she sprang out of the taxi, leaving Charlie to pay the driver. He followed the lady flier, watching amused as she swiftly introduced herself to the first man she met.

The engineer escorted her towards the cavernous hangar and Charlie saw men and women in overalls hurrying to meet her. He headed for the administration block where he knew he could get a cup of tea. He had no wish to be deafened by the boffins' experimental engines again.

He had drunk several cups of tea, read his newspaper, done the crossword, and written three draft news articles in his notebook by the time the canteen door opened and Miss Earhart came in. Charlie half-expected to see her in overalls, but she was still an incongruous vision of Parisian elegance, in her long skirt and maroon wool coat. She was also beaming from ear to ear. Charlie signalled to the waitress for a fresh pot of tea.

'Jet engines,' she marvelled, as she dropped into the chair on the other side of the table. 'They've really done it.'

She unpinned her hat and put it beside the vase of flowers before rubbing her ears and grimacing. 'My head is still ringing.'

'Have some tea.' The tray arrived and Charlie poured two cups. 'Milk? Sugar?'

'Just milk, thank you. Though they'll need to learn to make coffee here, if American engineers are coming over.' She took the tea all the same and drank it thirstily.

'So you're interested in working with the chaps?'

'And how! That means yes,' the aviatrix clarified as she poured herself more tea. 'The sky's the limit, if we can get our airplanes and your engines working together. I can't thank you enough for bringing me here.'

She paused and looked at him, her gaze piercing. 'Why did you bring me here, Charles? The guys said you told them to expect me. This was your plan all along, even before you came to France. What gives?'

Charlie waved a casual hand. 'I was here a few months ago, doing a feature on the latest airship designs. I'm always on the lookout for a new story, so when I heard that incredible noise, I followed my nose, so to speak. We got talking and the chaps were saying it was all very well, them developing these new engines, but the teams working on an airplane that could use them were getting nowhere fast. Last month, I read about your transatlantic flight, so I did a bit of research and found out you're an expert in aeronautics.' He pronounced the unfamiliar word with care.

'So I popped over here and asked the chaps if they'd like me to see if you'd be interested in paying them a visit. The rest, you know.' He shrugged. 'I'm a newspaper man. We put things together.'

Miss Earhart wasn't so easily satisfied. 'Why do you need planes with jet engines?' Her gesture took in Charlie, the

Cardington works, and the countryside beyond. 'You said yourself that travel by zeps and trains suits Europeans just fine.'

The silence between them lengthened. Charlie made a swift decision. Miss Earhart didn't need to know about his chat with Johnny from the Foreign Office in St James's Park. No point in trying to explain to an American that a grammar school boy who got to Cambridge could expect a tap on the shoulder from time to time.

'Cards on the table? You remember what I said about India? Twenty years on and they've bounced right back from the Flu. So have the Chinese, thanks to the Flu hitting the Japanese so hard that they scurried back to their islands and have stayed there ever since. Add to that, the Chinese got rid of their Emperor well before it was the fashion hereabouts.'

Charlie turned to a blank page in his notebook and began sketching a map. 'That means we have the two most powerful countries in the world, each with millions of people and all the resources they might need, both with no good reason to trust outsiders, glaring at each other over the Himalayas. They're constantly wrangling over who has the whip hand over their neighbours to the south and east, so neither of them take kindly to anyone else's airships coming into their skies or steamships trying to cross the seas that they've claimed as their own.'

He finished his map and tapped the last outlines he had drawn. 'Which leaves our cousins in Australia and New Zealand cast thoroughly adrift. But you said it yourself. Fixed wing aircraft with the right engines can cross oceans and continents.'

Miss Earhart contemplated the sketch for a long moment. Then she looked up at Charlie and her eyes were bright with amusement. 'You haven't seen the latest engine prototypes these chaps of yours are working on, have you? They've been reading the journals from the universities in Vienna, Moscow, and Berlin.

Those professors have been working together, striking sparks off each other to fire up some great new ideas.'

'Such as?' Charlie said uncertainly.

'Rocket engines, they're calling them.' Miss Earhart's smile widened. 'They'll get you to Australia. Heck, give them ten years and they'll be ready to shoot for the moon!'

One cannot study history without coming across those points in time where if trivial events had gone slightly differently, we would live in a very different world today. It is remarkable how close the Great War came to not breaking out at all. Perhaps this fascinates me because I can recall talking about those years with my grandparents, great aunts and great uncles whose lives were shaped by that conflict, at the time and for decades after.

The Sphere

When he thought about it later, Henry Tall Deer realised the crash must have woken him. At the time, the only thing he knew was something had startled him awake. Sitting bolt upright in the narrow bed, his heart was racing. What the hell had just happened?

Conscious thought caught up with instinct and suggested there'd been a loud noise. Grabbing the flashlight from the bedside table, he searched the cabin with its beam. As far as he could tell, nothing had toppled from a shelf. There was no one here besides himself to knock over a chair by the scrubbed wooden table. No skittering claws betrayed some furry interloper.

Not that he expected one. The cabin looked as rustic as any other building in these remote valleys but the university ensured it was as weather and vermin proof as modern craftsmanship could make it. First and foremost, that was for the benefit of the costly instruments and computers recording and relaying vital data to the foundations and government departments whose grants paid for them, along with the pittance that just about covered Henry's bills back home.

Hooves outside, running. Not running, stampeding. Throwing back his blankets Henry hurried to unshutter the window. He glimpsed the stragglers as a herd of big horn sheep dashed down the valley towards the first suggestion of dawn.

Running from a bear? A pack of hunting wolves? Henry looked for some predator. At this time of year the nights were short, barely darkening beyond dusk before growing luminous with moonlight.

Instead, he saw a flare soaring up from beyond the ridge. A piercing mote of blue, rising ever higher into the darkness until he lost it amid the countless stars. It wasn't until much later that he realised he should have wondered about that. Weren't distress flares usually red? At the time he was too busy finding a compass and taking a bearing before he lost sight of the sapphire speck.

Turning on the lamp, he dragged on clothes and boots. Checking that the satellite phone was fully charged, he found the first aid kit, substantial enough to warrant its own backpack. Henry grimaced as he slung it on his back and tightened the straps. Hopefully it held whatever he might need to deal with whatever he might find. Calling the emergency services out here still meant waiting for hours. The retired Mountie who'd run Henry's wilderness survival course must have said so twenty times. As if a Nakota who'd grown up on a Montana reservation needed telling. But the university insisted everyone got certified before coming all this way.

One last check. Backpack, flashlight, handheld flares of his own in case he needed to scare off a bear or a bobcat. Water bottle, energy bars, all-purpose knife. Henry unlocked the door and headed out.

He went carefully. He might be familiar with the valley's trails after ten weeks but he'd be no use to anyone if he missed his footing and broke an ankle. There was also no knowing what local wildlife had been disturbed by whoever sent up that flare.

Henry allowed himself a moment of irritation. Who was stupid enough to get themselves into trouble before the sun had even risen? Some small aircraft's pilot? An idiot in a microlight? Hikers seduced by the notion of a night time walk, only to fall down a ravine?

His annoyance rapidly turned to apprehension. Was he going to find himself out of his depth? He was a field biologist, not a medic. His doctorate was on small rodents retreating up mountains to escape climate change.

He kept walking regardless, mentally running through everything he remembered the grizzled Mountie saying about emergency first aid. Really wishing he hadn't seen that movie about the hiker forced to cut off his own arm.

All such concerns evaporated when he finally reached the ridge line. Henry checked his watch and his heart sank. For all his urgency, it had still taken him nearly an hour to get here. The

'Golden Hour' when it came to saving a life, he remembered that Mountie saying.

On the other hand, the sky was light enough by now to give him a clear view of a broad, black scar seared through brush and saplings. He could taste char on the breeze and he spared the local spirits a moment of fervent thanks that the whole valley hadn't gone up in flames.

Something large and metallic lay at the end of the burned gash; angular and artificial and wholly out of place in this landscape. A passenger plane had crashed? He couldn't see anything immediately identifiable as cockpit windows or tail fins though. Was it some piece of a fuselage? He really had no idea. Henry had never paid much attention to planes beyond checking how much leg room he'd get.

As he scanned the rest of the valley, nothing else caught his eye. None of the things he half-remembered from news reports about airline disasters. No pitiful scatter of luggage. No rows of seats ripped free. No yellow emergency slides deployed in vain.

Did that mean the aircraft had broken up in mid-air? If it had, then surely everyone would be dead. There was certainly no sign of movement anywhere near the wreckage. He swallowed hard and wondered what he might find if he went down for a closer look. Sights too gruesome for even the greediest network chasing ratings to show on the nightly news?

He began picking a path down the slope, regardless. If there was someone lying there injured, someone who could still be saved, he didn't have a choice, did he? Though he was guiltily relieved to hear a total absence of anyone crying out in pain as he got nearer.

By the time he was halfway there, he was twice as puzzled. This really didn't look anything like an aircraft, large or small, or even a section of one. Though not all airplanes looked like something from Boeing, he reminded himself. Hadn't early stealth bomber test flights prompted a rash of UFO sightings? Was this something from an experimental, secret research project?

He paused for a moment to study the whole thing. Because it was still pretty much whole. Henry was sure of that now. It was crushed and crumpled around the edges and the impact must have torn off whatever had been attached to those stubby brackets along one side, but overall, this wasn't a piece broken off anything else.

There was also no sign that flames had engulfed it, from burning fuel or some other source. Henry looked again at the path of destruction scorching the valley. Whatever this was, it must have been white hot when it landed, to cause so much damage. Even though its own silvery metallic skin was barely discoloured.

Was this a satellite come crashing to Earth? Some of them were huge nowadays, weren't they? Well, if that's what this was, there couldn't be anyone inside it to be injured. His moment of relief was short-lived. He was still going to have to call it in. Satellite technology cost millions of dollars. Even a field biologist knew that. So the peace and natural rhythm of these woods would soon be shattered by trucks or helicopters or whatever whoever owned this sent to recover the wreckage.

He frowned. Hadn't some Russian satellite scattered radioactive debris all over Saskatchewan in the 70s? Better not get too close. Better alert the authorities as soon as possible. He reached for the satellite phone and hit the emergency speed dial button.

'Hi there, yes –' He quickly identified himself and explained.

The emergency operator didn't sound convinced. 'There's been nothing on the news.'

'Maybe NORAD is still writing their press release?' Henry suggested.

'Maybe a meteor strike –'

'I'd know one of those if I saw it,' Henry interrupted. 'This is definitely man-made. It's the size of a shipping container!'

'You're sure?' the voice persisted.

'Do you think I'm an idiot? Or making this up?' He hadn't expected this response.

'We get a lot of hoaxes,' the voice said repressively. 'Hold please.'

Henry stared at the sat phone with disbelief as tinny music seeped out of it. Could this be a set-up? He looked back down the valley. All the way out here? Who would possibly go to so much trouble? Why would they? To create some internet sensation?

He studied the silvery object. Then he looked for some sign of whatever had been ripped loose in its tumbling crash. Coppery gleams in the undergrowth rewarded him, now fingered by the inquisitive sun. Maybe one of those carried some identification which he could relay to the authorities. Who might this thing belong to? NASA? The Chinese? Didn't India have a space program now?

Or if he found something to prove this was a hoax, he could rip apart the rest of it until he found the webcam or whatever. Then he could tell whoever was responsible exactly what he thought of their stunt damaging this pristine wilderness. Let them put that up on YouTube.

Either way, he wasn't going to stand here on hold. They had his information. He cancelled the call and began to search for some answers.

To his intense disappointment there was no writing on the closest panel, or the next one, or the one after that. Which wasn't to say there were no marks. All the metal was scuffed and gouged and not just from this impact.

As his search took him nearer to the wreck, he felt lingering heat warm his face in the morning chill. Henry looked up to assess how close he'd come to any potential radiation. An instant later, he registered that the darkness in the corner of his eye was a black pelt. Cautiously he turned to get a better look, slowly reaching for the pocket that held his flares. The creature didn't move.

Henry blinked. Then common sense told him that the downed satellite must have hit some unfortunate animal. Except this wasn't some mangled carcass. Whatever it might be, it was strapped into a sizeable chunk of technology. He realised that looking for panels in the undergrowth had taken him around the end of the angular craft. Now he could see where the impact had ripped it open to reveal a hollow interior.

And this had fallen out? What on earth was it? Henry took a step closer. A chimp? A dog? What country was sending animals into space? Maybe that's why there'd been nothing on the news about this thing crashing. Whoever was responsible knew the public outcry would be horrendous.

He reached into a pocket for his own smart phone. A few photos would offer proof, in case anyone in authority tried to cover it up. He focused on the creature and then slowly lowered the phone.

Not a monkey. Not a mammal of any kind. Not any sort of creature that Henry recognised. It had a roughly rectangular body and what looked like four limbs but he couldn't see how they articulated under its fur and there was nothing he could readily identify as a head or a tail. The pelt seemed to have a thick fringe of long black locks with a golden metallic sphere caught up in a tangle on one side.

Was it dead? It wasn't moving but could it just be stunned? Unlikely. If this was some sort of ejector seat, whatever should have slowed its descent didn't seem to have worked. The cradle-thing had hit hard enough to dig deep into the mossy ground and Henry could see several big cracks. It had to be dead. Iridescent in the sunlight, blow flies were now arriving to explore the alien carcass.

There, he'd said it, even if only inside his own head. This was an alien. Which meant this was an alien spaceship. Henry sank to the ground, abruptly breathless. It wasn't only these remote valleys which would never be the same again. He sat still for a long moment, unable to move past that thought.

Gradually he became aware of the familiar sounds and scents of the woodland. He drank some water and ate an energy bar. What now? Well, he was a scientist. That meant gathering data. Then there'd be independent proof this had really happened, whatever the military or whoever else turned up might do when they heard about his phone call.

As he began taking photos, Henry felt profoundly sad. Humanity's first contact with extra-terrestrials had been thwarted by a fatal impact. However far this creature had travelled, it had come so close only for disaster to strike. He really wished things could have been different.

Prestige internship, my ass. David Mendlesohn had been thinking that for days now, though he was sufficiently prudent not to say so out loud. He still held out hope of a transfer to a project more worthy of an MIT student.

It's why he'd crossed the country, goddammit! Why wasn't he working on the intricacies of the alien lander's propulsion system? How about letting him see if he could crack the principles underpinning its communications protocols? After a decade and a half, so much still remained to be done, for all the progress made so far. Fresh eyes might make all the difference. He could be the one to see some vital connection.

He consciously set his irritation aside. He wouldn't get any meaningful opportunity if he shot his mouth off, so he'd bide his time and do what he was told. Even if that meant another tedious afternoon in this empty lab checking that these dusty boxes still held all the scraps from the crashed craft which no one knew what to do with.

He put the lid back on the one he was done with and slid it along the work bench. Flipping over the page on his clipboard, he checked that the number at the top of the typed list matched the label stuck on the next carton.

Okay, that was the first tick. Then he frowned at the entry on the next line. 'Gold sphere – query personal adornment.' What the hell kind of description was that?

He lifted the lid off the box. Okay, there it was, among the scraps of alien alloy and moulded polymer that had never been successfully pieced back together in a way that fit in with the rest of the buckled craft's instrumentation.

David lifted the gold sphere out. It fitted comfortably into the palm of his gloved hand. Personal adornment? Whose dumb idea was that? Necklaces, earrings, brooches, buckles; they had to be attached to whoever was showing them off. There was no sign of any such thing. No loop for a chain, no setting for a hook or a pin.

He weighed it in his hand. There was no way this was solid gold. On the other hand, it didn't feel light enough to be hollow. David turned it this way and that, to take a closer look. No, there was no hint of a seam, still less any hint of how to open it.

He stiffened as his phone vibrated in his pocket. Putting the golden sphere down on the lab bench, he fished it out. A swipe of his finger across the screen was no use. Goddam latex gloves. He hastily stripped them off and managed to answer before the last ring.

'Hey, Rebecca.'

'How's California?'

He could hear the smile in his sister's voice and grinned back as he gazed out of the window at the verdant landscaped grounds, the ochre hills in the far distance, and the cloudless blue sky above. 'Pretty cool.'

'Listen, are you bringing a plus one to Leah's bat mitzvah? I need to let the caterers know final numbers by the end of the week.'

David's phone interrupted with a beep. He looked at the screen to see the low battery warning.

'Yes, yes, I'll bring someone.'

'Someone or just anyone to stop Mom asking about your love life?' Rebecca countered. 'That's a lousy thing to do to a date, Davy.'

'So's shoving someone special in front of Mom and the aunts,' he retorted.

'So come alone.' Her voice softened. 'We just want to see you.'

The phone beeped again.

'I'll be there,' he assured her. 'And I'll let you know by the end of the week.'

'Okay, talk soon.' Rebecca rang off.

David found his backpack and dug out his charger. Thankfully there were unused electrical outlets all along the wall at the back of the bench.

He'd ring Sarah when he was finished here and ask her out for a drink. After he'd worked out how to invite her to a family event in a way that would show he wanted to spend more time with her – while making it clear it really wasn't any kind of big deal whether she said yes or no to this particular trip.

The gold sphere rolled across the bench. David snatched it up before it could fall to the floor. An instant of stomach churning panic subsided into relief. Catastrophe averted. He wouldn't be forever labelled as the klutz who'd broken some invaluable alien salvage. Because everything from the Kiruk Valley Lander was priceless even if no one knew what it might be.

The golden sphere buzzed and pulsed in his hand. In his *ungloved* hand. Sweat beaded his forehead in spite of the air conditioning. What the hell...?

David set the sphere back down with exquisite care. As it moved of its own accord, he stepped back, startled. The sphere wasn't following the lure of gravity towards the edge of the bench. It rolled over to the outlet and snuggled up to his phone charger.

What the hell...? He flexed his empty hand and looked at it closely, both sides. No weird sensations, no marks on his skin. He drew a slow measured breath.

Okay, so that happened. Now he had to decide who to tell and exactly what to say, to make absolutely goddam certain that he was one of the team set up to work out what it meant.

The computer completed its calculations and shared its conclusions with impersonal detachment. The numbers didn't match. So Namrita Kaur was the first to know that another exoplanet was conclusively ruled out as the origin of the universe's only other incontrovertibly-proven-to-exist intelligent life form.

Or rather, as the source of alien life bright enough to achieve near-lightspeed space travel, she corrected herself. Any number of these planets still might be home to less exalted creatures. And this was all progress, wasn't it? Another step along the way towards the ultimate goal. Sooner or later there had to be good news.

Of course, sooner would be better than later. What now? Namrita contemplated the data so painstakingly gleaned from over a quarter of a century's analysis of every scrap of information from the Kiruk Valley Lander's crash site. She didn't need to pull up the source file. She knew every line.

Leaning back in her chair, she stretched out her arms, grimacing as she felt the tension knotting her shoulders. Time to get up and walk around. Get the blood circulating. Maybe shake loose some new ideas.

Though a change was as good as a rest, wasn't it? That's what everyone's supervisors said, explaining why side projects were permitted, even encouraged. She accessed her personal drive and checked on the analysis she'd set running this morning before starting her official work.

Another dead end. Despite her determination to stay positive, Namrita felt a pang of disappointment. That meant the very end of this particular road. Whichever way you sliced, diced, or analysed those numbers, whether you converted the digital pulses into any and all numeral systems from binary on upwards, she reckoned she had now proven that the Mendlesohn Sphere's output bore no relation to any of the mathematical principles underpinning gravitational physics.

Or astrophysics or nuclear physics or quantum theory or anything else, according to the records left by those before her who'd been intrigued by this puzzle. Or chemistry: organic or inorganic. Or biology, for all Namrita knew. In the years since the mysterious artifact had so accidentally come to life, someone must have looked at its output in relation to whatever numbers were generated by the study of plants and animals.

Time for a cup of tea. She got up and walked to the far end of the long, hushed room. A few faces glanced up before concentrating once more on their own computer screens. The only sounds were the muted rattle of keyboards, the occasional creak of a chair, and here and there the soft scritch of paper on pencil. She'd never met a mathematician who could do without what her father always referred to as a 'thinking stick'.

She pushed open the kitchen door to be greeted by the cheery chirp of the drinks dispenser. Edmund looked around, stirring some frothy concoction.

'Tea?' He put down his mug and reached for another one. 'How's life in number crunching? Anything exciting to report?'

Namrita opened the cupboard, took out the canister and measured leaves into the small teapot she'd brought in from home. 'More planets ruled out. Of course, it would help if you telescope jockeys didn't keep finding new ones to add to the list.'

Ed grinned. 'You can't hold back science. How are you getting on with the Mendlesohn Sphere?'

Seeing the mischief in his eyes, Namrita narrowed her own gaze. 'Why do you ask?'

'It's just that I heard a rumour...' Ed held out a hand.

Namrita gave him the teapot. 'Go on.'

He pressed the lever and hot water hissed onto the tea leaves. 'Kate, over in Material Sciences, she was saying they reckon it's just a test.'

'The Sphere?' Namrita frowned, bemused.

He nodded. 'Ask around and you'll soon find out how many supervisors suggest it as a side project, whatever your particular discipline is. Kate and her team think they just want to see how long people will stick with it, before they realise there's nothing to be learned. Someone's probably running a pool.'

'It must have some purpose,' Namrita objected. 'Why else would it be on the Lander?'

Ed shrugged. 'Who knows? "Intelligences greater than man's" and all that.'

She challenged him with raised eyebrows. 'You're still expecting tripods and heat rays?'

He shrugged again. 'I'm just amazed someone hasn't taken a can opener to it by now.'

'What would that achieve?' she protested. 'We've got the output to analyse. Taking the Sphere itself to pieces would be as pointless as cutting into a tennis ball to try to find the bounce.'

Ed grinned. 'I'll see if I can get a bet on you sticking with it for a while longer then. See you in the pub later? A bunch of us are going to The Bird and Baby. Kate's got a cousin visiting.'

She nodded. 'I'll stop by.'

'Great. Well, better get back to it.' Finishing his drink with a few rapid swallows, Ed sketched a wave and left through the kitchen's other door, heading down the corridor.

Namrita poured her tea and stared through the kitchen window, past the twenty-first century's chrome and glass towards Oxford's ageless towers and spires. Mankind's finest minds had spent centuries in this city of golden stone solving the mysteries of the universe. The Lander and everything in it was just one more conundrum.

Though, of course, Oxford's scholars weren't only scientists. She frowned, sipping tea, as she tried to pin down an elusive memory, stirred by her conversation with Edmund.

'He that breaks a thing to find out what it is has left the path of wisdom.'

That was it. That's what JRR Tolkien had Gandalf say to Saruman in *The Lord of the Rings*. She'd have to remember that for the next time someone suggested cutting into the Mendlesohn Sphere.

Namrita headed back to her desk, thinking about journeys. Why did people take things with them? Sitting down, she opened the top drawer to her right and contemplated the contents. Pencils. A sharpener. Spare data chips and power cells for her handheld. Hair clips. A comb. Her expired digibadge for the Lucasian Professor's seminar when she'd visited Cambridge last month. No use any more but she wasn't about to throw it away.

Not everything was purely utilitarian. The picube her sister-in-law had sent from Sri Harmandir Sahib. Namrita shook it and the digital image of Variam with her nephews and niece in front of the golden temple floated to the top. Smiling, she put it down beside the earbuds for the musicube she'd got free with that gym membership she almost never used.

She carefully closed the drawer and woke up her computer with a tap on the fingerprint reader. A quick search of the Mendlesohn Sphere archive confirmed her first thoughts. Every possible way of turning the output into a visible image had long since been tried.

What about audio? It seemed various people had tried a few different approaches over the years. She called up their notes and began reading. After a little while, she reached for a pad and a pencil and jotted down some random thoughts. Soon after, she began working through a series of far from random equations.

'Time to call it a day?'

She looked up, startled, to see Padraig standing by his desk, easing his stiff neck this way and that. Glancing round, Namrita realised they were the last two left in the room. She hadn't even noticed the others leaving.

As Padraig had evidently observed. 'What's got you so ent'ralled?'

'Just an idea.' She contemplated her screen where she'd called up an array of sound processing software. Did she have everything she needed? Pretty much.

'Anything you're ready to share?' Padraig shrugged on his jacket and tucked his handheld into an inner pocket.

He'd be on his way any minute now. Should she try to explain or keep quiet until he'd gone, or maybe, just –

'Let's see.' Namrita caught her lower lip between her teeth as she hit a rapid sequence of keystrokes.

An instant later, melody floated through the empty room. It was definitely a tune, though subtly unfamiliar to her ears, and Padraig's, too, judging from his expression.

'What's that?' He looked at her, intrigued.

Namrita couldn't help laughing. 'The music of the spheres. Of the Mendlesohn Sphere, to be exact.'

'Oh look, it's ET's iPod!' a bearded man observed archly.

'How long have you been waiting to share that retro gem?' his companion mocked.

Namrita did her best not to scowl at the couple who barely spared a glance for the display case holding the golden sphere before wandering away.

Wasn't it worth noting the hard work and particularly the lateral thinking that had gone into discovering its purpose? Wasn't the alien music worthy of respect on its own merits? But every second person who'd commented on this particular exhibit had seemed to dismiss it as trivial.

Unwelcome suspicion soured the lingering taste of the reception's champagne. Was there something like that inanity written on the card inside the case? It wasn't as if any scientist had been included in the team putting this exhibition together. Diplomats, media experts, and public relations specialists had taken charge of making the arrangements months before.

They'd probably been planning it for years. Starting within minutes of the first signals from the Travellers' ship reaching the Hawking Probe, most likely. The success of tonight's gathering was doubtless going to make or break careers.

But before Namrita could get close enough to see what some communications genius might have written about the Sphere, another woman came up to peer into the glassy box. The stranger's face lit up with sudden delight, framed by long hair as glossily black as Namrita's grey locks had once been.

Despite her lingering irritation, Namrita was intrigued. Then she saw the name on the woman's digibadge. Approaching, she offered her hand.

'Laura Tall Deer? Any relation to –?'

'– Henry? My grandfather.' The American shook Namrita's hand and checked her digibadge. 'And you're the genius who unlocked the music! He was so thrilled. He always wondered what the sphere could be.'

Laura broke off as someone else approached. Another courtesy guest, according to the hologram on his badge.

He held up apologetic hands. 'Please, take your time. Don't let me disturb you.'

'Join us, please.' Namrita invited him closer with a gesture when she saw his name. 'Mr Mendlesohn.'

'Please, call me Simon, and yes, I'm his son.' He smiled ruefully. 'But no, I'm not a scientist. I'm a dentist.'

'Do they have teeth, do you suppose?' Laura Tall Deer wondered mischievously.

All three of them turned to look at the two closest aliens, of the eight that were currently wandering round the exhibits, discreetly shadowed by heavy-set, square-shouldered men with very short hair and expensively tailored suits.

'Are you a zoologist?' Namrita recalled reading somewhere that Henry Tall Deer had been something of that sort.

Laura shook her head. 'Astronomer. Grandad took me out to show me the stars from Kiruk Valley when I was six years old and told me about the night when the Lander crashed. I've been trying to find out where it came from ever since.'

She studied the aliens as they flanked a case containing a replica of the Hawking Probe. 'He'd have been fascinated to see them walking around.'

'Aren't we all?' Simon Mendlesohn laughed a little nervously.

Every biologist certainly was, if Namrita's professional-cloud tag-stream was any indicator. The questions were endless and the misconceptions extrapolated from the First Scout's corpse had turned out to be legion.

That black pelt? Not fur. A living Traveller was enveloped by a sensory organ composed of hundreds of thousands of filaments. However they perceived the world around them – and Namrita really didn't envy whoever had to find a way to ask politely for details about that – they responded with swirls and ripples of every possible colour and shade coruscating from head to toe.

So to speak, given they didn't have either heads or toes. It turned out the Travellers used all four limbs for walking on or manipulating things utilising each limb's four digits with equal ease. They would also head straight in whatever direction they wanted to without feeling any need to turn around. Depending on what they were doing, their overall body shape could be rectangular, square or trapezoid.

'Er, I think they're coming this way.' Simon unconsciously retreated a pace.

Laura stiffened. 'I hope I didn't offend them. Was I staring?'

She had been, but there was no point in saying so. Namrita reminded herself that she was the oldest of the trio and the only one who'd actually met one of the Travellers before, when the ship's navigator had visited Oxford ten days ago. Though that had been to discuss mathematics, not a trip for socialising or sightseeing.

She took a step forward and summoned up a welcoming smile. She only hoped the Travellers stayed on all fours, or on two feet at least. Last week, when the navigator had stood up on a single limb in order to use all three others at once, it had towered over the tallest man in the gathering in a distinctly unnerving fashion.

'Good evening.'

'Good evening.' The first Traveller's polite response came from the silvery translation box it carried in its – well, the biologists as well as the journalists were still arguing about what to call the fringe of what were now self-evidently not just passive locks of hair or fur. Each tendril was mobile, flexible, tactile, and Namrita had seen for herself how swiftly the navigator had worked out how to type with them on a human keyboard.

She took refuge in conventional courtesy. 'How are you enjoying the evening?'

'It is very pleasing to meet so many of the humans who have devoted their time, effort, and skills to making contact with our people.' The first Traveller's words were smooth, accentless and effortlessly fluent.

Namrita could only imagine the chagrin among the linguists who'd painstakingly developed the protocols for learning an alien language, when it turned out the aliens themselves had perfected a translation device capable of handling every widely broadcast language.

She didn't imagine the diplomats were any too pleased either. All the ones she'd encountered had naturally assumed they would control access to and communication with the Travellers. It turned out these aliens had other ideas.

The second one moved forward, waves of purple rippling towards Namrita. 'We are most honoured to meet you, Professor Kaur. May I take your hand?'

'I —' Namrita steeled herself. 'The honour is all mine.'

They're not tentacles. Not tentacles. Really not tentacles.

As she extended her hand, the second Traveller's tendrils enveloped it, colours shifting through the rainbow from scarlet at the tip to violet at the root. The firm caress wasn't in the least unpleasant, silky and comfortably warm.

'May I ask,' the alien enquired politely, 'what inspired you to study the sphere in your youth?'

'It was a puzzle.' What else could she say? 'I've always liked a challenge.'

Her reply prompted nearly identical flashes of silver across each Traveller's pelt. She wondered what that meant.

The first one had turned its attention to Simon Mendlesohn. 'And you are the son of the man who made such a fortunate discovery when the sphere lacked energy. There is great honour among our kind for those who are lucky.'

Perhaps it sensed his nervousness. It made no request to touch his hand before spiky waves of green indicated its focus shifting to Laura. 'While your ancestor was the first human to see the First Scout after death?'

'He was, yes.' Laura's answer prompted those same flashes of silver from each Traveller.

'Please —'

Was it Namrita's imagination or was there a note of urgency in the second alien's modulated, artificial voice?

'– did your ancestor ever say exactly where the sphere was found?'

Laura nodded. 'The First Scout had it – that's to say, he was holding it. Or she, excuse me,' she added hastily.

Questions of alien gender could wait as far as Namrita was concerned. She wanted to know why that answer prompted both Travellers to entwine a handful of tendrils and link with each other. Sparkling white surged from one to the other and back again.

She wondered how unnerving the diplomats found the realisation that these aliens could communicate in ways they had no hope of understanding.

'That's good news?' Simon Mendlesohn edged forward. 'Why? What's the thing for, anyway?'

The Travellers loosed their hold on each other and the first one addressed him. 'It is –'

His translation box emitted an incomprehensible garble.

Yellow swirled around the device each Traveller held.

The second alien tried. 'That is to say, it serves as –'

Once again, the translator burbled nonsense. Yellow swirls darkened to orange.

'Is there a problem, sir?' The Travellers' dark suited escort stepped forward with a warning look at the three humans.

Namrita wasn't bothered. She guessed that glare was the security detail's automatic reaction to anything unexpected. She was more curious about the translation device's failure. When the navigator had visited Oxford, his box had been perfectly able to handle every variation on academic titles and every possible distinction between various specialities in maths and physics.

'Forgive us,' the first Traveller said, and this time, Namrita was convinced she could hear irritation underpinning its words. 'We seem to have discovered a lack in our translators' priorities.'

The second alien chose its words carefully. 'The purpose of the music is to focus the mind on –'

Gibberish defeated it again but now the first Traveller found a solution.

'– to focus the mind upon the divine.'

'The divine?' Namrita hadn't expected that.

'The divine.' The second alien's closest tendrils twitched in her direction. 'Is that the correct word? You understand what we mean by that?'

'Yes, at least, I think so.' She hastily qualified her answer.

Each alien's shifting pattern of colours instantly stilled.

'Please,' the first Traveller invited, 'tell us what humanity knows of the divine?'

'Please,' the second echoed.

Namrita looked at Simon Mendlesohn and Laura Tall Deer and saw the same question that now paralysed her tongue was reflected in their eyes.

Where on Earth could they possibly start?

I have always loved science fiction, even though I have always found a great deal of actual science frankly baffling. The idea that mathematics is a universal language which will enable communication with aliens is an appealing one that often comes up, but I feel very strongly that the arts, languages and humanities need to be included in any first contact scenario.

Speak Softly and Carry a Big Stick

We were moving as quietly as we could. Thankfully the matt black flooring was designed to absorb as much noise as possible. The curved walls and ceiling were coated with soft blue anechoic paint. The last thing any of us need is the incessant bombardment of voices or the clatter of equipment or tools constantly bounced back by hard surfaces. There's enough stress on a space station, even for men and women whose tendency to claustrophobia is way below the minimum threshold for off-world deployment.

I raised a hand as we rounded a corner and everyone stood still. I strained my ears for sound up ahead. Nothing. That didn't mean he wasn't there, beyond the next pressure door. He could be lurking just out of sight, with the same noise suppression measures ensuring we couldn't hear his harsh breathing.

He must be somewhere in these Storage levels. Another team had finally reported checking the last of Technical, and Habitation had been cleared first of all. Now every door in those sectors was shut; every corridor empty. Everyone not directly engaged in this hunt had locked themselves in their own quarters, singleton or family unit, for fear of the killer loose in the station.

He had to be somewhere close. He was running out of places to hide.

'Doctor –?'

My head snapped around and I glared at the woman at my shoulder. Even Stanton's whisper sounded deafening in this silence. I could only hope it hadn't carried further than the pressure door. If our quarry heard voices, he'd know we were here. He already knew we were after him.

Then I saw the strain in the old warrior's eyes. She'd been a career marine and loved space too much to ever go back dirtside, but she'd been retired for over a decade. Besides, in all her deployments against Mars separatists, Asteroid Belt renegades and plain old-fashioned criminals, she'd never faced an enemy like the one threatening to kill everybody now.

Looking down the line of the search party, I realised Stanton wasn't the only weary one. Yamaguchi, Bradley, Ibn Kathir and Schmidt all looked as exhausted as Anders bringing up the rear where hopefully he couldn't do any harm. It wasn't as if Gowrie could be behind him. We were locking each sector we cleared, using a fresh door code Gowrie couldn't possibly know.

I checked my chronometer and was startled to see how long it had been since we'd begun this sweep, section by section, corridor by corridor. Why wasn't I as tired as everyone else?

Well, some things about being a surgeon have never changed, no matter how much instruments, scans or drugs have advanced since humanity escaped Earth's gravity.

You get used to spending long hours concentrating, no matter how many times you may have done any given procedure before. You take the operation step by step, never missing something out or cutting a corner. You make all the same checks you've made time after time to be certain that you'll catch anything unexpected. Then you can look your patient in the eye when they come round from the anaesthetic and you assure them that they're going to be fine.

But before I'd been sent after Gowrie, I'd spent ten devastating days tending patients who'd never opened their eyes as they'd slipped from delirium into coma and finally into cascading organ failure, no matter what combination of vaccine-emulators and bacteriophages we pumped into them.

I shouldn't be dwelling on that. I should be concentrating on the task in hand. What would this tell me, if I was evaluating a patient?

That I was more tired than I realised. If my thoughts were wandering, we were all overdue a break.

We had to pace ourselves. There were still plenty of sections, corridors and levels to cover. Titan Lagrange Four might look insignificant against the moon and that's dwarfed by Saturn itself but this station's population, habitation and storage capacity is still more than you'd find if you stuck all of a small town's buildings together back on Earth.

I nodded at Stanton and answered as quietly as I could. 'We'll take ten minutes here.'

I used my remote on the pressure door ahead of us. Once that was shut, we could talk more normally without worrying that Gowrie would hear us.

Anders was already flat on his back on the black decking. He was trying to ease the stiffness in his shoulders, torso and legs. I'd shown him some stretches when I'd realised he was going to cripple himself, skulking along, tense and hunched over the stun gun he'd been issued.

It wasn't Ander's fault. He'd never learned the muscle relaxation skills that were second nature to Stanton and to me, thanks to our very different training. Anders was a cargo-chucker and a junior one at that. At the start of his second half-year, he was still getting to grips with despatching his allocated drones to catch containers of elements skim-mined from Saturn's atmosphere and sling-shotting them through the hyper-gate for a skip back to Earth, Mars and the Belt.

In between times, he'd be catching containers of supplies coming our way; assorted fabricator-mediums and the luxuries so essential for morale. 3D printers can do a lot but they can't do everything. A bit like personnel.

Anders could never have expected to find himself on a manhunt, any more than the others would. Stanton, retired marine and now hyper-skip safety compliance officer: Yamaguchi, waste management engineer: Bradley, Oort Cloud astronomer: Ibn Kathir, sensor array analyst and Schmidt, zero gravity chemist.

Like me, they'd been drafted as soon as Command Echelon got permission from Earth to declare a State of Emergency. That made us all subject to Crisis Discipline. Though no one was inclined to argue. If we couldn't track down Gowrie and capture him, everyone on this station, men, women and children, would end up as dead as some oxygen-thief shoved out of an airlock in a suspiciously plausible accident.

I was the one leading this pursuit to make absolutely certain no accidents happened to Gowrie. Physicians still swear the same ancient oath. First, do no harm.

Yamaguchi sat on the floor and took a long drink from his belt bottle. He looked at me. He'd only joined us this morning. On our fifth day clearing these corridors we'd had word from Command Level. Tshuma's husband had fallen ill. Even though she'd only be able to hold his hand through four layers of plastic, she wanted to be at his side. Since I knew she'd be unable to concentrate with her thoughts constantly turning to Med Level, I'd immediately agreed to let her go.

'They said it was just Swap Flu.'

I could see Yamaguchi wanted to ask the same questions they all had, once they realised I was on detachment from Medical. 'It was, to begin with.'

We'd been ready and waiting, on Med Level, for the usual plague of sneezing, coughs, headaches and low-grade fevers. Swap Flu. The predictable result of a whole host of pathogens arriving with the new personnel and seizing their chance to mingle and mutate with each other as well as with the station's existing population of germs.

We'd been equally well prepared for the secondary infections that some unlucky few would succumb to; ears, sinuses and respiratory tract. Nothing life-threatening with modern medicine and with every newcomer pre-screened for genetic vulnerabilities. Everyone would be fully up to date with their mandatory inoculations.

Swap Flu is nothing new. No station's ever found a way to avoid it so now we accept it. It's even cited as one reason for standard assignments lasting six Earth months. The temporary dip in station performance is acceptable twice a year but the consequences of bringing in personnel more frequently would be problematic.

That and there's the eye-watering cost of bringing living, breathing human beings safely through a hyper-skip to the outer planets. So much more expensive than cargo or resources that can stand hard vacuum. I'm still not convinced that any government or corporation will ever finance a full-scale hyper-jump to establish an exoplanet colony. Even if the astrogators ever work out how to get there reliably. Any separatists who really want to leave this solar system had better find the money themselves.

I realised I was losing focus and snatched a swallow from my own belt bottle. It didn't take much of the energy drink spiked with my own personal cocktail of stimulants to sharpen my wits. At least I knew I couldn't be suffering from anything worse than tiredness. Not yet.

'It was just Swap Flu until Gowrie arrived.' And everyone sent on this hunt had already had this latest variant and recovered.

Yamaguchi interrupted. 'But surely you knew he was from Mars?'

He wasn't accusing me personally. But I was the closest thing he had to a representative of the station's management. I began to explain.

'From Mars, yes. Not from Ophyr.'

Stanton spoke up a second before Yamaguchi could interrupt. She was leaning against the wall rather than sitting down, not wanting to have to get all the way back up.

'His records had been falsified, back before he was even enrolled in primary school. According to the data on his ident chip, he was from Mangala Valles. No red flags there.'

I guessed I shouldn't be surprised she had found that out. Once a marine, always a marine and every soldier knows the value of good intelligence. Just like every doctor knows they need a full medical history. These days an ident chip is supposed to counter people's tendency to leave things out on account of forgetfulness and to counter the lies they tell out of shame or whatever seems like a good reason at the time.

Schmidt cleared her throat. 'What happened at Ophyr, exactly?'

I wondered what rumours she'd heard. There have been wild stories swirling around the grey and black Webs ever since the disaster. One of my tutors at medical school had delighted in horrifying us with half-baked theories and gruesome exaggerations before scientifically ripping them to shreds.

'The Ophyr settlers were Clean Living Advocates –'

'On Mars,' Yamaguchi scoffed.

I ignored him, not about to get sidetracked into the hypocrisy of people claiming their ethical beliefs demanded they cut themselves off from humanity. Other than maintaining contact with those people paying the costs of sustaining them in the hostile Martian habitat, obviously. I'd never understood how anyone could be suckered by the slick half-truths peddled by well-groomed professional ethicists on mass-channel video. All donations gratefully received, as they say, and swiftly obscured with barely legal accounting, as they never mention.

My thoughts were wandering yet again. I concentrated on answering Schmidt. 'These were real zealots; CLA separatists. Before Ophyr, one of the things they rejected was vaccination. Then the Ophyr Plague struck.'

'What was it, exactly?' Schmidt was hollow-eyed with apprehension.

'Honestly? No one knows. Our best guess –' by which I meant the entire medical profession '– is they stirred up some Martian virus latent in the soil when they were digging foundations and service trenches for their habitat domes. We don't know what pathogens some of the separatists were already incubating but a Martian virus found something it liked enough to join up and mutate with.'

'And it killed them,' Ibn Kathir said quietly. 'Horribly.'

I nodded. 'Some sort of haemorrhagic fever with a particular affinity for the lungs.'

Which is why the disaster response teams found so many corpses with blood-caked mouths. That's what sparked hysterical stories of vampiric Martian ghosts possessing the unlucky colonists. That appealed to the people who didn't believe this was biological warfare waged on the separatists by Earth's political echelons.

'But the plague didn't kill them all.' Yamaguchi sounded accusing again. 'Didn't the authorities keep track of the survivors?'

'They were supposed to but some of them obviously slipped through their fingers in the confusion. Kids, mostly.'

'Like Gowrie,' Bradley said grimly.

I answered with something between a nod and a shrug. That tutor in medical school had been a very junior member of the clean up team. He'd related the constant interference from CLA public relations pests arriving by hyper-hop barely a day after the news hit the Grey Web.

They'd been quickly followed by several contingents of so-called aid workers. Money was no object as they tried to conceal this disaster. Even if a hop is only a hundredth the cost of a hyper-skip to the outer planets, that still doesn't make it cheap.

Presumably CLA funds paid for the falsified ident chip in Gowrie's arm, once their activists smuggled the small boy to Mangala Valles and found a family willing to foster him, with more CLA cash to keep their mouths shut.

'How did he end up here?

'How come he isn't dead, if he's got Ophyr Plague?'

Bradley and Anders asked their questions at the same time. I answered them in turn.

'He got here just like the rest of us. Liked the idea of deep space work, loved the pay enhancements and bonuses, applied and got a job. He's not dead because he must have had Ophyr Plague as a kid and survived it. Except, as it turns out, it's one of those viruses that linger in the body, tucked away in the spinal column or somewhere, like Chicken Pox.'

I could see confused faces along the corridor. I waved that digression away.

'The Ophyr virus revived when Gowrie's immune system took a hammering from Swap Flu. Except all he had to show for it was an unusually persistent cough.'

That was according to his neighbours, when we finally identified him as Patient Zero, after tracking back the contacts of the first handful of people turning up in Medical coughing blood.

By the time we had done that, our few patients had turned into dozens. We escalated to Contagion Protocol but that didn't do us much good for the next few days. Knowing where this new disease had come from hadn't helped save people who'd already been exposed. All of those neighbours were dead now.

'He still had antibodies in his blood from when he was a kid,' I explained, 'so he was able to fight it off a second time.'

'So now we need his blood.' Ibn Kathir was as soft-spoken as ever.

I tried to make a joke of it, patting the med satchel on my hip, holding sterile needles, syringes and vials. 'You could say a vampire really is after him.'

No one laughed.

I pushed myself away from the wall where I'd been leaning. 'Come on. The sooner we find him, the sooner this will all be over.'

As soon as I was satisfied that everyone was ready, I entered the code on the remote. Pressure seals yielded with a gentle hiss.

We moved onwards, silent, alert as we could be after so long. More storage bays opened up beyond this next corridor and clearing them would be a nerve-wracking task.

We entered the first vast space. Schmidt and Anders stayed by the door; one of them to make sure Gowrie couldn't make a break for it if we found him in there. The other one would watch the corridor in case he tried to slip past while we were occupied.

That left me, Stanton and Yamaguchi, Bradley and Ibn Kathir searching the stacks of bulk containers. Each bay held sixteen stacks in standard formation, four by four. So Bradley walked down the outside on the left while Yamaguchi, me and Stanton took the aisles cutting between the stacks. Ibn Kathir shadowed us on the far right hand side. At each intersection, we all paused and looked right and left, to see if Gowrie was cowering between us.

Halting like this would also check we were keeping pace with each other. If someone got ahead of the rest, Gowrie might attack them. By now we'd done this so often we matched each other step for step without even thinking about it. As we reached the first transverse aisle, we stopped as if we'd been synchronised.

At my nod, we moved on, silently. I really hoped we'd catch Gowrie before our next scheduled downtime. That's when I'd have to report into Medical and deal with the latest brilliant ideas from Command Echelon's fevered brains.

Why weren't we tracking him using the station's sensor net? Because that's not designed for following people. It's there to monitor leaks and spills and changes in air pressure inside and impacts from micro-meteors outside. Anything that could indicate a compromised environment.

It's not as if strangers can just wander into a space station. Central records show who's arrived and who's left and while they're here, it turns out that people work best with minimal supervision. Knowing you're always being watched will spark claustrophobia in even the most well-balanced.

Yes, ident chips are programmed with individual access codes but that works on the principle of only locking people out of areas where they definitely must not go instead of only permitting them to access areas where they live or work. If some unforeseen emergency arises, no one is going to die here because a computer is locking them out of their only route to safety.

Yes, we might still have been able to use ident access to help us find him, except for two things. Firstly, Gowrie was a data-shuffler by trade. As soon as he knew we were after him, he'd given himself some sort of universal pass code. That's why we needed the handhelds to lock him out, portal by portal.

Secondly the one person with the skills to write a subroutine to show us which doors Gowrie had used was currently in an iso-tent on Med level, desperately trying to suppress the cough that was shredding his lungs. As we reached the second transverse aisle, I wondered how Ap Rhys was doing.

Over to my right, Stanton froze. I looked at her, eyebrows raised in a silent question. She tapped her ear and I strained to listen for whatever she had heard.

To my left, Yamaguchi hadn't noticed. He frowned at me, ready to walk on, until Stanton snagged his attention with a furiously waving arm. Beyond her, Ibn Kathir stood motionless. I checked left and saw that Bradley was waiting, poised, as well.

I listened again. There it was. Soft but unmistakeable. Someone trying to stifle a cough. We'd found Gowrie.

But where exactly was he? There was still one transverse aisle to clear and then we'd reach the wider space extending from the end of the bulk stacks to the bay wall. Which pair of us would he be caught between?

I stowed the door remote safely in a pocket. I carefully unslung the long, narrow bag I'd been carrying across my back all through this hunt. Slowly I slid the fighting stave out, making sure not to knock the hollow metal containers. Close as we were, Gowrie still might not know we were in here too. No sense in alerting him before we had to.

Even now, when we'd reached the most dangerous point in this quest, I couldn't help a grin as I slid the staff between my hands. Gannon's face had been a picture of bemusement when I'd described what I'd wanted from his industrial scale 3D printer; this was when I first arrived on the station and still had fabrication credits to spend.

As close an approximation to hardwood as he could manage; 1800 mil long and 30 mil in diameter. A quarterstaff, I'd explained. My hobby was Historic European Martial Arts and this was my preferred weapon. For one thing I could do solo drills with it, not needing a partner. It was a great way to keep myself fit and supple, to counter long hours spent at the desk in my consulting room, in the lab or in the operating theatre.

'I see,' he'd said unconvincingly. At least he hadn't protested that the staff was longer than I was tall, or wondered aloud why a slip of a girl like me had such a peculiar, not to say violent, hobby. I've become used to unguarded comments like that, though seldom from other martial artists, whatever their chosen tradition. Most who've trained for any length of time, however manly and muscled, have been soundly thrashed sometime or other, by a woman whose skills outstripped their own.

An ex-Marine, though? As I glanced at Stanton again, I could see she was still struggling to hide her scepticism. She'd been vocal in her opposition when I'd first put forward my plan, when we discussed how to capture Gowrie. What could I possibly achieve with a medieval weapon on a 23rd century space station?

There'd been so much I could have told her. How medieval authorities on close-quarters combat praised the quarterstaff's versatility and flexibility, against swords or any other weapon. It can be used effectively in defence as well as attack, switching from one to the other in seconds. It's a great weapon against more than one opponent. In 1625, a captured English sailor won his freedom from the Duke of Medina by defeating three Spaniards who attacked him at once. Why do you think medieval nobles were always so nervous about peasants' revolts?

Since none of that seemed likely to impress a Marine, I'd settled for a medical argument. We needed to capture Gowrie alive and if at all possible without stunning him. The original Ophyr Plague had attacked the heart as well as the lungs. We were seeing similar symptoms in our current patients and although Gowrie had survived, we had no idea what damage even a mild dose of this new, modified virus might have done. A stun could throw him into a potentially fatal arrhythmia.

Add to that, as effective as modern stun guns are, the shock still alters blood chemistry, raising carbon dioxide levels and acidity. This wasn't just about finding antibodies to synthesise a vaccine and vaccine-emulators. If I was going to understand what this disease had done to him, so I could find the best treatments to sustain the patients up in Medical, I needed his blood samples as untainted as possible.

We also wanted to capture him with the least close physical contact. We'd all had the latest Swap Flu but none of us had come into contact with Gowrie and this new Ophyr virus variant. That's why we'd been drafted for this mission. That's how we knew we'd stay healthy long enough to see it through. But we sure as hell didn't want him getting close enough to cough on anyone now.

I could achieve all this by taking Gowrie down with my stick, I had assured Stanton. Even if he was 200 mil taller than me. Her agreement was the very definition of grudging and she insisted she'd use her stun gun the instant she judged Gowrie was getting the better of me. From her tone it was clear she expected that would be a case of 'when' not 'if'.

Taking a deep breath, I held the staff loosely in both my hands, pointing front and back. Looking to left and right, I nodded. I was ready.

Gowrie wasn't in the final transverse aisle. Ibn Kathir, of all people, was so exasperated he forgot himself and swore loudly in the lyrical Arabic he'd learned at his mother's knee.

'Who's there?' Gowrie's screech was shocking in the silence.

'Anna Westwick, from Medical,' I called out.

'Go away!' He sounded hysterical.

'I can't do that.' Calm, just like dealing with any fractious patient.

'It's not my fault!'

'It's no one's fault. We still have to deal with it.' Leaning my staff against the metal container wall, I got gloves and a mask out of my med satchel.

'So go and deal with it! Leave me alone!' Now he was belligerent.

'We need you to come with us.' I put the mask on but didn't cover my mouth, so he wouldn't hear any change in my voice.

'No! You can't make me! You can't prove anything!'

That was what this was about. That's why he'd run, as pointless as that was on a space station nearly a billion and a half kilometres from the sun. Until we had his blood to prove he had Ophyr antibodies, until Ap Rhys or someone like him could pinpoint how and when his ident chip had been falsified, Gowrie couldn't be blamed for the catastrophe here. That's what he was trying to escape; the crushing guilt of being responsible for several hundred deaths and however many more were yet to come.

'I didn't realise. I didn't know!' Now he was yelling. 'I don't remember any of it. I never even suspected my ident was forged.'

Stanton clicked her tongue to get my attention. I could see she was impatient to get this over and done with. I frowned at her before answering Gowrie.

'We know.'

'Then leave me alone!' he raged.

'We can't do that.'

And Gowrie already knew it. When we'd identified him as Patient Zero, Dewell, Head of Medical Echelon, had led a masked and gloved team to his quarters, explaining the need for blood samples to help our other patients. No one had expected him to refuse, which is how Gowrie had taken them by surprise. Punching his way out, he'd gone on the run, leaving Dewell nursing a broken nose.

'This is nothing to do with me!' he snarled.

He was never going to come willingly, was he? Days of cycling through exhaustion and adrenaline surges had destroyed any chance of him thinking rationally. Now he was so deep in denial he was drowning.

I raised my staff, to show it to Stanton and everyone else, to remind them what we'd agreed. Then I nodded and we moved forward.

'You have to come with us,' I called out. 'You heard the Crisis Discipline announcements.'

'Fuck that,' he spat, 'and fuck you!'

I saw his shadow just beyond my exit from the container stack. He'd headed for my voice. Fine with me.

Raising my mask, I walked faster, my staff at the ready. As soon as I emerged, I swept the lower end round, aiming to scythe his leg out from under him.

Exhausted or not, Gowrie still had impressive reflexes. He sprang backwards with a curse. The end of the staff missed his knee by millimetres.

'You bitch!' He was astonished as well as furious. He'd never expected this.

I flipped the staff over, end to end, aiming for his shoulder to knock him down. He dodged again. Not a problem. Every step back took him closer to the wall and gave him less room to manoeuvre.

I slid my hands to the end of the staff and swung it around my head. Thinking I was about to crack his skull, he scrambled backwards some more. That was fine. I didn't want to have to knock him out, not unless I had no choice. Forget what you see on mass-video. A smack on the head is nothing like an anaesthetic.

I brought the staff back down to a ready hold, my hands equally set along its length, balanced on the balls of my feet.

Gowrie glanced over his shoulder, seeing how close he was to the wall. He made his move. Springing forward, he seized the staff with both hands, one gripping between my own, the other towards the upper end.

I heard Stanton swear and the swift whine as her stunner charged.

'No!' I hoped she realised I was talking to her.

Gowrie thought I was protesting, afraid he'd take my staff away. He grinned.

I smiled back and worked the weapon like a double-ended paddle. As my left hand dropped, backed by the strength in my hips and legs, he lurched forwards, pulled off balance. My right hand came up, driving the other end of the staff upwards and under his arm.

I rotated my body and the weapon as one. The butt end of the staff hit him hard under his shoulder blade. He was still being dragged forward at the same time. Letting go didn't help him. He was completely off balance so all he could do was use his outstretched hand to try and break his fall.

Another mistake, as any emergency medic will tell you. His right wrist snapped with an audible crack, unable to take his weight.

As he sprawled, face down on the decking, screaming with shock and pain, I held him firmly pinned, with my staff angled across his back and down over his shoulder with the end hitting the floor by his neck.

'Masks, gloves, restraints. Call it in.'

As I barked orders, the team obeyed. Everyone was safely masked in moments, Gowrie included.

The fight had gone out of him now. He lay there sobbing as Ibn Kathir secured his feet with rigid ankle cuffs and Bradley got on the comms to tell Command that we'd captured him.

'Yamaguchi, give me your stunner strap.' Stanton unclipped the sling from her own weapon. 'Cuffing his hands would be a bastard's trick if he's broken that wrist. We'll lash his elbows to his sides.'

She dropped into a squat near his head. 'Now, when she takes that stick away, I'm going to roll you over. Any nonsense from you and she'll smack you with it so hard, you'll be seeing stars without any optics.'

Gowrie nodded, mute. He lay there, unresisting, as he was trussed.

Bradley clicked the comms off. 'Gurney team's on its way.'

'May I?' Stanton reached out a hand for my staff.

'Of course.' I handed it over.

She weighed it thoughtfully in her hands. 'You think you could show me how to use this?'

I smiled. 'My pleasure.'

The science I find most accessible has always been biology. Disease also crops up a lot when you're studying history. So it should come as no surprise that the science fiction that I write from time to time often draws on such inspiration.

Do You Want to
Believe in Magic?

Gold is the Sun Goddess's gift. It's the colour of her bounty ensuring we all thrive. Grain from the southern wheat fields, reaching to the horizon. North of the great rivers' union, dairy women make golden butter and cheese from the creamy milk of tan cows roaming the hill country. All this and more brings in the gold coin that's made our city more prosperous than any town upriver or down. Such wealth signifies the Goddess's favour as she guards and guides us all, from the Paramount King on his throne down to the humblest urchin.

Silver is the Moon God's metal. Keeper of secrets, he hides it mingled with lead and other ores. Only those with the patience to study learn the secrets of extracting it from the darkness of the mines. Even so, hidden hazards still trip the arrogant or unwary. But those with the relevant knowledge can cure deadly maladies with those poisons bound to silver. Silver is the physician's metal in so many ways. As his priests in their schools and hospitals often remark; every coin has two sides.

So the poets and pious say, Ruvon reflected. But the men at this table had no time for such fancies. Gold or silver, coin was for spending.

'My purse is as empty as a marsh trader's promises,' Scop groused. 'Anyone got a proposition to fill it?'

A proposition. No one would say it outright, not even among friends. The truth was, if Scop wanted coin to spend he'd have to steal it, or steal goods that could be sold quickly and without questions. He wasn't alone in that. Ruvon reckoned the men and women who did an honest day's work for a fair day's pay could be counted on the fingers of one hand in this crowded and noisy tavern.

He wasn't one. Ruvon didn't lie to himself, whatever falsehoods he told the constables prowling these wharfs, whenever some merchant went bleating to the Justiciary about cargo pilfered from some barge or a warehouse where it was stowed.

At least he'd had no choice. He'd been born to this life, in this narrow spear-point of land where the great river Tane tumbled down from the hills to join the mighty flood of the Dore winding its way across the plains. Where the perpetual flow could wash away the blood and stink of tanneries, slaughter houses and dye works, so those upstream could enjoy sweet water and fresh air.

'I have a notion.' Alinar paused. Of course. He wouldn't share his scheme without sufficient entreaty.

Alinar had a choice. Ruvon studied him over the rim of his tankard as he drank. Alinar hadn't been born to a rag picker; scavenging washerwomen's leavings for linen to sell to paper makers. Ruvon had been sent to steal shirts and chemises as soon as he was big enough to climb garden walls in the fine broad streets upstream. He'd done so willingly, once he'd realised the alternative was his mother bringing barge hands back to their meagre home, to do whatever they wanted with her, as long as they left coin to pay the rent.

Scop rubbed filthy hands together with gleeful anticipation. 'This'll be worth hearing, lads.'

'You've not steered us wrong yet,' Haspel agreed, obsequious.

As every other man nodded, Ruvon forced himself to bend his neck in a show of assent. Haspel was right. Alinar was clever and he'd learned all manner of things from the Moon God's priests, at one of their schools for the sons and daughters of those whose houses Ruvon stole from. Alinar could name each one of the towns upstream and down, within and beyond the Paramount King's rule and list every noble who swore him fealty.

Ruvon had learned his numbers and letters from a man once crushed between a laden barge and a wharf's wooden pilings, never to walk again but still with children to feed. Those lessons had ended as soon as he could write his own name and read a notice posted by the constables, in case the description of a man sought might match him.

Ruvon only needed enough reckoning to be sure of his fair share from a night's thieving. So his father had said, reclaiming him from his mother once he grew too big to escape with a thrashing for stealing clothes. As the priests said, every coin has two sides. That meant Ruvon was old and strong enough to join his father's gang. Until the constables caught Erzet and the Justiciar hanged him.

Why hadn't Alinar joined his father's business? Ruvon longed to ask. The man bred and sold horses and that was a lucrative trade with the Paramount King's cavalry and garrisons always needing new mounts. Why had Alinar abandoned his comfortable life to play cock of the dunghill among the Spearhead's depraved and desperate?

He didn't ask. He never did. Besides, Alinar was sufficiently flattered to share his new scheme with the table.

'The new moon rises to shine on the last month before midsummer. Everyone wants their books balanced before the Goddess's shrines update their ledgers and the Golden Temple sends out writs for the King's taxes –'

'Everyone knows that.' Ruvon was tired of Alinar treating them like halfwits.

Alinar slid him a narrow-eyed look before continuing as though no one had spoken. 'That's just as true for the money changers. They'll be sending plateau coin upriver and marsh coin downstream to their partners who trade beyond the Paramount King's suzerainty.'

Ruvon watched everyone nodding sagely, even though they had no more idea than he did, what holding outlandish coin would mean when the Goddess's auditors assessed a man's taxes.

No one hereabouts ever banked coin with a shrine, not with the King's head stamped on it or the heraldic beasts that signified towns beyond his majesty's reach.

'A goodly number of strong boxes will be loaded on barges these next few nights,' Alinar went on.

'Aye, and locked up tight in the holds with guards armed with bows and hand-cannons up top,' Ruvon objected.

Alinar glared at him. 'So we hit them before they reach the wharfs, in the streets after they've left the money changers.'

'With an escort of constables?' Ruvon challenged. 'We've seen them shepherding such chests.'

But Alinar shook his head. 'Not those who don't want any Justiciar's men seeing how much coin they're dealing, in case some whisper finds a priestess's ear. Especially not Pallot Usenain.'

Ruvon didn't have an answer for that. Though everyone looked much less eager at the thought of robbing Pallot. Moneylender as well as money changer, he paid brutal men to deter undue interest in his affairs.

Not even Alinar's honeyed tongue would persuade them to risk crossing Pallot, Ruvon thought with sour satisfaction.

Then Scop cleared his throat. 'Just supposing we did snatch such a strongbox, what do we do then?'

'Take the coin to a money changer?' Ruvon scoffed. 'You don't think they talk to each other, to fix their rates and swap news from plateau towns and the marsh?'

Alinar smiled, smug. 'We take the strongbox to a tinsmith I know. He'll melt every last penny down, for a tenth share of the weight,' he allowed. 'We sell our share to craftsmen making brooches and rings for the nobility.'

'When they ask where you got this gold and silver?' Ruvon demanded stubbornly.

Alinar waved him away. 'Once coin is melted and cast into ingots, no one will ever be able to say where such bullion came from.'

'A priestess will, or a priest.' Ruvon spoke before he could stop himself.

Alinar crowed with laughter. 'Bless the boy! You truly believe your grandmother's stories of their magical powers?'

Ruvon ground his teeth. 'You try telling lies to a priestess, to convince her you're entitled to withdraw money from your mother's deposits at her shrine. See how far that gets you.'

Alinar stared at him with ostentatious wonder. 'You do! You honestly believe those tales! That the Golden Mother can really see into a man's heart and judge his honesty? That the Moon God truly tells his priests when a man's burdened by dark secrets?'

Such open derision for the divinities prompted shivers of unease round the table. Alinar spoke quickly before he lost them. 'I'll grant priests and priestesses alike can read the faintest hints in a man's expression They pick up all manner of news from folk visiting their shrines and sanctuaries. True, only a fool would try to deceive them, but we won't be doing any such thing.'

He laughed and the rest laughed with him. Only Ruvon sat stony-faced.

'Do you want to believe in magic?' Alinar challenged 'To give you an excuse for not playing your part? So no one can call you a coward?'

'I'm no craven,' spat Ruvon.

'Good, then you're in.' Alinar leaned forward, elbows on the sticky table. 'Now, here's the plan…'

It was a good plan, much as it galled Ruvon to admit it. He scouted ahead down the narrow alley, cudgel in hand and Beasel at his shoulder. Pausing at the far end, he glanced back.

Scop and Pinse lugged a strongbox between them and Cheffe and Narrias followed with another. Alinar brought up the rear with Vulse and Toka, armed with daggers and clubs in case Pallot's men recovered from their beating to follow.

'All clear,' Ruvon murmured to Beasel. They stepped out to guard the alley mouth as the men carrying the strongboxes emerged. They crossed the street together to duck down another dark entry. No one knew the Spearhead's shortcuts better than Ruvon.

This one opened into a cobbled yard overlooked by crowded tenements. Beasel looked up warily but Ruvon knew these folk wouldn't open a shutter whatever they heard out back.

He skidded to a halt all the same, seeing movement in the gloom ahead. 'Clear out,' he growled, 'if you know what's good for you!'

Something growled back. The bestial snarl sent a shiver down his spine. Ruvon readied his cudgel. Heavy and copper-banded, it was barely the legal handspan shorter than a constable's iron-shod ash stave.

'Ruv?' Beasel quavered. 'What's that?'

As the man tugged at his sleeve, Ruvon realised he wasn't looking at the snarling thing. Beasel had seen a long, sinuous shape in the muck to their right.

'What is it?' Alinar demanded.

'Not sure,' Ruvon shot back before he realised no one was talking to him.

'It's getting closer!' Vulse's voice cracked with apprehension.

Before Ruvon could ask what was going on, Scop and Pinse barged into him and Beasel. With Alinar and the others following, they staggered into the cobbled yard, strongboxes scraping on the ground.

'Watch –' Ruvon's rebuke died on his lips as the growling thing stepped into the starlight. It was akin to a giant cat though walking on its hind legs as steadily as any man. Its feathery pelt was edged with eerie golden light.

Ruvon gripped his cudgel in both hands. The creature's ruby red eyes fixed on him and it spread forepaws tipped with ebony talons.

'Ruv!' Beasel pressed close.

Ruvon snatched a frantic glance and saw a snake as thick as a man's thigh. Sickly, silvery light outlined every lurid green scale. As it opened its mouth and hissed, its fangs were as long as his forefinger.

'That's a gryphon.' As Alinar spoke, Ruvon heard a hunting bird's cry behind them and the rattle of bating wings.

He wanted to turn, not to see what a gryphon was, but to seize Alinar and shake loose some answers. Where had these creatures come from and what did they want? But that would mean turning his back and that giant cat was edging closer.

As he kept his gaze fixed on the creature, rainbow mist shimmered beside it. Another nightmare solidified, with a rooster's head and scaled, spurred feet. Only it stood as tall as Ruvon's waist and he'd never heard of any fowl so large. Besides, its body was scaled like the snake and it flapped bat wings, lashing a serpent's tail.

Beasel yelped. 'What's that?'

If there was truly no such thing as magic, what was this madness?

'What do we do?' rasped Scop.

'They tell tales of gryphons in plateau towns,' Alinar remarked, 'and that's a cockatrice. They're a marsh myth, I believe.'

Ruvon couldn't help looking round. He found himself staring at Alinar. The fool had turned to see what he and Beasel faced. The man might have been scoring casual points in tavern conversation, proving he was the best-educated as well as the quickest-witted.

Not tonight, he wasn't. Ruvon watched, disbelieving, as the fool turned back to face the advancing gryphon. The beast was as big as a dray horse, though it had paws rather than hooves at the rear and a long tufted tail besides. More incredible, it had the head and wings of a bird of prey, and taloned forefeet as massive as the rest. How could such a creature exist except through magic?

Vulse and Toka shrank away from Alinar. Scop and the rest huddled closer to the strong boxes, seeking the reassurance of standing shoulder to shoulder over their loot.

Ruvon snatched a glance at the cat-man. The creature was standing still, its glowing red eyes fixed on the gryphon. The cockatrice stood beside it, leathery wings folded, while the snake slithered back and forth behind them.

'This is just some dream.' Alinar waved a scornful hand at the gryphon.

The beast's head darted forward and bit clean through his wrist. Alinar's scream echoed back from the buildings as the gryphon tossed back its head to drop the morsel down its gullet.

Ruvon was deafened as chaos erupted all around. Alinar fell to his knees, screeching and clutching his spurting stump. The gryphon sprang at Scop and the others who yelled defiance and terror alike.

Their flailing blows didn't leave a mark on the beast but its quick beak and claws inflicted ghastly wounds. Narrias reeled away, pressing bloody hands to his ruined face. 'I'm blind! I'm blind!'

Vulse darted forward, dagger drawn, to stab the beast in the flank. His blade barely grazed its hide before a clawed hind foot raked his belly. His entrails spilled onto the cobbles.

Beasel yelled as the giant snake slid between his feet, intent on Toka or Cheffe. The cockatrice took flight, flapping high enough to rake Beasel's face with his claws. He smashed at it with his cudgel. The creature pecked viciously at his weapon hand. As it tore at his scalp, hair and skin tangled around its feet.

Ruvon wasn't fighting. He locked gazes with the red-eyed cat-man. The creature stood poised for him to make the first move.

'I won't fight you.' Ruvon extended his hand, cudgel loose in his fingertips. 'Not unless you fight me. Then I'll do my best to kill you, the Horned God is my witness. But leave me be and I'll let this fall and walk away, leaving every penny in those boxes.'

The cat-man retreated, lowering its taloned hands, still eyeing him intently.

Ruvon took a step away from the mêlée and dropped his weapon. None of the beasts paid any heed. If any of the gang condemned him for a coward, Ruvon didn't hear their voices in the uproar.

He walked across the courtyard and went on his way without a backward glance.

The gang's remnants soon scattered, leaving Vulse and Cheffe dead on the cobbles. The cockatrice capered on the blood-spattered strongboxes while the giant snake's maw gaped to swallow Cheffe's booted feet.

'No,' a woman chided, emerging from a doorway. 'It's back to the Unseen Realm for you.'

She wore a hooded cloak and the gleam of a sunburst amulet illuminated the lower half of her face. The snake retreated in a sullen coil. As she gestured, it vanished in a sparkling mist.

A tall man in black followed the priestess. Starlight shone on his silver mask. He turned to the gryphon. 'Thank you.'

The beast preened for a moment and sprang into the air. By the time it reached the rooftops it had faded to transparency. With the next beat of its wings, it disappeared. The cockatrice and the lion rampant had already returned to wherever they dwelled.

The priest contemplated the strong boxes. 'What will Pallot Usenain say when we return his property?'

The priestess snorted. 'How will he explain such discrepancies in his ledgers?'

The priest looked towards the alley Ruvon had taken. 'Why do you suppose he was so desperate to believe in magic?'

The priestess shrugged. 'Just be grateful that he was. It drew the creatures to him. We'd never have got wind of this plot otherwise.'

The priest cocked his masked head. 'You know him?'

'I knew his mother.' The priestess hesitated. 'Can you see to this?'

As the priest nodded, she ran after Ruvon, light-footed in her billowing cloak.

He didn't know where to go or what to do. He couldn't say how long he wandered through the dark streets. After the night's shocks, it was hardly a surprise when he saw a spark of light ahead blossom into a white dove. He halted as the bird hovered in front of his face.

A woman's kindly voice whispered in his ears. 'Break free. Seek a new home and a fresh start. Go, tonight.'

Ruvon couldn't see who was speaking. He didn't look. He simply watched the bird circle upwards and fly away. Then he turned to head for the wharfs. He'd take the first barge to hire him, whether it was heading upstream or down. He'd go as far as he could, way beyond the Paramount King's rule.

He'd often longed to leave his sordid life and the Spearhead behind. He'd never dared to try. But after everything he had seen tonight?

Now Ruvon knew he could believe in magic. Now anything was possible.

We all want to believe in magic. Humanity's earliest stories that we have recorded, the tales first told around campfires, feature heroes, mages and monsters. Individual responses to magic, especially when someone first encounters sorcery, have always fascinated me.

The Wisdom of the Ages

'Today we will study the schism between Colaye and Esro.' Miss Ashbur stalked across the raised platform, her gown as black as the chalkboard behind her.

She never stood behind the brass-bound lectern. If she did, no one would see her. Her head didn't top her shortest student's shoulder, even with that greying crown of plaits lending her height as well as authority. Well, there was always the split leather strap hanging beside the framed map on the wall.

Gillart still wondered if she would really use it, if the students chose to ignore her one day. Like him they were grown men, or as good as. Some even had whiskers.

If their fathers had been craftsmen or shopkeepers, they'd have been working for their families' benefit these past two years. Since they were merchant born, their mothers had ambitions. They'd be educated as befitted future councillors and guildsmen. In the mornings at least, before spending their afternoons among ledgers and storerooms.

'Master Herste.' Miss Ashbur raised her voice above the murmur in the lecture hall. 'Distribute the artefacts.' She gestured to a box on the table below the map.

The youths sat up, straight-backed, attentive on their tall stools. Once the rows of desks had been scarred with pen nibs through lessons' endless tedium. Now all that had changed.

Herste shivered as he picked up the box. So that was an artefact too. Gillart watched Herste hand out trinkets to the first row. Buttons, guild tokens, a silver-gilt tiepin, a loop of woven cord to secure a neckerchief. That same frisson ran through the boys as they received the relics.

Gillart flinched when his turn came, seeing Herste about to drop a musket ball into his hand. Herste had never liked him. At least the lead was undamaged. Miss Ashbur wouldn't allow a pupil to handle something dug out of a dying man's flesh.

The shock was still bad enough. As the sphere rolled in his palm, Gillart could see the autumn field churned by scrambling boots. He smelled black powder tipped down the barrel, felt the cold ramrod driving home wadding, musket ball, more wadding. The crack of the shot deafened him in the silence of his own head.

His blood surged with the passions of that long-dead soldier, grandsire to one of his classmates' grandsire, if he had lived through the battle. The man was fighting for Colaye, for their share in this newfound shore. Esro's scoundrels couldn't claim the best harbours and the most fertile land. They had all crossed the ocean together, escaping the crowded squalor of Yanmor. That alliance was at an end if Esro's thieves sought only their own profit.

By the time the noon bells sounded, Gillart's head was ringing. Every time he exchanged an artefact with another pupil, another man's hopes and hatreds assaulted him.

'Think on all that you've learned.' Miss Ashbur smiled thinly. 'Tomorrow we continue with journals and letters.'

'Journals?' Kenthe grinned as he slid from his stool. 'How quaint.'

No one kept journals now, not since The Charm had been perfected. Why bother to commit your thoughts to paper when words were so awkward and imprecise? The Charm meant your every impression, your innermost emotions, could be instantly understood by whoever held something which you'd once owned.

Gillart managed a meaningless smile before he forced a way through jostling boys to the sunlit spring air.

Would he ever get a chance to ask Miss Ashbur? Why were the tales from journals and letters so often at odds with the visions that The Charm drew from them? He knew the usual answer. People would hide behind words. They'd paint a more flattering self-portrait or downplay danger or shield deceits. That's what The Charm stripped away, revealing the past's true essence through the unguarded thoughts of those who'd lived it.

Gillart began walking home. He longed to dispute that. Weren't words chosen and polished, written after calm reflection, worth far more than hasty first impressions? Couldn't one man's reasoned conclusions reveal more fundamental truth than a dizzying panorama seen through a thousand incomplete glimpses? Perhaps he would speak up tomorrow even if it earned him a stinging leather slap.

He paused before crossing the street, to allow a laden dray to go past, wheels grumbling across ruts dried hard in the muck. He wasn't the only person standing still. In front of shop fronts hung with everything from sides of bloody beef to little baskets of fresh apricots, men and women would pause. Their eyes grew distant as they reached into a pocket or to some jewel at wrist or throat. It was so commonplace that no one remarked on it.

Gillart fumed. What fool had first claimed that The Charm didn't merely convey visions? That artefacts could actually respond to unspoken questions? Were these people truly stupid enough to believe it? Why couldn't that woman in the green worsted cape decide whether to dine on lamb or veal without appealing to her grandmother's ring and trying to find the answer in some random image?

A rattling carriage approached. As Gillart let it pass by, he looked up to the forested mountains. They framed this broad, sheltered bay where Colaye's founders had first made landfall. Gillart had seen it for himself; the ground as yet unmarked by spades and ploughs now sanctified by The Charm. They'd all seen the gradual growth of the town from clustered wooden homesteads ringed with pigsties, chickens and vegetable plots to these broad thoroughfares with the merchant guilds' stone halls standing proud amidst workaday brick houses.

What lay beyond those peaks? More forests, granted. Miss Ashbur once brought a box of buckles and straps and flints from gunlocks carried by hunting parties. Gillart had felt their uncertainty, those men searching the trackless trees for deer or boar. Valuable meat in Colaye's markets. Nearly as valuable as any Esro spies they might get wind of. If they didn't get their own throats cut first. Undoubtedly brave men, the hunters would nevertheless be glad to get safely home.

They always came scurrying back. It infuriated Gillart. What lay beyond those far forests? Hunching angry shoulders, he shoved his fists into his jacket pockets as he strode across the street. His knuckles struck his keys, cold and hard.

Charmed sensations assailed him. His grandmother's love for hearth and home as she locked her spice cupboard. His uncle's satisfaction as he secured his strong box. Some nameless ancestor's resolve as he bolted the door that defended his family from wolves or worse prowling down from the heights.

Gillart snatched the bunch from his pocket and hurled it into a steaming heap of horseshit. He was sick of being told to revere such guidance, ordered to yield to the judgment of those who'd gone before him. Those people had lived in such different days. Why must he let these echoes of past lives shape his own hopes and dreams?

Worse still, Gillart was convinced, The Charm stopped people thinking for themselves. Why should he detest every man of Esro, just because he'd held a musket ball fired by some frightened footsoldier three generations ago?

Gillart began walking. Not heading for home. He fixed his gaze on the mountains and took whichever road led most directly that way.

By the time the sun began to sink, he'd left Colaye far behind. Walking through the densely leaved forests had been such hot and thirsty work that he'd nearly discarded his sturdy twill jacket. Now he was glad of its warmth, scrambling up these rocky slopes.

He paused to cup a handful of water from a spring moistening a crevice. Gillart sat on the dusty ground and contemplated Colaye far below. The first lamps looked like distant fireflies. With sunset nearly here, could he make it home before dark?

Twisting around, he considered the cliffs. He couldn't scale those but surely that tree-lined cleft was a pass? Could he get that far without a hunter's equipment or supplies? Not before he lost the daylight. But if he went home to fetch what he might need, Gillart knew that would be the end of it. He'd be paying the price for disappearing this afternoon until midwinter at least.

Could he possibly go on? He searched his trouser pockets to find a grimy kerchief and his grandfather's folding knife. That was one Charm he valued. Gillart smiled as he heard the old man's voice relating one of his youthful exploits.

Grandpa had been a boat builder and trader. Well into his old age he'd shaped furniture for his sons and daughters now that his wealth had shaped their futures. Gillart had watched and learned and heard all his thrilling stories time and again.

With a sharp knife and common sense, a man could always survive, so Grandpa had insisted. Gillart resolved to go on, at least far enough to see what he could see beyond the mountains.

The unexpected uses which people find for technology intrigue me. So do the unexpected consequences of the correct use of some technology which no one predicted. For example, the widespread availability of the bicycle improved the genetic health of European populations by increasing the 'marriage radius' for ordinary people from around seven miles historically to twenty one miles or so in the late nineteenth century. Why wouldn't unexpected consequences happen with magic as well?

Patience,
A Womanly Virtue

'Mother Valdese! Thank Her Radiance you're here.'

Breathless, newly-vowed Lansa broke into a run along the path through the herb garden.

Valdese glanced through the open door of her workshop. 'Peace, my daughter,' she reproved mildly, continuing to grind astise seeds with her pestle.

'Forgive me, my mother.' On the threshold, Lansa shifted anxiously from one bare foot to the other. 'Baron Shautier is worse.'

Valdese looked briefly upwards. 'May Her mercy shine upon him.'

Lansa plucked at a loose thread hanging from her coarse devotee's dress. 'People don't die of onionskin fever.'

Valdese hesitated before replying. 'Sometimes they do, my daughter,' she said regretfully.

'But King Orete –' Lansa bit her lip.

Valdese raised her brows. 'What of him?'

'Nothing, my mother.' Lansa's unattractive blush mottled cheeks already scarred by a disastrously pustulent adolescence.

Valdese concentrated on grinding the seeds. Lansa was new enough to the Sun Goddess's Circle to be well aware what Baron Shautier's death would mean. She, on the other hand, had spent nearly thirty years in sanctuary, vowed to Her Radiance as a child by pious parents. It wouldn't do to betray any knowledge of politics beyond the encircling walls, still less any curiosity about the fate of the kingdom. Her realm was this herb garden and the medicines she made from its bounty.

'What did you want, Lansa?' she prompted.

The girl was slow-witted as well as ugly enough to curdle milk. No wonder her parents had persuaded her into the life of sanctuary. Saving the cost of her keep would swell the bridal purse her brother could offer, and no man with eyes in his head would offer a bent penny for Lansa. Not outside a brothel and the girl's parents apparently cared enough to save her from that fate.

Lansa snapped off the loose thread. 'Mother Frasete asked for scarlet sage tincture.'

'His fever still hasn't broken?' Her brow furrowed with concern, Valdese turned to the cabinet where she stored her medicines. She decanted a pungent tincture into a smaller bottle. 'Are you wrapping him in damp muslins?'

'It does no good,' Lansa said unhappily.

Valdese set the stoppered bottle of tincture on her table. 'Let's try rabbitsbane.' She took a woven-straw box from a shelf. 'Use half at sunset and the rest at midnight. Let the leaves steep in hot water till the steam stops rising, then add that to the cold water soaking the muslins.'

'Will it break the fever?' Lansa accepted the straw box and the tincture bottle with shaking hands.

'We'll know by tomorrow.' Valdese shrugged. 'We must commend the poor man to Her Radiance.'

'Thank you, my mother.' Fresh hope in her eyes, Lansa scurried away, ochre dress flapping around her bare calves.

The girl would take the death of her patient hard, Valdese reflected. But that was a lesson she must learn. Not everyone could be saved and no illness respected rank or virtue.

Even a man as rich and powerful as Baron Shautier could be struck down with a childhood ailment like onionskin fever, to sweat and thrash in a sickbed till the gossamer surface of his skin sloughed off leaving scarlet tenderness beneath, with days of weakness to follow.

But Baron Shautier wouldn't recover. He would sink into the moonless night of death. Instead of rabbitsbane cooling his fever, marshtongue's insidious malice would seep into his blood as he lay wrapped in the poisonous muslins. Lansa wouldn't suffer more than a headache. She wasn't dosed with scarlet sage. It was the combination that would inexorably slow Baron Shautier's heart.

Valdese tipped the powdered astise seeds into a lidded pot and looked through the unglazed window. The sky was still richly blue though the spring sun had slipped behind the high tower. The garden was fragrant as evening's cool approached, the many hues of leaves and flowers an intricate tapestry against the grey stone walls.

There he was, slipping through the gate from the outermost gardens, where the laundresses bustled each morning. Valdese shuttered the window and spread a woollen blanket on the dusty floorboards.

'Valdese.' He was already hoarse with passion when he arrived.

She bolted the door securely. 'Elif.'

One hand sliding around her waist, urgently kissing her face, her hair, he grabbed at her skirt. As he pulled up the coarse wool and her linen shift, she tugged at the string around her waist. Kicking away her drawers, she sank onto the blanket and lay back. He pushed up her clothing, exposing her thighs, her belly, her breasts. His breath was hot on her skin, the brush of his beard tantalising.

'My love.' She wove her fingers into his curly hair.

His reply was stifled by her nipple in his mouth. Anticipation had hardened his ardour; he barely unlaced his breeches before he thrust into her. Valdese arched her back and matched him move for move. Normally she would take her own pleasure. But today, the quicker, the better.

He soon collapsed against her, spent. Through his shirt, she felt his heart hammering. Could he feel her racing blood? No matter. He'd think her passion was for him.

'Did you get it?' she breathed into his neck.

'I did.' Elif withdrew to kneel between her thighs.

She could still see the fearful wonder in his eyes; that he was slaking his lusts in the heart of Her Radiance's sanctuary. That this holy woman had gifted him with her virginity, spurning sanctioned marriage to an acolyte of the Moon God.

In truth, King Orete's henchmen had stolen her innocence, leaving her bleeding in agony even before that vile apothecary violated her with his pastes and probes. Not even old enough to wed, by the time they were done, she would never bear a child.

Or rather, Princess Utralda would never bear a child cursed with royal blood. Utralda, thrown into that distant sanctuary between pest-ridden marshes and the deadly chill of the mountains. Orete wouldn't risk Her Radiance's punishment for outright murder, so he trusted deprivation and disease would soon kill the girl, like the rest of her cousins.

It was all in the past. Now that desecration merely meant she could buy Elif's services with her body without fear of bearing his brat.

'Did you get it?' She raised herself onto her elbows.

Grinning at his own daring, Elif hauled up his breeches to find a pocket. A golden pendant slipped down the finely wrought chain looped over his hand. 'Does that repay the sanctuary for the medicines spent on him?'

'Is it the least of his trinkets?' Valdese had been specific. Even with Baron Shautier's attendants distracted, his belongings left unguarded, this had been her most hideous risk. Even though no one would take a sneak thief's word over her own, if Elif had been beaten into betraying her.

'No one will miss it.' Elif tucked in his shirt.

'But the poor will see their bellies filled and that's fair recompense for his nursing.' Valdese closed her fist around the pendant. It bore Baron Shautier's crest, as she had requested. 'Still, we must wait half a season till you turn it into coin.'

'As you think best.' Elif shrugged, unconcerned.

It was thieving that gave him a thrill, not the spoils. Valdese had seen that the first time she caught him breaking into her workshop. Any town apothecary could offer more potent euphorics than she distilled. The challenge was getting in and out of the sanctuary. So she'd given him spurious justification for his adventures and bound him ever more closely to her.

'How long will he be sick?' Elif wondered, tidying himself.

'Another ten days or so.' Valdese rose to her feet and opened her cabinet.

'It's not the best of omens,' he observed.

'A glass of cordial?' She filled two little glasses, filling the workshop with the heady scent of plums.

'He's been named as King Orete's successor.' Elif persisted.

Valdese savoured the richness on her tongue. 'I pay no heed to the crown's affairs.'

That was all the prompt Elif needed. 'There was a great ceremony. The king swore to treat him as a son, before the Horned One's very altar.'

Valdese let him ramble on about the Moon God's acolytes, stern-faced beneath their crescent headdresses as they demanded binding oaths. These men took their right to rule so seriously, with their rituals and pledges. While women saw everyone fed and clothed, nursed and nurtured, thanks to Her Radiance's bounty.

'Now everyone's wondering who he'll wed and when – '

As Elif drew a breath, she interrupted.

'You must go, my love.'

He drew her close. 'Can I call again tomorrow?'

She turned her cheek for his kiss, not her lips. 'At dusk.'

As usual, when everyone else was heading for the refectory in the sanctuary's central hall. Only the senior devotees could arrive late unchallenged, on the assumption their duties delayed them.

'Till tomorrow.' She unbolted the door and confirmed he could make his escape unseen.

Valdese watched him go with mild regret. He had been a considerate lover and the most useful of all the helpers she'd manipulated over the years. But Elif would be dead before dawn, struck down by apparent apoplexy. Unusual in a young man but not unheard of. A merciful death; he wouldn't expect it, any more than he had suspected she would offer him poisoned wine. But now she had set her long-cherished plans in motion, she couldn't risk any inconvenient slip of his tongue.

The bronze bell in the gatehouse tolled the day's final knell. Valdese dropped the pendant in the jar of astise, reclaimed her undergarments and locked the workshop door behind her. Her pace composed but brisk, she followed the spiral path in through the concentric walls of the sanctuary.

The last junior devotees were filing meekly into the pillared refectory that occupied the ground floor of the central hall. Valdese took her place in the line and accepted her bowl of lentils and hunk of coarse bread with dutiful thanks for the cooks.

As she took a stool at one of the tables encircling a pillar, the girls barely glanced in her direction. Comfortably dressed, they weren't devotees but noble maidens sent here for safe and chaste education.

'He's not the king's son. So how could the curse – '

'But the Icicle Witch's prophecy – '

'Such delusions are snares for the foolish.' Valdese raised her voice just enough to be heard at neighbouring tables. All around girls blushed guiltily and applied themselves to their food.

Once out of earshot, though, they would gossip and speculate as long as Baron Shautier lay sick. When he died they would send urgent letters to their families. The replies would be full of conjecture. Differing interpretations of prophecy were all the more tempting for being forbidden.

Inventing spurious predictions had been petty revenge at first, as Valdese moved from sanctuary to sanctuary. Then gradually over the years, she heard her spite echoing back. Those fallacious rumours of the Icicle Witch had taken on a life of their own.

People were far more willing to believe in some oracle, instead of assessing the true likelihood of King Orete's sons being slain in his interminable border wars. They weren't inclined to note how often women died in childbed when they married their cousins, as the king's daughters had done, like their own parents and grandparents before. Some mysterious fate unfolding was far more intriguing.

So as the king's choice of successor steadily narrowed, Valdese had deliberately concocted dread omens. She had spread them through these credulous girls by means of tartly explaining precisely why they shouldn't be believed.

Who could think this sworn daughter of humble peasants had any ulterior motive? No one living knew the real Valdese was buried under Princess Utralda's headstone, thanks to those distant mothers deciding to free their brutalised charge of her birthright's burden.

She scraped the lentils from her bowl and softened her bread with the broth. Grateful though she was to those holy women, now passed away beyond the north wind, that hadn't been their decision to make. Young as she had been, she had sworn she would never forget her true name. She would see justice for her slain family. So young. So foolish.

Swallowing her last mouthful, Valdese took her bowl and spoon to the scullions' basket by the door. All around, devotees were returning to their duties while the schoolgirls anticipated an evening's leisure.

What should she do now? She wasn't going near the infirmary. Baron Shautier would die without her ever laying eyes on him, still less tending him herself. She wouldn't risk drawing the most fleeting glance of suspicion.

It had taken so much time to establish herself here; a respected senior devotee in this sanctuary that controlled the river crossing that the baron must naturally seek out, travelling between his own estates and the capital. Because she had guessed long ago that Baron Shautier would be left standing, his loyalty unquestioned, when paranoia had driven King Orete to lop every other branch off his family tree.

Accordingly, she discreetly applied herself to learning everything she could about the baron; his virtues and vices and crucially, what ailments he had, and had not, suffered. As she plotted how she might kill him before he begot any heirs.

Valdese headed for the stairs to the round hall's upper levels. With onionskin fever within the walls, no one would remark on her visiting the foundlings' dormitory.

The little ones were already abed, drowsing in the shadows of the shuttered lanterns. She walked between the narrow cots, smiling fondly at those few still wakeful. The children adored Valdese. Strict, she was scrupulously fair. Demanding their best efforts, she never set impossible challenges.

She picked out two particular faces. The son of that woman who had sought treatment at the paupers' gate, not knowing she was dying of silk palsy. So Valdese had numbed her pain and promised her child would be cared for till she recovered. Pliant under the euphoric medicine, the woman agreed to sneak into the baron's lodgings, when he paused on his way to be honoured by King Orete. Who gave a maidservant a second glance?

She had tucked the kerchief that Valdese gave her inside his tidily folded nightshirt. The kerchief that Valdese had used to mop the brow of every onionskin fever patient this past year. The journey was just long enough for the disease to seize the baron on the road home, as Valdese knew it would be. Where else would he seek treatment but within this circle of sanctuary?

The second boy caught her eye and sat up. 'Mother Valdese– '

'Go to sleep,' she said firmly.

A heartbeat and he thought better of protesting, snuggling back into his blankets.

Yes, he would do very well. He was bright and biddable and of all the foundlings left in the outer wall's covered cradle these past few years, he most resembled Baron Shautier. He could even be some bastard slip from the baron's stock.

No one would dispute her word, when she went to Sanctuary Mother with the token that had been left with the child. That's to say, with the pendant Elif had just stolen, and the pitiful note she would forge, from the unknown mother beseeching Her Radiance's protection for the baby.

Naturally Valdese would do penance for concealing the child's origins. It would hardly be severe. Sanctuary Mother knew how ruthlessly the baron would have dealt with any bastard who could challenge his later, legitimate heirs.

Quietly content, Valdese walked to the far door and sought her own modest cubby in the devotees' dormitory. Kneeling by her hard bed, she recited her evening devotions and contemplated the future.

She would give it four or five years. Baron Shautier's claim to succeed King Orete clearly outstripped all the rest but, with him dead, no one had an advantage. The kingdom would be locked in fruitless bickering. As the nobles squabbled, perhaps even taking up arms against each other, the surrounding countries would steadily encroach upon the borders.

The Moon God's acolytes would call that calamity, regarding their carefully drawn maps as sacred as holy writ. The barons were nearly as obsessed, their heavy boots measuring every pace of their domains. So the acolytes would rebuke and cajole and desperately seek compromise which the barons despised as weakness.

That meant the acolytes would be the first to welcome an unknown heir promising renewal of Baron Shautier's line. It was the stuff of heroic fable and, more importantly, the child had been reared in the disciplines of sanctuary. If not quite one of their own, the boy was close enough. Senior acolytes would bring all their influence to bear.

After another year of murders and stealthier assassinations, Valdese reckoned the surviving barons would be sufficiently weary to accept a fresh start with a youthful king. They'd see the potential advantages of seats on a Regents' Council and begin jostling for positions of influence.

Let them dream. By then, she would be that child's most adored attendant. His nurse, his confidante, his spiritual advisor. Valdese would be with him when he woke, when he retired to bed, and close at hand throughout the day, preparing his food and tending to his needs and comforts.

Standing up, Valdese pulled her coarse dress over her head and hung it on its peg. She would continue to wear it, she decided, as she guided the young king's decisions without anyone being the wiser.

Because women had no power in the kingdom. Silent, demure, they served Her Radiance or the men of their families, as ornaments, as bargaining chips, as mothers of valued sons and of daughters whose only worth was measured by their marriage.

Would that be justice for her family, for her sufferings? Slipping into her bed, Valdese dismissed the question. She would rule, and that would suffice.

Magic is a tool. It can be used and misused, especially by those who lack other means to redress wrongs or to get what they want. Tales of princes and the fates of kingdoms are great and I enjoy reading those. As a writer, though, I'm always interested in people outside the inner circles of the powerful.

Unicorn Sandwiches

I don't know who decided that unicorn sandwiches are the official, sacred, royal food for a coronation but that was the kingdom's tradition and kingdoms like their traditions. The king's mage said it had to be done and that was that.

The thing is, unicorns are bloody lethal. Horses are dangerous enough with hooves and teeth and kicking. Unicorns have that horn as well, and it's not just for show.

The other thing about unicorns is only a virgin can tame one. I was the princess and thus was uniquely qualified by virtue of royal birth and being untouched by human hand. That's what the king's mage said, and that was that. Bloody wizards.

So the night before the hunt, I cut up my sheets and plaited and knotted and made a rope, and tied it to my bedstead and hung it out of my window. And Sir Pelin climbed up.

And the next morning, I wasn't qualified to go hunting unicorns, and the king's mage couldn't do a thing about it, and that was that. They say once a king, always a king. Well, sometimes, one knight is enough.

Juliet E. McKenna

One of the scariest things I have ever done is take part a flash fiction contest in front of an audience at a convention. This was my winning entry in the round prompted by audience suggestions, where 'unicorns' and 'sandwiches' were shouted out simultaneously. I include it here as an example of the creative inspiration to be found by taking classic genre ideas and flipping that template. Though I recommend working under a lot less pressure!

The Land of the Eagle

'... and the brass eagle stood proud on the highest pinnacle of the castle gate, overlooking the town grown up around the margrave's walls. Flying high on our flags, it was the token of our luck and so the eagle itself was carried into battle against the River Kingdom's army...'

Nedirin ducked his head to hide a yawn. He'd had a tiring day, herding obstinate goats in these gullies and thickets between the river and the uplands. Now that the herds were penned for the night with the dogs on watch, he wanted to wrap himself in his blankets and yield to his weariness. He'd heard old Thulle's stories so often that he could recite them in his sleep.

They all could, from the dog boys younger than Nedi to the grey-bearded herd masters as old as his grandsire. Their town had yielded to the men of the River Kingdom when Thulle was still a babe in arms.

If someone other than Thulle were telling the tale, the brass eagle had been cast into a charnel pit with the battlefield dead, or fallen into the river, or been stolen by the Paramount King's men to be thrown in their furnaces far away to the south, in their capital city where the ruddy brown Tane flowing from the upland plains met the pale silty waters of the mighty Dore. That distant river cut through grasslands bounded only by the horizon to east and west and by mighty forests to the south. So folk said but no one from Hatalys had ever travelled so far to seek their fortune and returned to confirm such stories of woodlands without end.

Still, listening to old Thulle was the price which Nedi must pay for a seat by the fire pit, and the weather was growing colder as the hazel and ash trees turned to autumn gold. So he hid his boredom and edged closer to the embers.

'If the eagle ever returns,' Thulle continued, 'Hatalys will be free.'

That was the one thing which all the tales agreed on, though ever since he was small Nedi had wondered how that could happen if the bird had been melted down and turned into door knobs or buttons for fancy waistcoats.

'Give it up, for pity's sake,' growled Uderil from the far side of the stone-lined pit.

Some of the men who had already forsaken the fireside for their bedrolls murmured agreement. Nedi's mother's youngest brother and his father's next elder were among them. They had promised to watch over him as he tended his family's goats while his father's broken ankle mended. They couldn't afford to abandon this last trip into the hills to fatten the billy goats born in the spring and now destined for salting and smoking after autumn's slaughters.

Uderil was still speaking. 'I'll take the River Kingdom's grain and fine horses and black powder weapons to keep moor dogs from killing my goats over foraging for nuts and fruit and hunting hill elk with bow and arrow.'

Seeing Thulle's eyes widen with outrage, Nedi gazed mutely into the flames, keeping his face as blank as a freshly wiped slate. Antagonising the spiteful old man was never a good idea. Nedi would wager his best gloves that Uderil's most highly prised goats would lose their bells and stray over the next few days or fall victim to stinking flux. Not that anyone ever caught Thulle wreaking such revenge.

'It's worth it, is it?' A new voice spoke up from the shadows on the far side of the fire. 'Paying for black powder and lead shot carried a hundred leagues upstream? Paying tithes in coin and in kind to the Paramount King to feed and clothe the garrison who watch over us? Bending our necks to the justice of strangers?'

'Getting our necks stretched, more like,' Plore said quietly.

Nedi remembered his father and mother talking in low tones, sitting in their chairs on either side of the stove at home, the evening after Plore's cousin had been hanged. They hadn't realised Nedi was listening, crouched behind the curtain hiding the stair to the loft where he and his brothers and sisters slept, four to a bed. Nedi had got too used to sleeping alone in his blankets now that he was old enough to go herding goats with their father through the summer, only returning to the town each market day.

Plore's cousin had been a violent fool. His parents agreed on that. But did he deserve to hang for being the only man caught by the troopers after a drunken brawl where another bully had died? Any one of twenty men could have struck the fatal blow. Even the dead man's brothers and wife had said so.

Father recalled the old margrave's lesser sentences. A man got a chance to mend his ways if he was punished with a flogging or a spell in the stocks or the pillory. But the new margrave had gone south and the castellan handing down judgements stamped with the Paramount King's seal only ever sent men to the gallows.

Nedi's mother was more distressed to hear that the hanged man's body had been given to the Horned God's temple, for the masked priests' secret rites before he was buried. Plore's family would have laid him out in a funerary gully, she wept, to be unmade by the beasts and birds of hill and valley to release his soul.

Nedi had crept silently back to the crowded bed, privately vowing to never fall foul of the Paramount King's garrison.

'Granted, there's bitter to go with the sweet.' Uderil glanced at Plore, apologetic. 'But we have to live each day as best we can.'

'Do we?' the voice challenged. 'Can't we make our own choices?'

'How?' Zanner, his mother's brother, sat up.

Nedi was startled to hear the hope in his young uncle's words.

'We look to our own lore,' Thulle said robustly. 'We know that the eagle flew away when the Horned God's priests conjured

151

monsters to break down the castle's gates. The king of the skies went to rally the beasts and birds to fight with our forefathers. Before he could bring them salvation, though, the fools had surrendered for lack of faith!'

Along with everyone else, Nedi looked at Thulle. Only the crackle of burning wood broke the silence around the campfire.

Did the old man truly believe that the Horned God's priests had summoned up ogres to smash the city's defences? That griffins had soared up to the ramparts, rending the brave defenders with deadly beaks and talons?

'The eagle could win back our freedom, together with our own courage and resolve.' The stranger walked into the soft orange light, carrying a heavy sacking-swathed bundle.

Uderil shuffled aside and the man knelt to begin unwrapping whatever it was. He was dressed much the same as everyone else; buff leather breeches and high topped boots to foil the thorn thickets, a leather jerkin over woollen shirts layered to keep out the cold. He had sturdy gloves tucked through his belt and a knitted cap warming his head. His complexion was weather-worn, his brows and stubble dark and his eyes brown, like everyone Nedi had known all his life.

The herdsmen gasped as the last fold of sacking fell away. A statue shone golden in the firelight. It was an eagle rearing upright with mighty wings outspread and its head turned to one side. Flowing lines marked every detail of its feathers while carved facets gave the eye turned towards Nedi a piercing glint.

'The king of the skies has returned!' Thulle was so ecstatic that he almost fell into the fire pit as he scrambled to his feet. As it was, he brushed so close to the flames that Nedi smelled leather scorching. Tears glistening on his wrinkled cheeks, the old man dropped to his knees before the brass statue.

It was a sizeable thing, at least a cubit tall, with the bird perched on a square pedestal which had four stubby feet. Thulle stretched out a trembling hand only to snatch it back before his fingertips touched the gleaming metal.

'Where did you find that?' Uderil wondered aloud.

'How is that effigy going to restore our liberties?' Uncle Zanner demanded. 'Who are you?'

'My name is Sincai,' the newcomer told him, 'and I believe this statue can help Hatalys regain its freedom if you men are brave enough to follow me to the town.'

'We will follow you anywhere!' Thulle still gazed at the statue, rapt.

'Speak for yourself,' Uderil snapped.

'Hear me out before you make any decision.' The newcomer surveyed the assembled men. Even those who'd already fallen asleep were tossing aside their blankets, wide-eyed and open-mouthed.

'The River Kingdom has overreached itself.' Sincai rose and tugged a long stick from the firewood piled close to the pit. He scraped swift lines in the dirt.

'Here is the Tane coming down from the plains and here is Hatalys. Here is the Dore, cutting the grassland from sunset to sunrise.'

Then, to Nedi's surprise, he drew a second river joining the Dore far to the west.

'This is the Fasil and the town of Gotesh.' Sincai dug a little hole in the ground where the two rivers met. 'That has been a River Kingdom town for five generations but Hedvin and Bastrys—' he marked two more towns some distance further upstream on each river '— they drove the Paramount King's armies away in their grandfathers' day and the plainsmen have never returned.'

He swept the stick across to the other side of his dirt map and scraped four rivers fanning out eastward from the River Dore. 'You've heard tell of the Nalgeh Marsh? It's bounded by three cities, Scafet, Julach and Avelsir. They have never fallen to the plainsmen. The most westerly River Kingdom town is here.' He stabbed the dirt a good way short of the sprawling marsh. 'Usenas.'

'What has this to do with us?' Zanner asked impatiently.

Sincai drew a slow circle around his map. Nedi saw the stick's tip pass through the marks signifying Gostesh in the east and Usenas in the west. It cut through the writhing line of the Tane to the south and east of Hatalys. The triangle of land between the Tane and the Dore, where the capital city ruled over the bridges and all river trade up and down stream, was at the centre.

'Here's where the River Mothar joins the Tane.' Sincai drew a second line coming down from the north. It met the Tane just where the circle crossed the river. 'Where the plainsmen hold Mithess.'

Nedi longed to visit Mithess. The town was only four days travel down river by barge. Three days, so Uncle Zanner said, when the spring swelled the Tane with snowmelt from the mountains far beyond the high plains. When he was older, his father said. If his mother agreed.

'Wait.' Nedi's Uncle Isom walked forward to study the scrawled map. 'We're the only town outside that circle which is under the River Kingdom's heel?'

Sincai nodded. 'Anything beyond is too far from the Kingdom's heart, as the folk of Hedvin and Bastrys showed and so did the men and women of Scafet and the Nalgeh Mire. When their people rebelled, the Paramount King's cavalry couldn't arrive in time. Not before the townsfolk drove out those sworn to the Paramount King.'

Sincai raised a warning finger as the men murmured surprised approval.

'They let them leave with food for themselves and their horses. They didn't put the River Kingdom castellan or garrison to the sword or drag them to the gallows. They didn't ravage the Horned God's temple or tear down the Sun Goddess's statues. They simply restored their old rites alongside the new.'

He raised his voice over Thulle's muttered outrage.

'They chose trustworthy men to serve as constables to keep order in every district and to make up a jury for an assize at every third full moon, with a judge chosen by drawing lots among them. Merchants honoured their agreements with traders up and downstream. They proved that they did not need the Paramount King's rule to secure peace and prosperity so he had no excuse to send his cavalry against them.'

'Good for them,' one of the old men sneered.

'We could do the same,' Sincai assured him. 'Winter is nearly here. Drive out the castellan and his men and even if one of them sends a pigeon flying with the news, the Paramount King's army won't get here before the first snows fall.'

'The castellan in Mithess could send his cavalry to join forces with the men we've thrown out,' Uderil countered.

'As long as Hatalys men hold the walls and gates, all they can do is sit outside and battle the frosts,' Sincai insisted

'While they wonder if Mithess' people are contemplating their own rebellion,' Isom mused, 'while their garrison's elsewhere.'

'Quite so.' Sincai grinned.

'The harvests are in,' someone beyond the fire observed. 'Even if we couldn't go hunting for fear of the Paramount King's men, we wouldn't starve within the town.'

'The storehouses will only stay full until the castellan starts sending barges downstream,' Zanner said abruptly.

Nedi saw the men stiffen and glanced at each other, grim-faced. Nedi remembered the hungry days at the end of last winter when the snows and the river ice had endured for a full half-moon longer than usual.

Even the thriftiest bakers had run out of flour so there was no bread and the men couldn't hunt or fish to ease their wives' struggles to eke out their pantries' dwindling supplies. Old Mistress Tigad, who ran the dame school where Nedi had learned his letters and numbers, had been found dead and cold in her bed.

'Who are you?' The question was out before he realised he had spoken aloud.

Sincai smiled. 'I'm the man who's spent these past eight years sneaking out beyond the walls to search every nook and gully for the place where the eagle must be buried, after hearing my grandfather's tale of his father carrying it away for safekeeping.'

He looked at the rest of the men. 'My family name is Dorsin. We're leather workers and we live around the Aspen Gate.'

'I've sold hides to a Rever Dorsin,' Uderil said thoughtfully.

'The eagle wasn't carried off. It flew away.' Thulle was still gazing, entranced, at the statue.

No one paid him any heed. Uncle Isom looked at Plore and Nedi saw something pass unspoken between them.

'What do you have in mind?' Isom asked cautiously.

'Men were hanged for talking treason in the old margrave's day.' Plore tossed another log into the firepit sending up a shower of sparks.

Sincai nodded. 'We cannot debate and discuss our plans in the streets and taverns. Word will get back to the garrison and the castellan will send ten men to seize each one of us. We need to strike as unexpected as lightening and in as many places as we can. Let the garrison try stamping out ten different fires when twenty more have sprung up before the first is quelled.'

'Fires?' Thulle looked around with unnerving eagerness.

'No one will be lighting real fires, you old fool,' Uderil said scornfully.

'Just kindling a lust for freedom in people's hearts.' Challenge shone bright in Sincai's eyes.

'Fine words,' Uderil observed. 'What do you actually want us to do?'

'Raise a cry for Hatalys and the eagle,' Sincai said promptly. 'Rouse everyone to come to the castle and see it for themselves. Then we'll tell the castellan and his men that they're no longer welcome. If they come out to confront us, they'll be outnumbered and we can drive them to the gates. If they hide behind the castle's walls, we bar the gates to keep them inside until they've emptied their store rooms. Then the price of food and drink will be leaving the town.'

'Why should we be the ones to start this landslide?' Zanner demanded.

'Who goes around the town more unnoticed than goat herders and their wives?' Sincai grinned.

He was right, Nedi realised. Day in and day out, men too old to endure these hills drove freshly purchased beasts to each district's butchers, from the tender and sweet-fleshed kids to the aged nannies destined for the stew pot. The women sold milk and cheeses from door to door each morning, leaving the dogs and younger children watching over the milking flocks grazing around the town walls.

'The townsfolk will laugh in our faces,' one of the grey beards prophesied.

To Nedi's surprise, Sincai shrugged. 'Then what have you lost? What have you risked? Calling folk to come and see a marvel isn't treason. You won't even look foolish when the mockers learn that the eagle is there for all to see.'

Uncle Isom raised a hand. 'How do you propose to get something that size back up onto the gatehouse pinnacle?'

'We need someone who can climb.' Sincai looked around the fire. 'That's my other reason for coming out here.'

Muted laughter eased the tension a little. Goat men were well known for their surefootedness. They had to be as nimble as their charges, given the beasts' perverse ambition to scale the steepest crags in search of forage. Come the winter, when the snows penned everyone up within the town, Nedi's father and uncles mended leaking roofs and rebuilt unsteady chimneys.

Abruptly he realised that everyone was looking at him. Despite the heat from the fire, Nedi felt chilled to the bone.

'The lad's the best climber here.' Thulle's unblinking gaze was profoundly unnerving.

Nedi silently cursed his own readiness to help the old man rescue a cragfast goat the day before last.

'The garrison would just think some lads were larking about,' Uderil observed slowly.

'I couldn't!' Nedi's voice rose embarrassingly and he swallowed hard. 'Not without my father's say-so.'

'Your father would agree in a heartbeat.' Plore looked steadily at him and Isom nodded.

Zanner grinned. 'You'll be up there, back down and away before any River Kingdom man can find a foothold.'

'If we're to do this, let's do it sooner than later.' Plore rose to his feet.

Half the other men joined him, their faces eager in the firelight. Did that mean it was agreed? Was there to be no show of hands? No further discussion? Nedi wanted to ask but the words froze in his throat.

'If we leave now, we can be at the gates by daybreak,' Sincai said swiftly. 'You can go and wake your wives and all spread the word.'

'We'll tell your father and mother,' Isom assured Nedi.

'If they forbid it, we'll come at once to call you down,' Zanner promised.

'We'll keep the goats penned until you come back,' one of the greybeards announced. 'The dog boys can cut fodder and shovel shit for a few days.'

Nedi saw the other men were already rolling up their blankets and securing their few possessions in the bags which each herder carried. He rubbed a shaking hand across his face and felt the prickle of bristles. So much for his pride in those. At the moment, he'd give anything to still be a smooth-faced dog boy.

'Come on, young hero.' Sincai was at his side. 'Don't you want to be the man who restores the eagle to Hatalys?'

Nedi supposed that would be something, since it seemed he had no choice. He gazed at the statue. Thulle was wrapping it in the sacking again, as gentle as a man swaddling a baby. 'Who's to tote that weight back to the town?'

'I will,' Sincai assured him.

Nedi looked up at him. 'Where did you find it?'

Sincai grinned. 'In the last place I looked.'

Before Nedi could press the stranger, Isom came over. 'Your father will be proud of you.'

And that was that. The rest of the night passed more quickly than Nedi could have imagined. The men all knew the path and then the familiar road and the air was cold enough to turn muddy ruts sufficiently firm for them to find sure footing. The moon rode high in the sky, round and full, to light their way.

By the time the sky paled, the town's walls cut a jag-toothed line of darkness across the horizon. Nedi was stumbling with exhaustion but he still kept pace with his uncles at the head of the straggling column. Though his fear of falling behind and being lost on the road was fading, dread at what was to come took its place.

Someone cried out from the rearguard, chagrined 'The gates won't unlock till dawn!'

'They'll open to me,' Sincai shouted over his shoulder.

Nedi caught a glimpse of his face in the strengthening light. The stranger had carried the eagle's great weight all this way yet his pace was unflagging, his certainty undimmed. Nedi began to wonder if this madcap plan might actually succeed.

Reaching the gatehouse, Sincai knocked with a brisk triple rap on the porter's door cut into the great double oak gates.

Like every boy, Nedi knew that opening the gate was completely forbidden between the dusk and dawn horn calls from the castle. Get locked out, their mothers warned, and you'll be cold and hungry all night, if the moor dogs don't eat you for their own supper.

But the porter's door opened up and a man greeted Sincai with a fervent smile. He ushered them through the portal before locking it securely again.

The goat herders quickly dispersed, each man heading for home. Zanner clapped Nedi on the shoulder. 'We'll meet you at the castle. You need not climb if your parents forbid it.'

Before Nedi could answer, he hurried away to catch up with Isom.

'What's the matter?' Sincai murmured.

Nedi turned to see the gatekeeper drawing Sincai close to say something in urgent low tones. Nedi couldn't make any of it out.

'Let me take that.' Thulle had been following Sincai so closely that he'd been all but treading in the younger man's footprints. Now he reached out to slip the rope sling supporting the sack-swathed eagle from Sincai's shoulders.

'I'll take the boy to the castle. No one will look twice at an old fool like me.'

Sincai let the old man take possession of the bird before looking intently at Nedi. 'There's something I must attend to. Can you see this through without me?'

He's asking me, Nedi realised with nervous pride. Not old Thulle. He nodded jerkily, his mouth dry and not just from the long night's journey.

'Come on.' Cradling the eagle in his arms, Thulle forced the boy onwards like a grizzled dog herding a young billy goat.

Nedi didn't need any old man chivvying him. He knew the quickest routes to the castle through the town's back alleys, up the sloping streets to the highest point of the wall-girt hill. More than once, he glanced over his shoulder to see Thulle labouring under the eagle's weight and had to slow to let him catch up.

All the while, the daylight was strengthening. Nedi saw the first signs of households waking; threads of smoke from chimneys and upper shutters unlatched as chamber pots were emptied into the gutters below.

The castle's gates were still firmly bolted when they arrived in the cobbled square in front of the ancient stronghold. Twin towers, as round as a drum, stood on either side of the peaked arch of the gate. Above the iron-bound oak, the wall linking the towers stretched upwards high, as sheer as any cliff. Rising like steps on either side, the stonework rose to a pinnacle above the wall-walk which circled the castle's battlements. The highest point was the plinth where the eagle had once stood.

How was he supposed to get up there? One slip and he would plummet to his death. Nedi turned to Thulle. 'I can't –'

He gasped as Thulle's knife prodded his belly. The old man had set his burden down and drawn the long, square-ended blade that every goat man carried to hack a path through brush or to cut fodder.

'You will,' Thulle assured him.

'Or you'll gut me?' Nedi cried, incredulous. 'Who will carry the eagle up then?'

'I'll say a cavalryman killed you.' Mad cunning lit the old man's eyes. 'While the townsfolk raise a hue and cry, I'll slip inside and go up the stairs.'

He was, Nedi realised, quite crazy enough to imagine he could succeed.

'So climb,' Thulle snarled, 'before your fool of a father arrives or your uncles.'

Could he yell for help, Nedi wondered, if the castle gates opened? Not before the old lunatic killed him.

Trembling, he studied the angle between the curve of the closest tower and the wall spanning the gateway. The stonework had been coarse when it was first built and long years of rain and frost had crumbled the mortar away. Moss outlined useful ledges and tufts of yellow grass were seeded here and there. Nedi and his friends had climbed just such weathered stretches of the town wall when they'd been supposedly herding milch goats in the pastures.

'Take it up!' Thulle jabbed his arm with the blade.

Nedi felt a sting like a wasp. Had the lunatic drawn blood? 'All right! All right!'

He grabbed the loop of rope and slung it over his shoulder. The eagle wasn't as heavy as he had feared but it was still a substantial burden. He worked his other arm through the second loop to pull the lump of sacking tight between his shoulder blades.

'Let me look for the best route,' Nedi snapped as Thulle advanced his menacing blade again.

He contemplated the round towers. They were only two storeys tall, albeit high-ceilinged within. If he could get as far as the top, he could climb up the stepped side of the stonework rising behind the wall-walk easily enough. It wasn't so far. Not as far as he had climbed before in the hills, at least a few times.

Nedi reached for a handhold on the gatehouse wall and found another on the side of the tower. As he pulled himself up, he wedged his toes into convenient cracks. He was grateful for his sturdy boots, though he knew his mother would scold him for scarring the leather.

More handholds presented themselves. Nedi climbed as quickly as he dared to get beyond Thulle's reach, pressing himself close to the masonry.

'You have two hands and two feet. Keep three of the four firmly planted all the time.' He recalled his father's words when he'd first been sent up a crag to chivvy a young goat who saw no need to be penned for the night.

Moving more slowly as he climbed higher, the cold stones numbed Nedi's hands. Perversely though, his fingertips felt scoured raw. He should have put on his gloves.

As he stopped for a moment, his foot slipped on sodden moss. The eagle on his back swung sideways, nearly dragging him to his doom. The ropes cut deep into his shoulders, agonising. Heart pounding, Nedi scrabbled desperately at the masonry. Finally his boot caught on some foothold.

Breathlessly, he tested its strength. Would it bear his weight? He clung to the stones with one hand and forced his other toe deeper into its own crevice. Snatching for the next handhold, he pulled himself upwards.

Someone exclaimed below in the square, only to be cut short by a warning murmur from a handful of people. Nedi could not look down. He wasn't even sure he could climb back down. He had no choice but to continue with this madness even though his arms and legs were trembling with exertion and fear.

Nedi pressed his face against the cold stone and craned his neck, trying to see upwards without fatally unbalancing himself. He was heartened to see he was closer than he had imagined to the dubious safety of the tower's crenellations.

He could hear baffled voices within the tower. Narrow windows overlooked the approach to the gate and along the length of the castle wall to either side. Nedi guessed that more windows overlooked the courtyard within the gate. The garrison had woken up. What would happen when someone roused the castellan?

Was there someone already up on the tower roof keeping watch? Nedi couldn't see. Would he get to the top only for grasping hands to drag him onto the leaded roof, demanding to know what he was doing?

Then they would seize the eagle and he would have risked his life for nothing. Thulle would never forgive him. Whatever Sincai and the others might say, the old madman would cut his throat one dark night, Nedi was sure of it. Or the castellan's men would throw him off the tower to fall to his death, smashed and broken on the cobbles below.

He began climbing faster regardless. He must climb up onto the gatehouse pinnacle as soon as he possibly could. His only hope of safety was getting higher than bigger and heavier men dared to climb.

There was no one on top of the tower. Nedi hauled himself up and toppled forward between the upthrust masonry to land painfully hard on his numbed yet aching hands. The eagle's weight bore down mercilessly between his shoulder blades.

He scrambled across the tower roof. The stepped facade of the wall spanning the gateway seemed impossibly narrow. How could he hope to do this?

How could he turn back? Hearing shouts in the castle's courtyard, Nedi looked down to see men pointing upwards. He unslung the eagle from his back and looped his arms through the ropes again so that the ungainly bulk was held against his chest. He began climbing up the stepped stones rising behind the wall-walk on his hands and knees, even though the wall itself was barely wide enough.

He kept his gaze fixed on the next step and then the step after that. If he slipped, he would try to fall sideways towards the gatehouse's outer face. He might just land on the wall-walk. Capture and a broken arm or leg would be a fair trade for his life.

Nedi reached the top, breathless and sweating despite the cold air. Agonisingly careful, he sat astride the last stone below the plinth and gripped the wall with his knees and ankles. The sacking-wrapped bundle sat safe within the circle of his arms as he clung onto the plinth for added reassurance.

Now he dared to look down. Outside the castle, he saw a crowd with their pale faces turned upwards and hands pointing just like the garrison men. They had come to see the eagle returned. So Nedi had better oblige them.

He began picking at the ropes with his sore, cold fingers. His breath came faster, harsher, as he broke his nails on the knots pulled tight by the eagle's weight. Finally the hemp yielded and Nedi could unwrap the coarse sacking to reveal the eagle's head.

Close to, it was crudely made. Rough edges on the cast metal hadn't been filed smooth. The incised lines marking its feathers were uneven and incomplete. Its head and beak looked more like a crow than an eagle and Nedi had never seen any real bird spread its wings in such ridiculously rounded fashion. Its legs were slightly different lengths with clawed feet seemingly melting into the square pedestal.

The crowd below began cheering nevertheless, as the strengthening sunlight struck golden fire from the brass. So now Nedi had to secure the thing in its plinth. He could see the four holes where the brass pedestal's stubby feet would hold it secure. He held on tight with his knees and feet as he lifted the eagle up.

His arms burned, already so tired from climbing. Nedi was seized with terror. He wasn't going to be able to do this. At the last moment, with his last despairing effort, he lifted it a little higher and further. As his strength failed, the pedestal's brass feet slid into their sockets.

A triumphant cry rose up from the crowd below the gate. Newcomers were swelling the tumult. Now pots and pans clashed loudly together, punctuating a rhythmic chant.

Rough music. Nedi had heard it a few times. When a man persisted in beating his wife. When a mother let her children go hungry and barefoot. When some adulterous couple dishonoured their vows and their spouses. When remonstration had failed. When help was rejected or abused. Then the clamour would start. It would last night after night until exhaustion wore away defiance and the guilty sneaked away with nothing but the clothes on their back.

Did the River Kingdom men understand? Did they realise that the Hatalys folk were telling them to leave? That they would brook no refusal? Nedi looked down into the castle's courtyard and shuddered so violently that he almost lost his balance. He clung to the stone, pressing his cheek against the eagle's plinth.

The garrison had drawn up in serried ranks. They were loading their hackbuts with black powder and lead shot. Nedi saw faint wisps of smoke rising from the coiled lengths of alchemist's twine which each man would clamp in his weapon's serpentine lock. Uncle Isom had shown him how a pull on the trigger snapped the curved lock down to ignite the priming powder in the flash pan. That prompted the black powder in the iron barrel to fire quicker than blinking.

Nedi was aghast. The cobbles would run red with blood. Why hadn't the older, wiser men foreseen the castellan ordering his men to fire on the crowd? Was Uncle Isom going to be killed?

Uncle Zanner? Where was his father? Was his mother among the women drumming on cook pots with their ladles?

Raucous shrieks closer at hand suddenly deafened him. Nedi was completely surrounded by fluttering wings and screeching birds of every size and colour. Had they been startled from their roosts by the noise?

As he ducked the countless scratching talons and piercing beaks, he froze, astonished. All his terror of being so high above the ground, all his fears for his family's fate vanished like morning dew. He could see the eagle despite the swirling cloud of birds. Only it wasn't the rough-hewn brass effigy which he had carried up here.

The golden metal bird was a thing of beauty, precise in every lifelike detail. It perched, wings raised and angled, ready to plunge from the sky to seize some unsuspecting prey. Its hooked beak gaped. Its eyes shone bright as diamonds. It turned its head to look at Nedi with a fierce hunter's gaze.

The other birds swooped down to fill the castle courtyard. The garrison men shouted and cursed, flailing with their hands and hackbuts. It did no good. From hedge sparrows to crag crows, the birds clawed and pecked and shat all over the River Kingdom men and their weapons.

When the flock dispersed as suddenly as it had appeared, the courtyard was deserted. Nedi saw that the men had fled back into their barracks. Some had held onto their weapons but more had let the precious hackbuts fall to the ground. Powder spilled over the cobbles along with lengths of alchemist's twine, now soiled and useless.

Someone had opened the castle gate! He saw the townsfolk crowding into the courtyard. Soon the men were banging on the doors all around. The garrison emerged with their hands raised in surrender. A knot of richly clad River Kingdom men were swiftly surrounded by Hatalys's leading craftsmen and merchants. They broke into several earnest conversations.

Nedi looked down outside the castle again. The crowd was still growing. More and more people were coming to see this marvel and to join in the triumphant cheering.

They were pointing up at the eagle. Now it looked just the same as it had done when it was first revealed. It didn't matter. From that distance no one could see it was ugly and crude.

Nedi contemplated the effigy. Had he imagined the living bronze's magical beauty? No, he hadn't. He could go to his deathbed as an old, old man, quite sure of what he had seen. Though he didn't think he would tell anyone. Not and be mocked for a fool like Thulle.

Firstly though, if he was to live to be a greybeard, he must get safely down from this perilous perch. Nedi considered his options and decided to climb slowly and carefully down to the battlements and wait there until someone came to show him the proper route through the castle.

It wasn't until he was safely on the wall walk that a profoundly unnerving thought struck him. If the eagle's magic had summoned the birds to overwhelm the garrison, did that mean the rest of Thulle's tales were true? Could the Horned God's priests truly conjure up monsters?

Nedi looked up at the eagle and a golden shimmer blinded him. For an instant he thought he saw the bird transformed once again. As he blinked, he fervently hoped that was a promise of the eagle's aid, if the River Kingdom's masked priests could really call on such sorcery and try to reclaim Hatalys for the Paramount King.

They say history is written by the victors. That's very true. Frequently, folklore is created by the vanquished. Myths rooted in grievance and rebellion are passed down to subsequent generations in stories told by the fireside, heard by children listening at their grandmother's knee. Belief is a powerful force and in a world where magic is real, that's going to have dramatic results.

A Stitch in Time Saves One

Sometime around mid-afternoon, Clella was satisfied that her ledgers were up to date. She closed the account books and stretched her arms wide to ease her stiff neck and shoulders. She rose from her chair at the polished table and locked the ledgers away in the oak chest that was bolted to the wall beside the door.

As she left her office, she found Kinsen in the hallway by the door to the storerooms at the back of the manufactory. Meticulous whenever he checked a delivery, he had opened the first of a stack of sacks to count the skeins of freshly spun yarns and verify their colours.

He arched one grey and bristling eyebrow. 'Mistress?'

'Carry on.' Clella ignored the fidgeting spinner's boy waiting impatiently for Kinsen's signature on his master's delivery note. Then he could push his empty handcart out to the cobbled yard at the back. Only paying customers used the splendid entrance at the front of this impressive building overlooking the market place.

Straight-backed in her plain blue gown, Clella walked up the broad staircase. The bannisters were polished and the brass rods holding the carpet secure gleamed golden. Not every customer for Diepen House's famous tapestries left after enjoying wine and cakes in Clella's office. Many of them wanted to see the artisans at work, after they had made their choices from the house's array of exclusive designs. These requests came as often from merchants paying for a single forest scene as they did from nobles investing in a sumptuous set of floor-to-ceiling hangings depicting some famous fable.

Upstairs at the front of the building, the tall, south-facing windows were unshuttered. No passer-by could see the tapestries being woven on the sturdy high-beam looms. To the right of the stairs, Edra and Lowri were deftly slipping multicoloured bobbins through the pale curtain of warp threads. Remar's hands might be bigger, but he was equally skilled. He was working in shirtsleeves and had shed his stockings and shoes, while the women wore loose-fitting, lightweight gowns. The midsummer sun made these weaving rooms stifling hot.

They were progressing well, Clella noted, building up the shadowed hollows and pale rock faces of the Crag of Jarral which would loom over The Trial of Alafit. Experienced weavers, they had the design fixed in their minds and barely needed to glance at the vast pattern pinned to the wall opposite, even though they were working at the back of the tapestry. None of them paused for an instant as Clella watched from the doorway.

She crossed the landing to the other work room. A breeze from the open window overlooking the market place teased a wisp of her silvered chestnut hair which had somehow worked itself loose from her coiled and pinned braids.

Osia looked over to the door and offered a reassuring smile. Clella answered with a nod of approval, even though the pace of work here was visibly slower. Osia was taking care not to outpace the boys working on either side of her, as they wove the trees of the forest. In the centre of this tapestry, Alafit's fatal encounter with Sishin of Jarral had already been created by the house's experts. That drama would draw every eye, not any slight irregularity in the backdrop.

Not that Clella or the other weavers would ever say so to Lin or Adis. The two apprentices were intent on getting every twig and leaf correct, helped by the mirrors opposite. Those showed them the front of the work, every time they referred to the pattern pinned to the wall below. Clella noted that someone needed to break Lin of that habit of tilting his head every few moments, before he ended up with a permanent crick in his neck. The boy simply had to get used to the way tapestries were woven with the design running from side to side. Neither Alafit nor Sishin or any other participant in this famous drama would be standing upright until the skilled work of so many hands was taken off the loom, given a quarter turn, and hung from what now became the top of the tapestry.

A giggle drew Clella to the back room where Kinsen's wife Rayley sat on a bench, weaving slowly on a low beam loom. White-haired, she was now too old to spend long days working on warp threads stretching down from the high beams. Her wrinkled hands were still nimble, though, and if she could no longer see to the far side of the market place, her eyesight was fine for close work.

Diepen House's two newest apprentices had helped her prepare, serve and clear away the soup and bread that everyone shared at midday. Now she was showing the girls how she tamped down the wool as she built up colourful flowers on what would become a window seat cushion. Understanding the basics of this craft came much more easily from watching smaller, simpler pieces worked from the right side of the design. There was always a market for a touch of Diepen House luxury in some prosperous tradesman's home.

Noticing Clella in the doorway, Vanna and Emish sprang to their feet. Emish blushed like a schoolgirl caught in mischief. Well, the child had still been learning her letters and numbers until the turn of her tenth year last midwinter. Though Clella found it hard to imagine this meek little mouse had ever got into trouble. Unless Vanna had drawn her into it. The glint in that bold young lady's eye reminded Clella of herself at that age, running up and down these stairs. When her father had been master of the manufactory and Kinsen had still had a full head of dark hair.

She smiled at Rayley. 'I take it all is well?'

'Very well.' The older woman gestured at the baskets of bobbins wound with the coloured wools which the other work rooms would soon require. This was always a new apprentice's task, to accustom them to the weight and feel of the yarns, as well as teaching them how to wind bobbins smoothly. Soon the girls would be introduced to the costly silks which were used to add lustre or fine detail where extra warp threads were introduced into a design.

'Have you –?'

Whatever Rayley was going to ask was lost as a clatter of horses' hooves cut through the murmur of townsfolk going about their business outside. A scream of terror made Clella's blood run cold. She hurried to the landing window at the front of the building.

Shocked shouts echoed back from the tall buildings around the market place as she looked down.

A young man sprawled motionless on the cobbles, wearing only breeches and a bloodstained shirt. Clella saw that his face was covered in blood before anxious townsfolk blocked her view. She looked after the horsemen, now galloping away as their task here was done. From her lofty vantage point, she could see they wore Baron Brehane's livery. What was this all about?

She hurried down the stairs and opened the front door. That turned heads in the throng gathering around the unknown youth. If any of these townsfolk ever had business with Diepen House, they used the rear entrance.

Clella strode down the steps and searched the crowd for a face she recognised. She snapped her fingers at Ettick, the baker's delivery boy. 'Fetch Doctor Naith. Quickly!'

As Ettick ran off, the crowd parted to let her see the wounded youth. Clella saw relief on several faces. Someone else had taken charge.

'What happened?' she asked no one in particular. 'Does anyone know who he is?'

'The baron's men, they just dumped him.' An ancient idler was mystified.

A goodwife stooped to study the youth's battered face. 'Isn't he Widow Sabin's youngest?'

After a moment, a chorus of voices agreed, suggesting his name was Mathy or perhaps Mathin.

Clella clapped her hands. 'Who knows where she lives? Someone should fetch her. No, don't move him,' she added sharply as two burly men stepped forward. 'Not until the doctor's seen him. Not unless you want to answer for making his ills worse.'

The market traders looked at her, disconcerted. Clella met their unspoken questions with the same level gaze she used when some lordling tried to haggle over the price of a tapestry as if she were a costermonger.

The burly men stepped back and two women hurried off. The crowd thinned as people drifted away, recalling their own concerns. Barely ten onlookers remained when Ettick reappeared with Doctor

Naith. The physician's new apprentice followed, wearing a tightly-fitted gown despite the heat with a full skirt swishing above polished buttoned boots. Clella couldn't recall her name.

'What's amiss?' Seeing Clella beside the lingerers, Naith was confused. He glanced at the manufactory. 'The lad said there had been some accident.'

'We don't know what's happened, but this boy needs a doctor.' She gestured at the bloodstained youth.

Naith knelt to examine the boy with no thought for muck which might stain his breeches. That was merely one reason why Clella favoured him above the town's other doctors, if some over-hasty apprentice fell on the stairs, or a weaver trapped an incautious finger as a finished section of some tapestry was wound around a loom's beam. Naith was as thorough as he was skilled. She also knew he would come quickly. When his apprentice presented her with his bill, they would leave with the silver owed as soon as Clella could count it out.

The doctor looked up. 'He's taken an unwholesome beating, but there are no bones broken. The bleeding's all but stopped so he can be washed and his worst hurts bandaged. As for his wits...'

Naith pursed his lips, dubious, as his fingertips searched through the young man's light brown hair, sticky with blood. 'His skull is whole, but there's no way to tell if he'll wake up addled until he opens his eyes. He needs to be watched until then, in case he sinks into a stupor. Where –?'

'We'll take him in.' Clella turned to snap her fingers at Kinsen who was standing at the top of the steps. Tamin and Bose, the thickset brothers who did the manufactory's heavy lifting stood behind. 'Carry him into the end room out in the yard.'

They knew where she meant. Diepen House served customers the length and breadth of the realm. Servants coming any great distance to collect a commission needed a bed for the night. Providing such accommodation was simply good business.

The doctor rose to his feet and brushed dust off his knees. 'Shryan will bring a salve to ward off festering in these cuts and scrapes.'

'Thank you.' Clella could see the doctor had as many questions as she did. As Naith walked away, she wondered if she would have any answers for him, by the time his apprentice arrived with that ointment.

Tamin and Bose picked up the bloodstained youth. She followed them up the steps and through the tiled hall. As they went out through the rear door into the yard, the stables stood on one side and the manufactory cart and her personal carriage were housed on the other. The empty room for visitors was at the end of that wing. Tamin and Bose shared the room opposite, in case any night-time miscreants were bold enough to scale the tall, spike-topped gates in search of whatever they could steal.

Before they reached the end of the yard, Rayley appeared with a roll of the coarse linen used for swaddling finished tapestries. Kinsen had wasted no time enlisting his wife's skills. Vanna followed, clutching a bundle of rags, and Emish carried a broad bowl so carefully it must be full of water.

'Don't you make a mess of that bed,' Rayley called out as Tamin and Bose paused for Clella to open the door. 'Keep hold of him till I get there.'

They waited obediently for the old woman to spread a double thickness of linen over the flock mattress on the iron bedstead. Tamin and Bose laid the bloodstained youth down and looked at Clella.

'Well done.' She thanked them with a brisk nod. 'You can go back to your duties.'

Tamin touched a hand to his forelock. 'Mistress.'

Bose, who didn't speak, made an attempt at his usual willing smile, but his snub-nosed round face was anxious. Tamin took his brother's blunt-fingered hand. 'The lad'll be fine,' he said, reassuring.

'Let's hope so,' Rayley murmured as the two men left. She looked at the girls and gestured towards the small table. 'Put everything down. Go and tell Osia I said to make yourselves useful.'

Emish couldn't leave fast enough, though Vanna was more reluctant. As she glanced over her shoulder at the doorway, her eyes met Clella's. The girl coloured and hurried away.

'No doubt they've seen their brothers naked, but there's no call to embarrass this lad.' Rayley was already stripping the stranger. He was covered with darkening bruises.

'Someone gave him a thorough beating.' Clella watched as the older woman used clean rags to wash away the blood where blows from fists or feet had landed hard enough to split skin.

'Someone who knew how to do that and still stop short of murder or maiming.' Rayley bound up the worst of the boy's injuries with strips of clean linen.

'Indeed.' Clella wondered what that might mean.

Rayley spread a worn bedsheet over the boy. 'Mistress?'

'I'll sit with him until his mother arrives.' Clella fetched the stool from the corner.

'Mistress.' Rayley's voice betrayed no hint of her knowing grin.

She tipped the dirty water down the drain outside the door and swept the bloody rags from the table into the empty bowl. She closed the door behind her and Clella waited for her steps on the cobbles to fade away.

'I know you're shamming,' she said, conversationally, 'and I know the baron's men did this. You owe me some answers, Mathy or Mathin or whatever your name is.'

She waited. After a long moment, the youth on the bed opened one painfully swollen eye. 'It's Macsin. What gave me away?'

'You went rigid for a breath when you thought she was going to wash your privates.' Clella guessed he'd taken a knee to the groin. She understood such bruises were particularly agonising. 'So what happened to you?'

'They said I was trespassing.' Macsin closed his eyes. 'Maybe I was, but I wanted to see – my girl.' His tongue found a split at the corner of his mouth. 'We had a row on her last full moon visit home. I wanted to say I was sorry.'

His shoulders shifted in what might have become a shrug, but he stopped with a sharp intake of breath as some unseen injury hurt him. A few moments later, Clella heard unfamiliar voices in the yard, growing louder until Rayley opened the door.

'Widow Sabin, Mistress.' She stepped back so the distraught woman could enter. A second woman followed the boy's mother, resembling her so closely they must be sisters.

'Oh my heart.' Fresh tears streaked the widow's damp cheeks.

'Mistress Diepen,' her sister said stiffly. 'We cannot thank you enough. What –?'

'Think nothing of it,' Clella said firmly. 'Rayley, find him a shirt and have Tamin and Bose harness the cart to take these goodwives and the lad home. Get their direction, to tell Doctor Naith's apprentice where to take his salve. Tell her I will pay his bill.'

The widow's sister protested, but Macsin chose that moment to make a convincing show of coming to his senses. Clella left them to it.

Inside the manufactory, she walked up the stairs. Edra, Lowri and Remar were still intent on their work. She doubted they had even paused. Vanna and Emish were watching Lin and Adis while Osia explained exactly what the boys were doing. Clella continued on up to the manufactory's topmost floor.

Her private apartment was on the right hand side. After her mother had died, Clella found their house far too big and empty. She had never had any interest in marriage or motherhood, so she was much more comfortable here. Her cousin Orday, Osia's father, made far better use of so many rooms with his sizeable family.

Clella crossed the landing. The first of this nearly completed set of tapestries hung on her personal work room's rear wall. Alafit was wooing his beloved Vetria at the longest-day dance, even though he knew full well she had been betrothed as a child to Sishin of Jarral.

Clella stepped close to study the lovers' faces, worked in closely graded hues of silk over three times the number of warp threads as the tapestry's background. Edra's work was excellent, as always. Now Clella would add the final touches with ink and paint, so subtly that most onlookers didn't realise how such detail was added.

As she sorted through her pens and brushes on the table beside her drawing board where she sketched ideas and drew new designs, Clella picked apart what Macsin had said. One of many things her father had taught her was to tease out any strands of truth when someone was lying.

Baron Brehane's men had caught Macsin trespassing, she had no doubt about that. The youth had been trying to see some girl, true enough. Not to make up after some tiff. That was clearly nonsense. So what had he been doing and why?

Clella mixed her paints and walked over to the tapestry. She started by giving Vetria's cheek the hint of a blush with a barely moistened brush. This was slow and painstaking work. Even more care must be taken when approaching the tapestry with a needle-nibbed pen dipped in black ink. The inkwell itself stayed well away from the precious result of so many days of skilled labour, over on the table.

The sunlight softened to gold. In the rooms below, Clella heard the others bid each other a good evening as they finished their work. Her father had taught her to allow experienced weavers to pace themselves instead of constantly measuring their progress. He was right. Trusted workers strove harder.

As she paused to assess her own efforts, she heard Kinsen shoot the bolts that secured the front entrance. A short while later, he locked the rear door to the yard. The manufactory was silent. Clella took her pens and brushes down to the basement kitchen and washed them clean. Then she ate the supper of smoked fish, salad greens and the last of the day's bread which Rayley had left for her in the north-facing pantry, along with a jug of light summer ale fetched from the brewery and set on the cool slate slab.

Clella returned to the topmost floor. The light was fading steadily, but her next task was simple enough. She went to her bedchamber to unpin and unplait her hair. Once she had brushed out the tresses, she plucked a single chestnut hair. She carried that carefully to her work room, wound around her forefinger. The needle case her grandmother had given her was tucked inside a battered basket holding a jumble of sewing notions, for catching up hems, restitching seams and replacing buttons. Clella twisted the age-darkened wooden case to open it and took out the single bone needle.

Her father had told her that wealthiest clients were often the slowest to pay. Some would default entirely, if they thought they wouldn't be publicly called to account. Few artisans dared to do that

177

and risk losing other noble patrons. Her father said he found it productive to drop a few hints that he knew more of a client's finances than they realised. Certainly more than the realm's tax gatherers knew.

Clella asked how he learned such secrets. He smiled and said remarkable things could be gleaned from women's gossip. Was that truly where he thought such secrets came from? Did he make sure he knew no different, in order to be able to swear to that, if he was ever challenged in court? Clella never asked. Meantime, her grandmother taught her the secret of the bone needle's magic.

She threaded the single hair from her head through the pale needle's eye. Standing in front of the tapestry, she studied the girls blithely dancing with their suitors in the background. Grandmother always said an unremarkable figure was best. When Clella created new designs, she made sure there would be someone suitable. Using the bone needle she wove the single hair from her head invisibly into a dancing girl's garland of flowers.

When she was done, she didn't return the bone needle to its case. Instead she went to the archive room overlooking the rear yard. The deepening twilight meant she had to find the spark maker on the mantel and light a lamp. She found the volume she sought among the heavy leather-bound tomes which recorded every detail of commissioned work. These books weren't only bulky with sketches and notes. Each entry was marked by a many-hued plait of yarns showing the colours that had been used, in case a tapestry was ever sent to the manufactory for repair.

Clella turned the stiff pages to find The Return in Triumph of Berakin. Baron Brehane was inordinately proud of his illustrious forebear, who had voyaged to a dozen unknown lands and returned with every one of the men and ships who had set sail, as well as valuable treaties and trade goods. Clella knew this particular tapestry hung in the not-so-noble baron's private sanctum. She also knew it was his habit to retire there each evening after dining with his family. He had married to benefit from his wife's connections, not from any affection.

Her hand hesitated over the plaited wool. Strands salvaged from the bobbins used in a particular tapestry could never be replaced so the bone needle's magic must only be used when absolutely necessary.

Was this necessary now? Clella recalled Macsin's brutally calculated injuries. She considered the way the baron's liveried men had dumped the boy in the market place, where so many townsfolk would witness his fate. Though she didn't think they had been given orders to drop him on her doorstep specifically.

It was seven or so years since the baron had commissioned his tapestry. He had paid up promptly, though for some unaccountable reason he had assumed that silver also bought him Clella's willingness to become his mistress. Caught unawares, she had turned him down flat, and thought no more about it.

Until the rumours had reached her, at least. Brehane was evidently not used to rejection, and he chose to retaliate. He spread word that Clella had tried to seduce him, seeking introductions to further noble and wealthy clients. Thankfully those who did business with Diepen House knew her character, and the gossip had blown away on the wind before the full of the following moon. But Clella had been wary of the baron ever since.

She teased a short, pale strand from the braided lengths of wool. Plucking another hair from her head, she wound the two together and stood as close to the lamp as she could, to thread them through the bone needle's eye. She went to her bedchamber and lay down on the covers. Once she was comfortable, she closed her eyes. It took her a few breaths to summon up the resolve to prick the palm of her hand with the needle. She closed her fingers around it to keep the point buried in her flesh. It was painful, but Grandma had always said magic must never be too easy.

The enchantment took a few moments to work, but Clella had grown used to that. Soon she was looking through the ink-dotted eyes of an onlooker on the quayside. The tapestry came to life all around her. Woollen waves lapped against the quayside and the sails of the adventurer's ships billowed in the breeze. The woven crowd murmured with pleasurable anticipation.

Clella forced herself to concentrate. She reminded herself she was merely part of a tapestry. Now her mind's eye could see Baron Brehane's private sanctum, even if her view was criss-crossed with threads like someone peering through coarsely-woven sack cloth.

She couldn't see the baron in the panelled room. Instead, she saw a servant girl, easily identified by her livery. She wasn't doing any of a servant's usual tasks, though. She was searching, though Clella couldn't tell if she was hunting for something in particular or simply seeing what she might find. The maidservant checked behind the portraits on the walls, and felt for anything that might be fastened to the underside of the table. She took the cushions off the sumptuously upholstered chairs that flanked the empty fireplace, in case something was hidden beneath them.

Clella could see her frustration as she stood there, empty-handed. Before the girl could decide where to search next, something drew her attention to the door. Now Clella saw the girl's fear. She fled and Clella's heart beat faster, as if she were the one pursued. A few moments later, the baron entered, along with a man Clella didn't know. Both were relaxed and smiling, so the girl must have made her escape.

The stranger was another noble. His coat and breeches were dull russet silk embroidered with black curlicues while his black silk waistcoat boasted crystal buttons. He was much the same age as the baron, though his dark beard and hair showed no grey.

'Cordial? To aid your digestion?' Brehane walked to a side table where goblets stood beside a collection of decanters. 'Plum or almond?'

'A small measure of plum, thank you.' The stranger made himself comfortable in one of the chairs. 'Are you sure that was wise? We don't want to stir up the townsfolk.'

Clella could guess what they were discussing. The stranger's next words confirmed it.

'You're sure the lad was up to no good? Not just trying his luck?'

'No doubt about it. His father was a notorious agitator for land reform, before he did us all a favour and broke his neck falling from a roof.'

Brehane handed his guest a glass and took his own seat. 'Regardless, the boy was trespassing. Townsfolk who don't know any better will simply assume I am issuing a warning to anyone else who might try hunting my deer.'

'And those who do know better?' The stranger's tone was light but his dark eyes were intent.

Brehane smiled, vindictive. 'Now they know what will happen to snoopers.'

The stranger sipped the potent plum spirit. 'And the girl, Varie?'

The baron glowered. 'We need to find out what she might have overheard, before we learned that she's a tattle-tale.'

Whatever the stranger saw in Brehane's face alarmed him. 'A lad straying onto your land and getting a thrashing is one thing. The maid is a member of your household. She cannot be found beaten bloody – or worse – without awkward enquiries coming to your door.'

Baron Brehane waved that away. 'I will tell my wife to bring her with us, when we travel to Zalisse.'

'You think she'll be willing to leave home?' The stranger had his doubts.

'What fool of a girl can resist the lure of our great realm's capital?' Brehane smiled unpleasantly. 'Especially a prying bitch who's proved so keen to stick her nose where she has no business. If she doesn't?' He shrugged as he emptied his glass. 'We bind her and gag her and throw her in the cart with the luggage. No one here will know any different. If anyone asks where she has gone, they will be told she's serving my wife on the journey. A last minute decision.'

The stranger sipped his cordial again. 'And once we have her in Zalisse?'

'We find out what she knows and who she has told.' Brehane's growl promised the girl far worse than Macsin's suffering. 'Then she can be stripped and dumped in a ditch. No one will discover who she is before she's rolled into a pauper's grave. I'll tell my wife I've sent her home, and we can tell her family here that she was swept off her feet by some suitor from a distant province. How are they to know different?'

'You seem to have thought everything through.' The stranger's tone was neutral.

'You haven't?' Brehane challenged him. 'When there's so much at stake?'

The stranger conceded that with a nod. 'Indeed. When do you leave?'

'Tomorrow morning, as soon as my wife can be persuaded to finish her breakfast.'

'When you reach Zalisse, you'll send word to Baron Queval?'

Clella wasn't interested in their scheming. She looked down. Inside the tapestry, her hands were mere nubs of pale wool but that didn't matter. She concentrated on feeling her own fingers and pulled the tip the bone needle free of her skin. A moment later, and she was back in her own chamber, resting on her bed.

Light-headed, she forced herself to lie still until the unpleasant sensation passed. While she waited, she blinked to rid her gaze of the lingering lattice of threads. As soon as she felt more like herself, Clella sat up and pulled the wool and hair out of the needle's eye. That did away with the last of the magic. She dropped the tangle into the empty hearth and headed back to the archive room.

Berakin's Return wasn't the only tapestry Brehane had purchased from Diepen House. A few years before that, he had celebrated his wedding by spending a sizeable amount of his wife's silver on a pair of hangings for the entrance hall. They were hunting scenes which Clella's father had drawn years before and used for a number of clients.

She found the reference pages. Before she removed a thread from the plaited remnants of wool, Clella wondered if there was any other way to save the girl. Could she send some message to alert her to the danger? Could she find words that would seem innocent to anyone else who might read them? Who would take such a message? Tamin? What reason could she give him? No, there was no time. Night was falling and no one would open the baron's gate after dark.

Was this worth the attempt? There was no guarantee that the maid would pass through the entrance hall while Clella was waiting in the tapestry, but this was her only option. No one adorned servants' quarters with costly hangings. She could only try to intervene if the girl was on her own. No one would believe Varie for a moment if she told them what had happened. Clella could not risk speaking to her if there was a witness who could corroborate such a tale.

She drew a resolute breath. She had to try, at the very least. Clella found the yellow wool of a groom's pointed hood among the graded shades of green. Truth be told, that was as much as she could remember of the bystander she had chosen for the bone needle's magic so long ago. She couldn't even recall which of the two tapestries he had been in, and she had to hope that the hangings hadn't been moved to somewhere else in the house.

She wound another hair from her head around the wool and rethreaded the bone needle. Returning to her bedchamber, she lay down and braced herself to endure the magic's effects again. She had never done this more than once in a day before. She had never used the bone needle twice within the passage of the same moon.

The speed of the transition caught her unawares. She had barely taken a breath before she was in the tapestry forest, surrounded by noise and movement. Now Clella remembered. The other tapestry showed the hunt in full cry. This one showed the pursuit's conclusion with a feast in a flower-studded glade.

Men gathered around a firepit where a slain stag was rather improbably roasting on a spit. They cheered as they congratulated each other. Servants hurried to and fro, carrying baskets of bread and jugs of wine. An ornate tent sheltered a handful of demure maidens. Clella looked around in wonder. Was this truly how the wealthy entertained themselves?

The woven horse whose reins she held tossed its head and snorted, irritable. It stamped and Clella wondered how much a kick from woollen hooves might hurt, since she was woven from similar strands. Then she felt the pain in her palm, where the bone needle still pierced her hand.

Abruptly, she recalled her purpose. This hunt had nothing to do with her. Clella quickly tied the woven horse's reins to the convenient branch of a nearby tree. A tree with several obvious errors in its trunk she noted. Whose work had this been? Orday's, before he decided against the weaver's trade?

What was she thinking? Clella shook off distraction a second time and hurried to the edge of the clearing. As she peered out through the warp and weft, she saw the tapestry was still hanging in the baron's entrance hall. That was a relief.

On the other hand, the hall was dark and silent. Clella could see that in the light of the tapestry firepit's flickering flames. The whole household must be abed. She had no idea how so much time could have passed and she didn't bother speculating. Now she could only hope the girl would be one of the servants who rose first in the morning.

She sat down on the emerald green grass dotted with bright blue flowers. Behind her, the jollity continued. Clella refused to look in that direction, in case she was drawn into the woven world again. She concentrated on the dark, silent hall.

Somewhere, some time later, a door creaked open. Clella saw a shadow moving through the stillness. Whoever it was carried neither candle nor lantern, relying on the starlight filtering through the hall's high windows. As they drew closer to the tapestry, the woollen firelight showed Clella the maid Varie's tight-lipped face.

She would know the baron and his wife were planning to leave in the morning. This was her last chance to search for whatever it was that might well cost this girl her life. Clella sprang to her feet. As Varie drew level with her, she snapped the fingers of her empty hand. Her other fist was closed tight around the bone needle. Her soft blunt hand made no noise at all. The maid walked on, intent, oblivious.

'Varie!' Clella shouted before she could stop herself. She didn't even know if the girl would hear her.

Varie froze, looking in all directions, and struggling to hide her fear, as she tried to work out where that voice had come from.

Clella ran across the tapestry, past the fancy tent and the roisterers circling the firepit. She pressed her pale woollen hand against the lattice of threads. 'Varie! Listen to me.'

Varie stared at the tapestry, open-mouthed. Clella could see the firelight reflected in the girl's eyes. The flicker dimmed then brightened again, as the huntsmen and grooms walked past the pit. There was no question about it. Varie could see the woven world as Clella could, vibrant and alive.

'Varie!' Clella summoned all the authority she commanded as Mistress of Diepen House. 'Macsin was caught by the baron's men and beaten half to death. The baron knows you are searching for his secrets. He plans to take you with him when he leaves, whether you're willing or not. His men will beat you to learn whatever you know and throw your corpse into a ditch.'

Varie stared at her, or rather at the yellow-hooded, woven groom. 'Who – what – how...'

'Leave. Now. At once. Don't delay to gather your belongings. Leave before they kill you.' Clella didn't know how else to convince her.

The girl retreated from the tapestry. She hurried away, heading for the baron's sanctum.

Clella was at the edge of the tapestry. She could go no further. Worse, she was distracted. As she reached out with both hands, the bone needle slipped free. Clella lay on her bed once again with an agonising pain in her palm.

This time it took an age for the magic's after-effects to fade. It was the dead of night before she rose and stowed the bone needle back in its case with numb, fumbling hands. She went to bed where she tossed and turned and finally slept, only to be woken by the market traders preparing to start their day.

Clella fetched water from the cistern in the basement which Tamin and Bose filled from the well in the yard every day. She washed and dressed and plaited her hair, pinning up her braids. By the time she had eaten some plum bread for her breakfast, Kinsen and Rayley had arrived. The apprentices followed and the manufactory's day began.

Clella went to her office and sat at the table, not knowing what to do. Should she send word to Macsin? Perhaps she could visit him, to ask if he had any news? But how could she explain that she knew Varie's name? That she knew they were searching for the baron's secrets? No skein of yarn had ever been as hopelessly tangled as her thoughts.

Someone knocked at the front door. Seizing on the distraction, Clella hurried to open it. She stared, dumbfounded, when she saw who stood on the steps.

Varie was dishevelled and dusty. She must have been walking all night. She had no bag that might hold her belongings, or even a shawl. But she carried something the size and shape of a ledger, wrapped in soft leather. She stared at Clella with wordless desperation.

Why had the girl come here? She couldn't have known it was Clella speaking through the woven figure of the groom. Then she realised the answer was obvious. Where else would Varie go to seek answers after encountering some mystery woven into a tapestry?

Clella opened the door wider. 'You had better come in.'

The increasing focus on social history in popular culture is revealing the considerable economic value and importance of yarn arts that were dismissed as 'women's work' for so long. When I was looking for inspiration for a new story, I happened to be reading a book about tapestries...

Coins, Fights and Stories Always Have Two Sides

As shadows lengthened across the camp ground, Erlin surveyed his fiefdom with satisfaction. Two tall tents of oiled leather were securely pitched at either end of a sturdy wagon, all embracing a sizeable hearth. A broad griddle and three lidded cook pots rested above the flames on an iron frame. To one side a spit rested on its uprights above an oval pan. That wouldn't be empty long. Korose was approaching with a plump young sheep's carcass over his shoulder.

The lanky lad grinned as he arrived. 'We'll do well tonight.'

'We will.' Erlin set the last of the flatbreads he'd been cooking in their linen-lined basket and moved it a prudent distance from the hearth. 'Get that fire stoked.'

He secured the beast on the spit with interlocked skewers. Customers would appear once the aroma of roasting lamb drifted through this Lescari mercenary throng.

Customers with coin in their pockets, so soon after the end of the fighting season. Aft-Autumn's shifting colours had yet to subside into For-Winter's unchanging calm and the weather had been kind thus far.

The camp would be a different place come Aft-Winter. Once the frosts bit deep, Korose would have to forage ever further afield for firewood. Hungry mercenaries would grudge every copper spent on barley broth. Erlin would need all his guile to persuade the Caladhrian villages across the river to part with their jealously guarded stores. He was already buying sacks of flour, beans and onions from farmers gloating over well-stocked barns.

Each day, as hungry mercenaries came to his fire, Erlin discreetly looked for those most likely to try stealing from him after the solstice; sneaking up to the wagon at night like a rat after cheese or threatening him with a sword, demanding the leathery remnants of a side of bacon.

'I'll want you out of your blankets early tomorrow,' he said as Korose fetched an armful of firewood. 'To practise with your quarter staff.'

'Maybe try some sword work?' the lad asked, hopeful.

Erlin smiled. 'If you impress me.'

He had every intention of getting his notched blades out from under the wagon's driving seat. These past ten days, this stretch of well-drained grassland between the river and a sprawl of coppices had been attracting ever more mercenaries seeking a winter haven. Time to show any covetous strangers that a grey-haired, weather-beaten old man was no easy prey.

Erlin had served his time in Lescar's interminable wars, as six rival dukes spent their silver and other men's blood on their ambition to be crowned High King. He still practised the skills that had seen him safe through countless battles.

He'd teach Korose, so the lad had some chance of surviving his first bloody season, once he'd put on enough muscle and height to catch a recruiting sergeant's eye.

Maybe the lad would come back years later, scarred and wealthy. Maybe Erlin would never hear of him again. No telling with such waifs and strays.

'Stir up the fire.' He set the laden spit on its uprights.

Korose threw weathered wood onto the flames. 'What news today?'

Erlin shrugged. 'Quicksilvers took a beating when Sharlac's duke challenged His Grace of Triolle. Greenhawks scattered to the four winds after the battle at Chinel turned against Draximal.'

'You reckon we'll see any of them here?'

Korose look dubious. That particular bloody fight had soaked the soil on the far side of Lescar. But Erlin had tramped the length and breadth of this blighted country ten or more times in his youth, loyal to his scrawl on various mercenary companies' muster rolls.

'Stranger things have happened.'

Korose tended the cook pots seething over the flames. Erlin turned the spit, making sure only the dull splat of fat dripped into the pan underneath, not the hiss of the meat's precious juices.

Dusk approached and more newcomers arrived. Some had laden horses or handcarts. Others had only the clothes and weapons they wore. Once they'd claimed a space, late arrivals wandered towards the cook fire in search of supper.

Korose served turnip pottage to a hungry warrior and replaced the pot lid. 'He'd be useful in a fight.'

A broad-shouldered and warmly-cloaked man with swords on each hip and carrying a bulky leather bag passed by their hearth.

'I'd say so.' Noting the lithe walk of an alert swordsman, Erlin fixed the man's face in his memory. If he wasn't hungry tonight, sooner or later their paths would cross and Erlin would learn his story.

The man's fine clothing and better weapons indicated he had no trouble filling his purse. So why come to this lesser camp instead of wintering in a larger stockade with some wealthy mercenary company?

Had he fallen out with the captain he'd mustered with last spring? Some quarrel over a wench or a wager? Never mind. Once the year had turned and For-Spring was on the horizon, Erlin would offer the stranger some introductions. By then the cook would know which war bands would welcome a swordsman who knew a rival company's secrets. Grateful coin would chink in the coffer Erlin kept well-hidden in his wagon's recesses.

Such profitable opportunities were merely one reason he liked to winter in these lesser camps. That, and the big mercenary company quartermasters ruled their cold season stockades with an iron hand. Free spirits like Erlin paid extortionate sums just to breathe the same air.

'That smells good.' Two leather-armoured men approached. One was tall and broad in a long jerkin with tarnished brass studs. He had a close-cropped head and eyes as dull as a dead trout.

The other was lithe as a snake in a short cuirass of oiled hide. Curly black hair and his sallow complexion spoke of Tormalin blood. He reached out with his belt knife to cut a slice from the succulent meat on the spit.

Erlin knocked the blade aside with his meat-jointing knife, as quick as he ever had been with a sword. 'I carve, and only once I'm paid.'

The snake withdrew, raising hands in mock surrender. 'I beg your pardon.'

'Granted.' Erlin made no move towards the spitted lamb.

A heartbeat later the snake reached for a purse tucked inside his leather breastplate. 'How much for two?'

'A silver mark each.' Erlin held out a hand. 'Silver, not Lescari lead.'

The snake cocked his head. 'Caladhrian or Tormalin?'

Erlin shrugged. 'Whatever you're carrying.'

The snake handed over two Caladhrian coin. Erlin slipped them into the pouch laced tight to his belt. 'Fat or lean?'

'Fat,' the croppy head growled.

'Lean,' his companion smiled.

Erlin trusted that like he'd trust a mantrap's grin but coin was coin. Korose offered a leathery flatbread in each hand. Erlin laid a generous helping of meat on each one and the lad handed them over.

'We'll see you again.' The snake tore off a mouthful and went on his way.

The croppy-head lingered to stare at Erlin before he followed.

'He thinks a lot of himself.' Apprehension undercut Korose's attempt at a laugh.

'He does.' Erlin pursed his lips.

He knew the snake's attempt to help himself had little to do with meat. When that sort got away with acting as though they had every right to take what they wanted, soon everyone would yield for the sake of a quiet life. Newcomers wouldn't even ask what gave such men such spurious authority.

He'd also seen the croppy-head taking in every detail of their little encampment, including the dun carthorse picketed on the far side of the wagon. Good luck to him trying to steal the beast or sneaking past to rob the wagon. Erlin had trained Pipkin to attack as readily as any guard dog.

He greeted the next man approaching the fire. 'What's your pleasure?'

'What's your price?' the Lescari countered.

Customers hurried up now they'd seen Erlin carving the lamb and plenty more wanted pottage. By the time the carcass was reduced to bones and gristle, all three cook pots were down to the dregs and the flatbread basket was long emptied.

'I'd say we're done.' Erlin weighed the silver in the pouch against his thigh with satisfaction.

Korose was looking out into the darkness. 'Do you –?'

He wasn't talking to Erlin. The cook saw a slender figure in the shadows, wrapped in a blanket doing duty as a cloak.

He beckoned. 'If you don't want to eat, you're welcome to warmth.'

'I'd like that.' The girl's hesitant voice betrayed her nature.

'Do you have a bowl?' Erlin tilted one of the cook pots. 'Otherwise I'll pour this away.'

'Thank you.' The girl's haste betrayed her hunger. As she rummaged in her bag and moved closer to the firelight, Erlin noted her shirt's ragged cuffs and her much-mended jerkin. Her purse must be as empty as her belly.

Erlin filled her age-darkened wooden bowl with the last splash of broth and snapped his fingers at Korose. 'Get those bones into a pot with a good tight lid and stow it in the wagon before any dogs come sniffing around.'

As Korose hurried to obey, the girl crouched down to drink her bowl dry.

Didn't even have a spoon to call her own, Erlin guessed. He scraped the drippings from the spit into an earthenware jar. As he stood up, he saw the girl look hungrily at the smeared pan.

He fetched one of the flatbreads he'd set aside for himself and the lad. Wiping up the savoury residue, he tossed it to the girl. 'Here.'

She caught it, deft as a pup leaping for a tidbit, and vanished into the darkness. Erlin saw Korose looking after her.

'Stir up that fire for one last blaze, lad.' He fetched juicy beefsteaks from the wagon along with a cast iron frying pan. 'Let's have an onion and those mushrooms from this morning.'

Korose was still trying to see where the girl had gone. 'Do you think she'll be all right?'

'What's it to us?' Erlin brushed windblown ash off the chopping block.

Though once they were fed, had tidied up and were settled in their blankets, his thoughts turned to the girl.

How old? Hard to say in the dying firelight. Not in the first bloom of maidenhood. That was some reassurance. If she'd been living around mercenary companies for a couple of years – and by her battered gear Erlin guessed she had – she must have learned a few tricks to save herself from rape or worse.

Not a whore. Skinny as she was, she'd worn a sword at her hip and made no offer to take his meat in her mouth in return for a meal. That was good to know. Satin Fantine's brothel tents were on the far side of the camp. The henchmen who guarded her girls would offer freelance trollops the choice of handing over half their earnings or taking a beating so bad that no man would come near them.

Maybe she was a scout, Erlin mused as he drifted off to sleep. He'd known a few such women in his day; nimble enough to spy out an enemy camp and get back alive to tell the tale.

Korose was up with the first glimmer of dawn to rekindle the fire. Erlin fed himself and the lad, then began serving griddled pancakes and bacon to those with silver to spend and porridge to those with copper.

Erlin was assessing the batter in his green-glazed jug when the broad-shouldered warrior from the night before offered Korose a shiny mark. 'Good day to you both.'

'The lad's Korose and I'm Erlin.' He mixed more ale and flour. 'What do we call you, friend?'

'Triggen,' the man said easily.

Young enough to still be friendly with strangers. Old enough and strong enough to stand his ground against anyone who tried to take liberties. Erlin wondered when he'd walked away from whatever plough or prentice bench he'd been born to. At least five years since, he guessed, maybe as long ago as ten.

'Looks like you had a good summer,' he observed.

'Up in Sharlac with the Sundowners,' Triggen agreed. 'Looking after the townsfolk of Welland.'

'Sundowners are a fine company.' Honourable, for the most part, though that wouldn't have stopped them extorting safe-passage money from any merchants taking the Great West Road. Erlin poured batter onto the hot griddle. 'What's your pleasure for breakfast?'

Triggen grinned. 'A couple of those wrapped around bacon. Nice and crisp if you please.'

As Korose served several bowls of porridge Erlin watched the swordsman wander off with his breakfast, stopping to chat with someone every few paces.

'Sundowners don't take just anyone,' Korose breathed.

'True,' Erlin agreed. 'And they'd slap a cook's boy silly for letting bacon burn.'

'Shit!' Korose hastily lifted the smoking pan from the grating.

'Good morning all!'

Erlin looked up as the snake greeted everyone present with an expansive gesture and a smile.

'Thank you for your attention! Now, I know Aft-Autumn's not even turned to For-Winter –' he held up self-deprecating hands although no one had said a word '– but a sensible man thinks two steps ahead. We'll need someone paying for our swords and skills before Spring Solstice. Better to have that agreement signed and sealed with a duke's ring sooner than later?'

He looked around but before anyone spoke, he nodded, as though satisfied with everyone's agreement.

'I'm Chellan, for those who don't know me. I've fought with the Shearlings, the Wheelwrights and the Red Dyed Men. My sergeant is Acuri.' He gestured to the croppy-head at his side.

'Show us your skills if you want to sign up. That's all, for the moment. Carry on.' The snake nodded at Erlin before strolling off, dead-eyed Acuri at his side.

Who was he to give Erlin permission to do anything? The cook gripped his ladle, wishing Chellan had come within reach of a hefty clout.

'Chellan?' A mercenary looked at his tent mate. 'What's his company?'

'Who's to say there's a company?' Erlin scraped a burned pancake off the griddle with his knife. 'A man swaggers like a captain, that doesn't make him one. If he's fought with those fine companies, why's he wintering here?'

But he could see several men were tempted. Learning to take orders, quick and unquestioned, was a skill which kept mercenaries alive. Following any obvious leader soon became a habit.

Erlin pondered as he cooked pancakes. Once their last customer was served, he hefted their biggest cauldron onto the grate's iron bars and filled it from the water butt by the wagon.

'Once this is hot, you wash the pots,' he told Korose. 'I'll take a turn around the camp before I scour the pans. See if anyone else is setting up a cook fire.'

Strolling among the tents, he was pleased to find he had no rivals thus far. Though as he'd expected a good few mercenaries had dug small pits to cook for themselves. Along his way he noted Triggen falling into conversations. The burly swordsman must be a companionable fellow.

When Erlin spotted a familiar face re-sewing a boot seam, he raised a hand. 'Marsis!'

The weathered warrior looked up, puzzled. His lined brow cleared. 'Erlin? It must be three years, you dog!'

That was invitation enough. Erlin sat down. 'What have you been doing?'

Marsis grinned. 'That's a story and a half.'

As he told it, Erlin learned some useful information. In return he shared a few insights to help Marsis secure a profitable hire for the next year's fighting.

'So what do you know of this Chellan?' he asked casually as their conversation wound to a close.

Marsis frowned. 'Nothing, for all he acts like everyone should know his name.'

'Wasn't there some trouble with the Red Dyed Men back at the start of the summer?' mused Erlin.

Marsis nodded. 'Near split the company down the middle. Rankers whispering round the shit pits, stirring up any fools who'd listen. Refuse to fight unless they got more of the Duke of Draximal's coin.'

Erlin raised astonished eyebrows. 'What happened?'

Marsis shrugged. 'The company didn't split. I guess the sergeants traced the stink to its source, beat those fools black and blue and slung them out on their arses.'

'Reckon so.' Erlin got to his feet. 'Good to see you. Come over when you want a meal.'

As he wandered back, Erlin wondered if Snake Chellan and Cropped Acuri still carried the scars of a Red Dyed sergeant's kicking. If he was a betting man, he'd wager on it. But Erlin took bets. He didn't lay them.

Back at the wagon, Korose was looking guilty. It wasn't hard to see why. The scrawny girl had scraps of scorched bacon in her bowl and the last crumbs of the burned pancake. As soon as she saw Erlin, she fled.

In the daylight she was definitely no poult. Past her twentieth year, by Erlin's guess, of an age to be wed with three or four brats if she'd stayed in whatever village bred her. Old enough to know her own mind if she chose to give Korose a thrill.

He looked up to check the sun. 'I'll scour those pans and we can try some blade work before we make a start on this evening's meal.'

Setting aside staffs and swords as the daylight faded, Erlin stirred and spiced while Korose chopped and sliced. A bull calf was on the spit this evening. Not worth costly fodder through the winter for a farmer but well worth fattening on summer grass to feed hungry mercenaries after autumn's slaughter.

Erlin noticed eager anticipation on the faces making their way to his fire. Though he soon learned it wasn't for his food.

'Thinking of trying your luck?' A scar-faced Caladhrian asked his Dalasorian friend.

'Depends what they're offering the winner.' The hawk-nosed man looked tempted.

'I got through the summer without shedding blood,' a solid Lescari said to no one in particular. 'I won't risk a winter wound festering.'

'Plenty of time to heal before spring,' countered the man beside him.

'A bout will only be to first blood,' a Carlusian agreed. 'They won't want anyone badly injured, not looking to sign the best fighters onto their muster.'

Erlin interrupted. 'What's this?'

A handful of excited voices answered him.

'A sword tourney?' Korose looked over the fire, bright-eyed.

Erlin sucked his teeth. 'At this Chellan's behest, and Acuri's?'

Before anyone answered, half the men by the fire turned as someone exclaimed.

'Here they come!'

The snake and his croppy pal approached, to be bombarded with questions.

'Will you make the winner a sergeant?'

'What about the runner up? You'll need more than one troop leader!'

Some seemed less confident of their prospects.

'You'll give everyone's skills a fair test?'

'You wouldn't write a man off for one unlucky slip?'

A vital question fell into one of those unaccountable silences that open up in the noisiest of crowds.

'How many days do we have to prepare?'

The snake squared his narrow shoulders, head tilted back as he surveyed the crowd like a rich man buying a horse. 'Three days,' he said tersely. 'From tomorrow. We draw lots on the fourth morning from now and then we'll see what you're made of.'

His last words were almost lost amid eager cheering. Chellan smiled thinly before he looked at Acuri, cold-eyed, and jerked his head towards the river. As Chellan turned and stalked away, the crop-headed man followed, scowling.

'What do you reckon?' Korose bit his lip as he looked at Erlin.

'No, I don't reckon you should try your luck,' he said firmly. 'You won't learn anything from a beating and you might be unlucky enough to catch a bad wound.'

He smiled to soften the blow of his words, seeing Korose crestfallen.

'Watch how the skilled men practise these next few days. You'll learn a lot from that. Once the tourney starts, look for what loses a man the bout, not just how his opponent wins. Here, you take charge of the spit. I won't be long.'

He handed the long meat knife to the lad and headed for the latrines. As soon as he was beyond the cook fire's light, Erlin changed direction. Cutting between tents and bivouacs, he headed straight towards the river.

As he saw his quarry ahead, he slowed and proceeded carefully. Thankfully the dusk was thickening and Chellan and Acuri were intent on their conversation.

'Why didn't you talk to me before telling half the camp your bright idea?'

'My idea?' Acuri growled. 'Everyone was telling me you spread the word.'

'Why?' spat Chellan. 'We've no coin for a victory purse!'

'So the notion sprang up like a toadstool?' Acuri challenged.

'More like some fool mixed one rumour with another like a drunk with white brandy and ale.' Chellan exhaled with a hiss. 'Does

197

it matter? If no one claims the notion, we can steal it. Has anyone definitely said there's a purse for the winner?'

'Not that I've heard,' Acuri said cautiously.

'So we say for certain there isn't,' Chellan mused. 'Offer sergeants' rank for the last two standing? Banner sergeant for the winner?'

'Where does that leave me?' Acuri snarled.

'Lieutenant,' Chellan said testily.

'Equal captain.' Acuri snapped back.

Chellan drew a resolute breath. 'We talked about that. Two captains means split loyalties and troublemakers always try to drive in a wedge.'

'I —' Acuri broke off to stare into the darkness.

Erlin stood as still as a tent pole, sliding his eyes sideways. Somewhere to his off hand, he saw a shadow move. He blinked. Or had he imagined it?

'Let's get a drink.' Chellan walked away along the river bank towards Jartan's wine wagon.

'We haven't agreed —' Acuri stood stubborn for a moment, before following with a muttered obscenity.

After waiting to be certain that neither glanced over his shoulder, Erlin took a roundabout path back to his hearth.

Korose was out of his blankets first the following morning and quick to do all his chores. He wasn't the only early riser. Clashing steel rang through the camp before they were halfway done serving breakfast, interspersed with angry shouts or startled yelps from someone caught unawares.

Erlin nodded when the lad asked for leave to watch the men practise for the tourney. Amiably resigned to doing the bulk of the day's work, he was surprised when Korose returned halfway through the afternoon, scowling.

Erlin stopped chopping cabbage. 'Who stepped on your heel?'

'Me? No, I'm fine.' Korose still looked troubled. 'How many swordswomen have you known?' he asked abruptly. 'How do they usually fare?'

'None so many, though more than a few.' Erlin paused to consider the armed and armoured females he'd encountered in his time. Most mercenary companies had a handful on their roster.

'For the most part they fare as well, or as badly, as any man. You don't last in this life without some talent for it. Some women rise to captain their own companies. You must have heard of Ridianne the Vixen?'

That was barely a question. Everyone had heard of her. Any man in this camp would clean her boots with his tongue if that was the cost of joining her roster.

'Do you know where she's camped?'

Erlin wasn't expecting that. 'You're thinking of leaving?'

'No.' Korose paused in his pacing. 'Do you think she'd look more kindly on a woman asking for winter shelter?'

Erlin laid down his knife. 'What's this about, lad?'

Korose dropped onto the turf and moodily poked the fire's ashy bed with a stick. 'It's Letsis. She wants to hone her skills, to make a decent showing in the tourney. Half the men won't spar with her and those who will just want to beat her bloody.'

Erlin guessed Korose meant the ragged girl. 'If she chooses to set herself up, she must know she risks getting knocked down.'

'It's not fair,' Korose protested.

'It's not your business,' Erlin pointed out. 'Who was giving a good showing? Who could you learn from?' He lowered his voice. 'Help me decide what odds to offer, when I take bets on the tourney and you'll earn a share of the profits.'

Korose still looked inclined to argue on the girl's account. After a long moment, he capitulated. 'That swordsman, Triggen, is a wonder. Wonderful light on his feet for all he's so broad, and quick as lightning with his hands.'

'Who else?' Erlin began chopping again. 'Stir up that fire while you're telling me. We can both do two things at once.'

By the time they had the evening meal ready, he was more than satisfied with Korose. The lad definitely had a good eye and a sound brain to go with it. Just as long as his head wasn't turned by that ragged lass Letsis.

Erlin caught a glimpse of her slinking past while Korose was fetching that evening's fat lamb from Rila Butcher. Looking for the lad, he guessed, and whatever scraps she could scrounge. He wasn't sorry to see her gone before Korose got back. The boy would be a danger around the fire, distracted by the sight of her battered face.

Seeing she carried herself stiff and careful, Erlin guessed she'd taken some hard falls, maybe even a kicking, leaving bruises hidden by her clothes. He hid his sympathy behind an impassive face. The sooner she learned this life showed no one mercy, the better for them all.

'I wonder –?' Triggen's voice broke into his thoughts. 'Might I have a cup of hot water for a copper?'

'Have it and welcome.' Erlin nodded towards the steaming cauldron. 'No charge.'

'My thanks.' Triggen carefully dipped a silver cup into the roiling water and dropped in a knotted scrap of muslin.

Drinking herb tisane like a fine lady, Erlin noted. 'Keeping clear of wine and ale until after the tourney?'

'Something like that.' Triggen grinned. Then he stiffened like a hound sighting prey.

Erlin pretended not to notice, concentrating on his flatbreads. But as Triggen strolled away, he covertly watched where the swordsman was going.

Not obviously hurrying, Erlin approved. Not making too much of his apparent surprise. Not one man in a hundred would have guessed his path crossing Chellan's was anything but happenstance.

He glanced around the fire. What might be stolen if he wasn't there to keep watch? Nothing he couldn't afford to lose. Knowing what Chellan was thinking would be worth far more. Erlin slipped quickly between two tents, getting as close as he dared. To his relief, Triggen and Chellan were still exchanging pleasantries. Naturally the snake wanted to stay friends with such a promising recruit.

'I hear you'll be the man to watch, come the tourney.'

'Don't believe all you hear.' Triggen chuckled. 'I'm just glad to know we'll see you fight. No better way for a captain to win a man's trust than showing his courage is equal to theirs.'

'I haven't said I'd take part, just yet.' Chellan cleared his throat. 'Who told you so?'

Triggen's brow wrinkled. 'The three-fingered man who fought with the Daybreakers? He was talking to Sergeant Acuri this morning?'

'Malhen?' Chellan forced a laugh. 'He never could keep a secret.'

'Everyone will be pleased to hear you'll show us your mettle,' Triggen assured him.

'Quite so.' Chellan nodded a brisk farewell and strode off through the camp.

Erlin glanced over his shoulder. He was still within sight of his fire and there was no one who shouldn't be prowling round his wagon. Though if he followed Chellan he wouldn't be able to see if a gang of robbers ransacked it. Where was Korose?

He yielded, though, pursuing the snake through the camp. At first he was poised to duck behind any concealment. Then he realised Chellan was so intent, he wouldn't have noticed a troop of Dalasorian horsemen on his trail.

Acuri was taking his ease outside a tent Erlin guessed was his own. Chellan strode up and grabbed the crop-headed man's shoulder, all but dragging him inside. Erlin's grin widened. It never failed to amuse him how people assumed a canvas wall was as solid and soundproof as wood or stone. Especially when they were angry. He strolled casually up to the side of the tent and knelt, as though to retie a bootlace.

'Why tell folk I'll fight in this fucking tourney?' Chellan accused. 'You're hoping I'll fall on my arse? Maybe get a knife in my ribs? So you'll end up captain?'

'I never said any such thing,' Acuri protested.

'You expect me to believe that?' Chellan's voice turned ugly. 'I remember Inchra.'

The whole tent shook with the scuffle inside. Erlin didn't wait to see if they brought poles and canvas down. He hurried off, discreetly pleased. Better yet, he found Korose at their hearth, standing guard.

The day of the tourney dawned crisp and clear. Korose was up and about before the sun rose over the coppices. Erlin took his time preparing a modest pile of griddle cakes. No fighter would want a full belly and the rest wouldn't linger for fear of missing a good bout. He saw Chellan and Acuri approaching. The croppy-head carried a bucket while the snake's leather armour gleamed with fresh oil.

'First bouts!' Chellan shouted. 'Stand forth or fight in your nightshirt!'

Acuri slapped a tent in passing. 'I've got your token, Vendrish, so swap that cock in your hand for a sword hilt!'

'How many in that bucket?' Erlin asked Korose quietly.

'Near enough full, yesterday evening.' The lad looked anxiously at the gathering mercenaries. Searching for the girl no doubt.

Erlin watched the crowd swell with mixed feelings. Having his fire become the camp's meeting place would be profitable but he didn't like Chellan and Acuri deciding that without a by-your-leave.

Still, Erlin could get a good look at the men he'd taken most bets on, as Acuri drew pottery shards from his bucket and shouted out the men's names scrawled on each one. Women were competing too. Letsis wasn't the only female fighter in the camp, though two others trying their luck and skills overtopped her by a head.

Several of the heavily backed men looked none too bright. Erlin had seen them over-indulge in ale last night. Overconfident.

Triggen had stuck to drinking his tisanes, always ready to chat by the cook fire with whoever might be passing. The young warrior looked formidable, shirtless in a leather jerkin.

The man called to fight him looked distinctly nervous. Unlike the warrior who'd face Letsis. He could barely restrain a laugh.

Acuri called out the rules of engagement. 'Find clear and level ground. Square off and fight on the count of three. Best of three touches if nobody yields but I don't want anyone maimed. We'll call witnesses to agree on a victor if there's any dispute.'

The crowd scattered into fighting pairs, eyeing each other warily, surrounded by knots of eager onlookers. Acuri took Erlin's chopping block for a stool. 'I'll take a stack of those griddle cakes, and find some honey to go with them.'

Erlin ignored him, watching Chellan stalk off. The snake was glancing sideways at a bull-necked bruiser from Ensaimin. Did he wonder if Acuri had palmed that particular token, setting him up against someone forewarned of his strengths and weaknesses? The two of them had barely exchanged a glance, still less a friendly word this morning.

'Did you hear me?' Acuri snapped.

Erlin looked levelly at him. 'Did you pay me?'

Acuri's lip curled but after a breath, he tossed a silver mark onto the turf. Erlin made no move to fetch it. When Korose took a step, he stilled him with a glance. 'You go see the bouts. Come tell me all the news.'

He had been planning to watch at least some of the fights himself. Not now, and leave dead-eyed Acuri unwatched around his tents. Not with the camp's gamblers' stake money hidden beneath his wagonload of sacks.

Erlin fetched more firewood from the stack by the water butt. When he returned, Acuri was holding out a silver mark. Erlin didn't need to look to know it was the one he'd thrown onto the grass.

He served the man a handful of griddle cakes, expressionless. 'No honey.'

He'd barely had time to wonder how Acuri would respond when the first roars indicated a sword bout was already over. The chagrined loser trailed back to the fire after the crowing victor, both surrounded by friends and strangers offering congratulations and commiseration.

Erlin left Acuri collecting the winner's potsherd while he went to the wagon to fetch his ledger of wagers. Soon they were both too busy to quarrel over cakes or honey.

The tourney was half done, by Erlin's reckoning, before Korose reappeared. Dismay and elation chased each other across the lad's face like clouds scudding across a bright sky.

'Triggen just took two wounds –' he began.

'Sorry to hear it.' Erlin made sure not to show his elation. A lot of men had just lost their stakes.

'But Letsis has won again.' Korose shook his head in wonderment. 'Though barely,' he allowed.

'Really?' Once again, Erlin kept his face impassive.

Though it wasn't long before he could express his amazement as openly as anyone else. The skinny girl came back time and again, to tell Acuri she'd won. Several times she had to shout to make herself heard above the men arguing over what they'd just seen.

'She's no skills. She's just lucky.'

'She's quick and that counts for a lot.'

'He slipped, that's all there was to it.'

'Too soft-hearted to skewer a pigeon, the fool.'

Korose was the first one back when the tourney was down to the final four. He raced up, barely stopping short of the hearth. 'She did it!'

'Well, well.' Erlin feigned astonishment, then concern. 'What if she fights Chellan next?' Much as he disliked the snake, the man's formidable skills had seen him safe through the tourney.

'Will she –' Korose broke off as the horde of mercenaries surged through the tents to the fire.

A circle formed and Chellan faced the girl. So he had won his last bout. But Erlin noted the blood smeared on his arms. He'd taken a few flesh wounds on his way to victory.

To be fair, so had Letsis, from the stains on her shirtsleeves. But she looked a different girl to the timid waif who Erlin had seen cowering around the camp these past few days.

Not that Chellan had noticed. He took a rag from Acuri and wiped his arms clean, scowling. Whatever he said provoked his supposed ally into a hostile sneer.

Letsis had barely taken guard before Chellan launched a storm of blows. Not that any hammer-stroke touched her. Letsis didn't bother trying her strength against his with any show of locked hilts. Chellan barely made contact with her deftly parrying blade. She dodged, nimbly retaliating with thrusts to slice Chellan's wrists or knees.

Recoiling robbed Chellan's swordplay of power and rhythm. Now he was on the defensive. Darting ever quicker, Letsis forced him backwards, unbalanced. A cry rose from the crowd, somewhere between a groan and elation, as her questing blade sliced into his forearm.

'Yield?' She grinned.

Chellan didn't even answer before assailing her. He didn't even allow her to take a proper guard. The crowd's murmur turned concerned as everyone saw her forced back towards the fire. That was hardly fighting fair.

That wasn't the worst of it. Erlin guessed Chellan's plan an instant before the snake ducked low and snatched up a burning stick with his free hand. He threw the searing brand at Letsis, provoking a howl of protest.

Breath caught in Erlin's throat. But Letsis was quick enough. She dodged it. More than that, she denied any instinct to parry the flames with her blade. What threat was mindless wood, after all? Instead she lunged, her sword thrust at full stretch.

Chellan was caught unawares, already coming forward to follow up his advantage. He was an instant too slow to realise she wasn't cowed by his unexpected assault. Her blade bit deep into his thigh.

Now the crowd's cheer was all congratulation for Letsis. Chellan's dishonourable ploy had robbed him of any sympathy. She stood still for a moment, before turning to Acuri and winking at him.

Stooped, clutching his wound, Chellan gasped. 'Shithead!'

'What?' Acuri spat.

'You're in it together, you and her?' Chellan staggered forward, sword raised.

Acuri drew a dagger, teeth bared.

The surging crowd closed around them before Erlin could see who landed the first blow. Then the throng parted just as quickly. Some were heading for their tents. More were escorting Letsis towards Jartan's wine wagon for a celebration. Chellan limped off in one direction, more bloodied than before. Acuri stalked towards the river, hand pressed to a wound in his side.

Someone tapped him on the shoulder. Erlin turned to see Triggen smiling at him.

'Come to collect your winnings?'

'Whenever suits you best.'

Erlin cocked his head, contemplating the younger man. 'So she's your lover?' He realised that was wrong before the words left his mouth. 'Your sister?'

'Big sister.' Triggen's grin widened. 'Taught me everything I know.'

Of course. Why else would he have wagered such a sum on her? Erlin chuckled despite himself. 'Including how to fight like a girl? Precious few men can do that so well.'

Triggen spread innocent hands. 'I don't know what you mean.'

Erlin nodded. 'As you wish. Come and see me tomorrow morning and I'll pay you what I owe.'

He watched Triggen stroll away. Would Letsis have won without her brother's aid? Perhaps, but it would have been a far closer thing without Chellan's suspicions distracting him.

'He fights as staunchly as any man,' Korose was still defending Triggen.

Erlin briefly considered explaining. Maybe later, when Korose had some chance of understanding how devastating spreading calculated rumour and starting precisely targeted gossip could be. Those tactics could undermine the strongest men and their alliances, like a tunnel dug under a castle's foundations.

Erlin never underestimated women, with or without a sword in their hands.

I started my career as a novelist writing epic fantasy. I have always adored tales of swords and sorcery, wizards, dragons, and dirty work at the crossroads. It's such fun when a short story commission gives me a chance to go back to the world of Einarinn which I created over my first fifteen books.

That could easily never have happened. My early attempts at getting published got me rejection letters from agents and editors saying things like 'There's nothing to distinguish this from the six other perfectly competent fantasy novels that have crossed my desk this week'.

Then I went to see an editor giving a talk, who explained how publishers are always looking for 'the same, but different'. I realised I had to find a new and original perspective on the genre that I love. I've done that in my writing ever since.

Win Some, Lose Some

The Martagon is one of those taverns which, while not a brothel, always has enough lasses idling about in low cut bodices to catch a man's eye through its hospitably open door. And there are always plenty of men passing the door, given it's in the middle of a street of rooming houses that cater to country folk on some long anticipated visit to this splendid city of Selerima. Such folk always include plough boys desperate to quench their youthful ardour without the risks of sowing their seed in some local furrow. And then there are the older men whose marriage bed has long since staled. They can often be tempted into a slice from a fresh cut loaf.

'Livak, there's a man asking for you.' One of the lasses sauntered over, hips swinging, hem of her pink gown hiked up to show the golden lace on her petticoats and fine white stockings above her soft yellow slippers.

I swept up the rune bones I'd been casually rolling on the table in front of me. 'Send him for a walk down the Andelane. He'll find what he's looking for there.'

Even dressed in a man's breeches and boots with shirt and jerkin loose enough to disguise my curves, getting the occasional offer is one of the prices of setting up in an inn like the Martagon. Some mistake me for a lad in the candlelight, half blinded by guilt or anticipation or both. Others just see my red hair and green eyes and remember the whispered stable yard tales about the insatiable appetites of Forest women. Such whispers had mortified my respectable housekeeper mother once I'd reached girlhood, just when she'd thought the gossip about her ill-starred dalliance with the Forest minstrel who was my father had finally faded.

'Tell him she's with me.' Halice was sitting behind me, apparently asleep in a round-backed beech wood chair, long, solidly muscled legs stretched out in front of her. She was booted and breeched like me but where I wore a cheerful blue jerkin and breeches she was wearing muted brown and grey, the better to go unnoticed in the shadows. 'If that doesn't put him off, give me a nod. I'll come and get some more ale and set him straight.'

There are precious few men who'll cross Halice. For a start, she'll look all but the very tallest straight in the eye and can stare down most of those. For any who won't back down, she carries a sword in those places that permit it and carefully hidden knives for towns and cities where the Watch say otherwise. Add to that a face as plain as an overcast sky and it's hardly surprising she doesn't get many importunate offers.

'He's not looking to ease his urges.' Tirian shook her head, golden ringlets dancing around her white neck. 'He says he knows a friend of yours.'

'Does he?' Halice's chair scraped on the floor behind me as she sat up straight. 'Who might that be?'

Tirian's brow wrinkled prettily. 'Lady Alaric? Does that sound right?'

'Who is he? Point him out,' Halice demanded.

Tirian obliged and I saw a middle aged man of middling build dressed better than most in this particular taproom. He wore a fine linen shirt with lace at its collar underneath a full-skirted, long-sleeved coat of soft black leather. His breeches were black too; fine broadcloth with silver buckles at the knee, sturdy black cotton stockings below to mask the filth of the streets that nevertheless spattered his square-toed black shoes.

'Merchant's clerk?' Halice hazarded.

'No ink stains on his cuffs or wear on his elbows.' I tossed the yellowed rune bones with their three deeply carved faces from hand to hand. 'Upper servant, I'd say, in a house where he gets

208

silver and gold slipped in his hand by grateful guests, not just copper.' I glanced back over my shoulder to Halice. 'Well?'

'Tell him he can come and drink his ale with us, Tirian' said Halice cautiously. 'Bring us another flagon while you're at it, please?'

Tirian shrugged and for a moment I thought her dainty pink dress was going to slip right off her shoulders. 'I've nothing else to do, I suppose.'

Halice took the hint and had a silver mark ready when Tirian returned with the flagon and this mysterious stranger in tow. We could afford to be generous to the lass. We were having a most profitable stay in Selerima.

'May I?' The stranger gestured towards one of the empty stools around my table.

I nodded, scanning the tap room as I did so. It was still early enough in the evening for Tirian to have no more than her thumbs to twiddle, so it would be a while before anyone could be tempted into a friendly game of chance with me. A game where they'd put their ill-luck down to distractions like Tirian catching their eye. Most evenings that was even true.

'You reckon we've got acquaintance in common?' I shifted my stool aside a little so Halice could swing her chair around to face this unknown newcomer.

'Indeed. The incomparable Lady Alaric.' He sat on a stool, knees together, both hands cupping his goblet of wine. Me and Halice might merit a second glance in a place like the Martagon but this chap stuck out like a cut finger needing a bandage.

'You've served her on some visit hereabouts?' I was right. This man was definitely an upper house-servant. I'd seen the type often enough, growing up as bastard daughter to a prosperous merchant's housekeeper.

'Let me introduce myself.' The man smiled. He had a thin mouth and circumspect brown eyes beneath black hair showing just a hint of grey and close cropped to disguise its thinning. 'Arle

Cordainer.' He held out an uncalloused hand bare of rings. I shook it without comment.

'A name that means nothing to me.'

Halice folded her arms, which showed up the muscles of her forearms at the same time as emphasising the width of her shoulders. I'd seen wrestlers envy those shoulders.

'I assure you it's good enough for Lady Alaric.' Cordainer paused then leaning closer, lowered his voice. 'And for Mistress Heraciol.'

'And what would those good ladies have to tell us about you?' Halice's expression didn't alter and neither did mine. When you keep yourself fed and shod through gambling, you keep a straight face or go hungry and barefoot. All the same, we were playing a different game if he knew two of our mutual friend's many faces.

Cordainer took a moment to sip his wine. 'Lady Alaric would remember me as house steward to Lord Elwyl, when she found herself benighted on the road between Peorle and Duryea. I was able to be of service when she asked me for a direct route to Trebin that would nevertheless keep off the highroads.' He took another drink of wine. 'And to be discreet about her plans.'

I exchanged a glance with Halice. So our distant friend had spotted this man wasn't above taking a little gold to help her out, with a little more besides to keep his mouth shut once she'd made her escape with whatever she'd blackmailed or bamboozled out of his employer.

'As for Mistress Heraciol, we've been correspondents for a year or so now,' Cordainer continued blithely.

Perhaps his finery had been bought with the gold marks she doubtless sent hidden in the seals of her letters, thanking him for snippets of information about the great and the good and the gullible of Selerima, titbits garnered as he waited on table or fetched and carried linen from closet to guest chamber. Who bothers to guard their tongue when a servant is no more to be remarked on than the furnishings? Less so in fact, if some rich merchant or minor noble has some new expensive tapestry brought all the way from Toremal or glittering crystal goblets from the fabled Aldabreshin Archipelago. Mistress Heraciol habitually drank from just such costly glassware in her expensive house in Relshaz, thanks to her talent for turning insubstantial gossip into solid coin.

'So what has she seen fit to tell you about us?' I wondered aloud.

'And why,' added Halice, her voice hard.

Cordainer smiled again and sipped at his goblet. 'When I wrote to wish her a fortunate Winter Solstice, I asked if she knew anyone who might be travelling this way in the first half of summer. Someone who had certain particular talents and none too many scruples about using them. She mentioned your names.' He looked Halice straight in the eye. 'In my youth, I spent some time in the Duke of Marlier's household. I can quite believe any daughter of Lady Lifinal more than merited your chastisement. I only wish I'd had the spirit to give her ladyship a slap in the face myself.'

'Heraciol told you about that?' Halice sounded amused but her eyes stayed wary. 'Well, I'd had about enough of playing watchdog for the duchess anyway. Being turned out to take to the road again was no great hardship.'

'But you didn't go back to the mercenary life,' Cordainer remarked with a glance at Halice's dun coloured hair which she still kept cropped as short as the soldier she had been. 'You've been travelling with your charming companion here.' He made me a half bow remarkably elegantly for a man sitting on a stool. 'And I gather you also know the trials and tribulations of the servant's life.'

'Enough to know it was never going to be the life for me,' I answered with a sunny smile. Not that I'd had a notion in my foolish head as to what I might do instead, when I'd fled my mother's fate. Setting my face against Tirian's trade, I'd been barely scraping a living playing games of chance in grubby inns when I first encountered Halice working her way from town to

211

town teaching swordplay or challenging the locals to wager their purses on their boasts that they could beat her. Both our fortunes had improved since then, now we had a practised routine for shading the odds in our favour over the course of a game of runes.

I gestured around the Martagon's taproom before throwing a spread of bones on the table. 'This is where we do our business and while it's pleasant to reminisce about old friends, you're keeping us from getting a game in play, so unless you've something more to say?' I raised my brows at Cordainer as I leaned forward to gather up the runes.

He sipped at his goblet and set it down, losing his amiable smile as he leant closer once more and lowered his voice to a murmur. 'I've been house steward to Master Barazon since the turn of the year. He's head of the Tailor's Guild and the richest liveryman in this city. He has a beautiful young wife whose fondness for him is equalled only by her fondness for jewels – and I've noticed if he wants her to open her bed curtains to him, she expects to close her fingers around something more lasting than his manhood.'

'Which may interest Mistress Heraciol,' said Halice with distaste wrinkling her nose. 'What's it to do with us?'

'Master Barazon has decided it's time he got himself an heir,' Cordainer replied crisply. 'And he has some concerns about standing at stud, given he's wed two wives already and neither had so much as quickened before they quit his house, never mind borne a child. He intends to cover his new filly as often as he can and that has meant dazzling her with something truly spectacular.' He paused and looked from Halice to me and back again. 'Something that would fund a nice retirement for me and set you ladies up with fine houses and servants of your own.' He looked back at me, dark eyes penetrating. 'I gather your fingers are as nimble with locks as they are with rune bones and with upper story window catches besides.'

'Is that so?' I said, non-committal. 'But you'll have keys and permission to be in the house. Why should you share the spoils with anyone else?'

'Because I would be the first person Barazon would set the Watch hunting, if I disappeared in the same night as his wife's newest treasures. I need to be there lamenting with the rest of the household.' Cordainer spread his hands. 'And while I know how to turn chance heard words into coin thanks to our friend Mistress Heraciol, I've no notion where to sell gems without awkward questions. That's one of the talents I believe you ladies have?'

'It depends if the gems are worth the trouble,' said Halice baldly.

'Diamonds.' Cordainer looked for a response. He just about hid his disappointment at not getting one. 'Of the first water and set in white gold. A necklace in the eastern Archipelagan style, hanging earrings to match and a crescent of diamonds fit for an empress's hair. I've seen them and believe me, Madam Barazon would lay down, hoist her skirts and let her husband take his pleasure on the steps of the Conclave Tower at noon for their sake.'

'Getting hold of them isn't half the task,' Halice pointed out. 'They'd have to be carried well away from here.'

'And still most likely broken up for sale,' I agreed, with a rueful shake of my head.

'And how do you know we won't just disappear with them, leaving you looking foolish?' asked Halice with cold malice.

'And have me write as much to Mistress Heraciol?' Cordainer leaned back from the table, picking up his goblet for a final swallow. 'I think we can trust each other to keep honest, given how widely she could spread the word we weren't to be trusted. Well, I imagined you'd want time to consider such a proposal. Perhaps we can share a drink and discuss it further later this evening?'

'Perhaps.' Halice inclined her head as Cordainer stood up.

We watched him walk over to the counter, confident without being confrontational as he asked a trio of men in country jerkins to let him by. He set down his goblet and turned to smile at one of Tirian's fellow flowers in a flame-coloured gown. Discreet silver changed hands and he left with the lass on his arm. As soon as his back was turned, Tirian swept up the goblet and drained it.

'Giving Mynna a quick joggle gives him a reason to be here,' I remarked to Halice. 'Just in case anyone's got their eye on him.'

'If we get a hint that anyone has, we don't touch this,' she warned.

'You think we should touch this in any case?' I looked at her, my surprise coloured with exasperation. 'Care to explain why?'

'He's obviously a friend of Charoleia's.' Halice studied one broad blunt fingered hand.

'Who doesn't know her by that name,' I pointed out with some asperity. 'I wouldn't call him much more than an acquaintance, if the only two faces he knows are Lady Alaric and Mistress Heraciol.'

'He's done her enough good turns for her to pass on our names when he went asking for help with this,' Halice countered. 'And if we do him a good turn, you know that'll be credit in our ledger with Charoleia.'

Which was always worth having. Among other things, Charoleia, who had more guises than a troupe of travelling players, generally knew which noble and wealthy sons had an exaggerated and consequently expensive belief in their own abilities at the gambling tables. It was remarkable how often they would fall into a friendly game of runes with a harmless red-headed lass who just happened to be stopping at the same respectable inn on some byway. If they took exception to their losses or felt inclined to try snatching their coin back, that's when they would discover I was travelling with that uncommonly tall, plain-faced and far from harmless woman who'd taken a seat at the gaming table once the runes were well in play.

I shrugged and snapped my fingers to attract Tirian's attention. She came over, eyebrows raised. 'I'm not your personal pot girl.'

'The old crow who just left with Mynna,' I jerked my head toward the door and then gestured towards the counter. 'How much wine was left in his goblet to quench your thirst?'

'More than half.' Tirian was puzzled. 'I don't know why he should be so fussy. That's a good vintage. Menk knows better than to serve bitter lees to someone dressed like that.'

'His loss, your gain,' I shrugged.

'I'll take all the luck I can this evening,' Tirian perched her rump on the edge of our table. 'It's cursed quiet, isn't it?'

'It is that,' I agreed.

'Not for long.' Halice nodded towards the taproom's outer door.

Two men entered, evidently brothers from their colouring and features but distinct in dress and manner. The first was stocky rather than tall and with flaxen hair that would be the envy of every girl lounging around the room. He was dressed with a style to catch the eye, boots brightly polished, breeches of dark green broadcloth, silver studs on the belt that circled his waist and his shirt of crisp new linen clasped at the throat with an emerald brooch. He scanned the room with sapphire eyes, well aware of the effect of his appearance.

'Doesn't he ever feel the cold?' I asked Halice. According to whichever Almanac you used, the season had turned from Aft-Spring to For-Summer three or four days ago but I still didn't find it warm enough to go around in shirtsleeves once the sun had set.

Halice shrugged. 'No, neither of them do.'

The second man was slighter in build than his brother and nowhere near as dapper in his dress. His boots were scuffed, his old leather belt was stretched, the brass tag from the end long since lost and his shirt was open at the neck. All the same, he was attracting just as much attention from the lasses around the room with his air of raffish charm, eyes as blue as his brother's and twinkling with impudence.

They came over and sat at our table. Tirian swiftly appeared with a fresh flagon of ale, two earthenware cups and a coquettish smile evenly shared between the two of them. 'Master Sorgrad,' she dimpled, setting a drink down before the taller of the pair. 'Sorgren.'

The rumpled brother slid a wiry arm around her waist and pulled her onto his knee. 'Good day to you, sweetness.' He used his free hand to brush the ringlets back over her shoulder and kissed her just below her ear. She blushed vividly.

'Give us a moment please, Tirian,' Halice asked. 'We've some business to discuss.'

'Gren caught up her hand and kissed it before releasing her. 'Later, sweetness?'

'I'll be waiting.' Tirian smiled at him with happy anticipation before returning to her position at the counter, more than one envious female gaze following her.

Sorgrad held out his hand and I dropped the rune bones into it. 'So, are we playing decoy pigeon for you?' It's a fact that men who'll baulk at proposing a hand of runes with a woman can be tempted when a table's already in play.

Halice shook her head. 'The evening breeze brought us the whisper of a richer game.'

'Runes? White Raven?' Sorgrad hazarded.

Halice lifted her drink to mask her mouth from curious eyes. 'Gems.'

Sorgren's eyes brightened. 'This sounds like fun already.' He leaned forward, elbows on the table, lacing his fingers together.

'This isn't a good city to fall foul of the Watch in.' Sorgrad sounded wary, unobtrusively checking to be certain no one was close enough to eavesdrop on this conversation.

'We've got a man on the inside,' Halice offered. 'Charoleia put him on to us.'

'Did she?' mused Sorgrad.

I hadn't known these brothers for long but I already knew he could count the people he trusted absolutely the fingers of both hands with a couple to spare. Charoleia merited the first forefinger when he made that count.

'What kind of gems?' asked 'Gren, persistent as always.

'Diamonds,' Halice answered simply. 'Aldabreshin. Of the first water and set in white gold.'

Sorgrad raised his golden brows. 'That's from your man on the inside?'

Halice nodded. 'House steward to the head of the Tailor's Guild.'

'Who sits and pretends to drink but leaves more than half his wine untasted,' I chipped in.

'You don't trust him?' Sorgrad looked at me, azure eyes piercing.

'I don't know,' I shrugged. 'And I don't know him.'

And I was still getting the measure of these two. While I will have various thefts to answer for when I finally face Saedrin at the door of judgement, at least I'll be able to plead I'd only ever stolen when the alternative was starvation. Well, mostly. But Sorgrad, Sorgren and Halice had quite a different attitude, having served together in various mercenary bands in the interminable Lescari civil wars. They wouldn't plunder peasants, not least because 'Gren said they never had anything worth taking, but if they came across someone rich enough to stand a loss without harm, they were never averse to weighting their purses at his expense.

Halice was telling the two of them about Cordainer. 'So he's trusting us to shift the gems for him,' she concluded. 'That should keep him honest.'

Sorgrad nodded slowly. 'Col, that would be the best place to take them. Each piece to a different merchant.'

I noted Sorgren frowning. 'You don't like the idea?'

'What?' He looked at me, brow clearing. 'No, it sounds like a fun game. I've been trying to think where I heard this man's name before.'

'Cordainer?' I queried.

'No, Barazon.' He looked at me exasperated before scowling again, eyes distant. 'He's more than head of the tailors' guild. He runs more sheep on the uplands than any other man in the city.'

'Does he now?' Sorgrad's otherwise handsome face turned ugly for a moment. 'Then he's got plenty to pay for.'

I thought about asking if they would be handing over their share of the loot to those uplanders dispossessed by the wealthy of Selerima eager to profit from the burgeoning wool trade. I decided against it. Their appearance marked them out as Mountain Men clearly enough but I'd never heard anything to suggest they ever looked back at whatever home they'd fled any more than I did.

'So we're agreed?' Halice looked round the table. 'We'll talk to this Cordainer when he's done with Mynna?'

Sorgrad and Sorgren nodded and I held my tongue. There was no point in finding myself outvoted three to one.

Guild Master Barazon lived in a part of the city where even the back alleys were paved and clean. Fortunately they were also deserted. Halice and I kept to the shadows as we approached the back wall of his sizeable dwelling, belligerently spiked against unwelcome intruders. There was the big main gate, wide enough to accommodate the biggest wagons laden with barrels and sacks of provender to keep his household fed and his guests impressed. Set into it was the narrow wicket door grudgingly opened to let the servants out to whatever hard-won leisure they spent their drudgery dreaming of. A slight shadow detached itself from a recess opposite.

'Are they all gone out?' Halice asked softly.

'Gren nodded, a hood hiding his fair head from the inquisitive moonlight. 'Every last one of them. Cordainer locked up himself.'

Halice nodded at me. 'Let's see what kind of lock Barazon spends his coin on.'

'Aren't we waiting for 'Grad?' I rubbed my hands down the sides of my dark grey jerkin to rid them of sweat.

'Here he comes.' Sorgren turned to watch his brother lope down the alley.

'All gone off in their carriages to enjoy,' he confirmed under his breath.

'Let's be about it, then,' Halice said tersely.

I slipped across the alley to press myself in the scant shadow afforded by the arch of the gate. My hands shook slightly as I sorted the lock picks Sorgrad had given me for a Winter Solstice gift. I took a deep breath and my hands stilled, my fingers deft as I felt my way through the unseen workings of the lock. It was a good one. Barazon might scorn the Mountain Men as he sent his shepherds and their bully boys to drive them from their pastures but he was still prepared to pay for their unequalled metalwork. Fortunately, Sorgrad had been picking Mountain made locks since his curiosity first outstripped what few scruples Maewelin has blessed his birth with. Better yet, he was an excellent teacher and I was an apt pupil.

With a last snick of well-greased brass, I had the lock open. Even before I'd turned to wave the others across from their hiding place, 'Gren was at my side.

'Have you got it?' I demanded under my breath.

'Just watch this.' Moonlight caught his mischievous grin.

I stepped back to let him slip through the gate, Sorgrad hard on his heels with a naked dagger in his hand. Halice stood at my back, glancing up and down the alleyway, hands seemingly casual in her pockets.

'Cordainer will get a flogging for this,' I said, not for the first time. 'For letting the porter go to the shrine dedication along with the other servants. I don't suppose Barazon will think much of such piety when he sees he's been robbed.'

'There are the dogs. Who'd have imagined thieves would feed them meat doused in some apothecary's draught?' Halice shrugged, unconcerned. 'And if he does get flogged, his cut of the proceeds should pay for plenty of salve.'

Sorgrad reached through the wicket gate to tug at my sleeve. 'Come on.'

I slipped through and Halice ducked after me. 'Lock it,' she ordered before following 'Gren across the clean swept cobbles of the yard.

I glanced at the motionless heaps that were the hapless watchdogs, dark against the moonlit ground. At least Sorgrad's blade had still been clean. 'Gren's friend the apothecary had unwittingly supplied something potent enough to save the poor hounds from a throat slitting to silence them.

The yard was ringed by single storied workshops and storehouses. By the time I had the wicket gate locked, Sorgrad and 'Gren were up on the stone slates of the roof closest to the windows of the main house. 'Gren was keeping an eye outwards while Sorgrad worked to foil the shutters' catches from the outside.

'Up you go.' Halice gave me a boost and I crept carefully across the treacherous slates towards the concealing shadow cast by the house. With surprising stealth for a woman of her size Halice swung herself up to join us.

Sorgrad eased the shutter open and now concentrated on the window within. I looked out across the yard, the roofs and out to the back alley beyond. There were more backyards, some butted up close to their neighbour, some separated by a narrow run giving access to the high road flanked by these expensive houses. A few windows in the garrets opposite were golden with candle light but they were too far away for anyone to pick us out of the shadows. Besides, the maids behind those meagre muslin curtains would hardly be staring idly out over the city. All they'd be thinking of was getting as much sleep as possible before the relentless sun called them to another day of tedious labours.

'In we go,' ordered Sorgrad, shoving the shutter back. 'Gren was in first, me next and then Halice. Sorgrad jumped lithely down from the sill and immediately turned to pull up the shutter.

Halice lit a small shuttered lantern to show we were in a neat sitting room furnished with a well-polished table that didn't match its chairs and an upholstered daybed whose silk was faded and worn at the foot. 'Housekeeper's domain,' she confirmed with a grin.

Sorgrad was lighting his own lantern. 'Let's find the stairs.'

The housekeeper kept her preserve guarded with a locked door but it was the work of a moment to undo that. Beyond lay a corridor carpeted with a strip of drugget to muffle servants' hurrying feet. I pictured the map Cordainer had drawn for us in my mind's eye. The house steward's room was off to that side, where our friend held court among similar cast-off furniture. That door on our other hand would lead to the servant's dining hall.

'Gren wrinkled his nose.

'What?' I demanded.

He looked down at his hands. 'I must have got some blood on my cuffs from that offal I fed the dogs.'

'Never mind that.' Sorgrad was already halfway up the first flight of the back stairs ahead of us. A short corridor with an expensive Dalasorian carpet led towards the front of the house and the expansive salons where Barazon would entertain his fellow guild masters and Selerima's richest merchants. We carried on up the back stairs, soft soled boots silent on the coarse carpet.

Sorgrad halted at the next floor. 'We'll take his study. You take her parlour. Then we'll hit the bedchambers.'

Halice and I turned to the double doors of Barazon's wife's personal sanctum. She was either too idle to lock them, or too confident in her servants' loyalty or in their fear of her wrath.

'Nothing too identifiable,' Halice reminded me as she set her muted lantern on a round table inlaid with florid marquetry.

'Silver for preference.' She was already breaking the beeswax fingers out of a delicate candle branch.

I tugged a soft cloth bag out of one pocket and began emptying the herbs from an array of silver canisters before dropping them inside it. Mistress Barazon would find her tisanes already blended for her when the maid brought hot water for her morning drink tomorrow. The herb canisters were fine work, modern but Tormalin made all the same. It was a shame to think of them getting scratched and dented as they jostled in the bag. Still, they were going to be melted down anyway. We weren't going to waste time trying to get a fair price for them, not when their theft was merely a feint to cover the fact we'd been after the diamonds all along.

'That'll do.' Halice caught up the lantern and headed for the door.

I followed, stifling a sneeze from the heady dust of the herbs.

Outside, 'Gren slipped like a shadow out of Barazon's study. 'I'll see you upstairs.' In sharp contradiction to his words, he ran lightly down to the floor below.

Sorgrad appeared at the study door, his own cloth bag bulky with their spoils. 'Let's get these gems.'

'Where's 'Gren going?' Halice demanded curtly.

'Thought he heard something,' Sorgrad shrugged. 'Let's get this done and get clear of here.'

I followed him and Halice up the stairs. My heart was pounding like a festival drum and my breath came fast and shallow. I rubbed one hand on my thigh to rid it of sweat and swapped the bag of tisane canisters over, so I could do the same to the other.

'I'll take the boudoir.' Sorgrad turned to me when we reached the floor where the master bedrooms were. 'I imagine the lady will have the best lock she can on her treasures. You go and see what the guild master might have to lose.'

'I'll wait for 'Gren.' Halice waited at the top of the stairs, frowning as she looked back down.

I took her lantern and hurried into Barazon's bedroom. His bed stood four square against the far wall, dark brocade curtains caught back with silken cords, linen pale where the sheet had been turned back for him by some dutiful chambermaid. The air was still and heavy with the scent of a sickly pomade just undercut by a sharp suggestion of the artemisia and the orris root that hid powdered in linen sachets to protect his clothes from vermin. There was a table by the window littered with oddments of parchment, a book with gold on the binding catching the moonlight cutting through a crack in the heavy drapes hiding the window. Somewhat unexpectedly, a glass fronted case of books stood against one wall.

There would be precious little in here worth taking. I cut across the caressing thickness of the carpet to the door of the dressing room. Ignoring the tall clothes presses set into the wall, and the marble topped washstand with its ewer and basin, I headed straight for the heavy painted coffer under the window. That would be where he kept his jewels; chains to add lustre to a chest already puffed with importance, brooches to adorn his hat and cloak, buckles for his shoes and breeches.

Unsurprisingly, the coffer was locked. I fished out my lock picks and, bending over it, I set to work. There had to be a few things in here a man this wealthy could stand to lose without too much pain.

'Livak!' Halice startled me. I jerked upright and caught her reflection in the tall looking glass where Barazon admired himself. 'Come on!'

I abandoned the chest and ran. Halice was already out of the bedchamber and on the stairs. 'Did 'Gren hear something?' I asked, abruptly breathless.

'He found something,' Halice replied grimly.

I followed her down the stairs, Sorgrad appearing at my elbow. 'Did you find the diamonds?' I demanded.

'I found the coffer,' he answered, voice tight with fury. 'Just where Cordainer said we would. Double locked, just like he said. I got it open and the cursed thing was empty.'

I was too astounded by that piece of news to say anything as we hurried down the stairs.

'Gren was waiting for us. 'In here,' he said tersely.

In there was the house steward's sitting room. In there was an acrid smell of blood compounded with voided bowels and the scorched polished wood of a side table where a candlestick had toppled over. The main table was thrown on its side, a chair splintered beside it. A body lay sprawled across a daybed the twin of the one in the house keeper's room. There'd be no saving the upholstery on this one and the whole room would have to be repainted besides. The walls were spattered with blood.

'So who do you suppose that is?' rasped 'Gren. 'Because it's not Cordainer. Look at those hands.'

One showed the unmistakeable indentation of a scholar's ring and there was the raised ridge of a pen callous on the middle finger of the other. The corpse was wearing the clothes we'd last seen Cordainer in, down to the last detail. That fine linen shirt wasn't crisp and white any more. It was ruddy with clotted gore. Whether or not the dead man was Cordainer was anybody's guess. His face was a nauseating pulp of torn flesh and smashed bone puddled with blood still wet enough to shine in the dim light of Halice's lanterns. Another glint showed up the poker used to do the murder tossed back into the hearth.

'Cordainer must be long gone, with the gems in his pocket,' Sorgrad breathed with ominous calm. 'We've been set up to swing for this.'

'Not if we get clear,' said 'Gren n fervently.

'Drop the loot,' Halice's bag dropped to the floor with a clatter.

We were back in the housekeeper's room when we heard the main door to the street below crash open, hobnailed boots screeching on the flagstones of the entrance hall on the floor below. Sorgrad smashed the window to get to the shutters and flung them open, heedless of a cut on his hand. We were out onto the low roof beyond as whoever was in pursuit came thundering up the stairs, their yells and threats indistinct. The voices in the alley beyond the backyard were all too clear.

'Stop where you are!' 'There's no use in running!' 'Hold for the Watch!'

Sorgrad looked one way, down into the yard next door. 'Gren considered the herb garden on the other side. It was no use. Candle lanterns swinging crazily on watchmen's poles threw light into every corner as they poured through the houses on either side. Barazon's neighbours' voices followed them with querulous questions and complaints.

The Watch had a key to Barazon's back gate. It swung open on dutifully greased hinges and a whole detachment of bully boys in their heavy coats and broad brimmed hats came flooding through. There was no escape. Sorgrad sat down on the roof and unobtrusively slid his scabbarded dagger inside his breeches while ostensibly ripping a length from his shirt tail to swaddle his cut hand. Halice pushed me down beside him, her hand on my shoulder inexorable. Then she spread her hands wide in the moonlight, in apparent surrender. 'Gren stood on the ridge of the roof, hands on his hips, defiance in every bone of him.

'You come on down and let's be having no nonsense.' A watchman with a white cockade in his hat peered up at us, quarter staff gripped purposefully in hands that could cover a dinner plate.

'Cry,' Sorgrad murmured beside me.

'What?'

'Weep, snivel, tell them how you never meant –'

'Shut your mouth!' shouted the man with the white cockade, his tone hardening.

He might have said more but uproar in the house interrupted him. The rest of his little army had found the body in Cordainer's room.

'All right, captain, we'll come quietly.' Sorgrad got to his feet and as he did so, quite deliberately trod on my hand. That was enough to startle tears to my eyes and by the time my turn came to clamber down to the waiting watchman and their manacles, I was grizzling quite convincingly. Not that it saved me from the same chains as Halice. I traded a swift glance with her. Her stolid face was unreadable but I could see apprehension in her eyes as well as her warning. Then she was shoved on towards the gate by guards who held their quarter staffs ready, just in case this woman who topped most of them by a head should try something unexpected.

'Gren was the last one down from the roof, jumping lithe as a cat to land beside his brother.

'Give us your hands,' barked the watch captain.

'Make me,' 'Gren challenged.

Sorgrad said something in what must have been the Mountain tongue and looking mutinous, 'Gren held out his wrist for the irons.

'Where are you taking us?' I wailed as we were ushered towards the gate, a solid wall of brown coated watchmen surrounding us.

'Lock-up, copper top,' said one behind me, with an unpleasant relish in his voice.

It wasn't the first lock-up I'd been in. There had been selfish market towns here and there on the road where being caught without the price of a bed for the night made you a vagrant. Such refuse wasn't allowed to clutter up their doorsteps or ginnels. Some would simply send you on your way whatever the chime of day or night, with a kicked arse if necessary. Others would throw you in a cell till morning, one deliberately filthy and cramped enough to be no kind of welcome lodging.

The Selerima lock-up was comparatively clean by contrast; a large cellar in the watch house divided up with walls of lath and plaster, each pen with a door of iron bars. A watchman dozed on a stool by the door we'd been dragged through earlier, oblivious to the drunken maunderings of some other inmate.

I ignored him as well, my attention on the stairs beyond the outer door. 'Where do you suppose they've taken him?' At least the rambling drunk's lament covered my words.

'Somewhere where they can wash the blood away easier.' Halice was lying on one of the two palliasses we'd had tossed in to us. The sackcloth was grubby and stained and the straw within was crushed and rank. 'Can you see 'Gren?'

'He's still just lying there.' I couldn't keep the anxiety out of my voice.

'He's tough as old boots,' Halice assured me.

'He's covered in blood,' I retorted, uncomforted.

Unsurprisingly Sorgren's uncrushed cockiness made him the watch captain's first choice for questioning. He'd swaggered out as if the men flanking him were some escort rather than guards. They'd carried him back in between them a while later, his fair hair plastered to his forehead with blood, his lip split and bruised, one eye swollen shut. His jerkin was gone and there were boot marks plain as day on his soiled shirt.

Then they'd taken Halice, who'd come back unbloodied but walking stiffly and dropping down to lie on her palliasse without speaking, not even turning her head as they dragged the limply unresisting Sorgrad away.

At least they'd taken the punishingly heavy manacles off us in here, along with every blade we'd carried between us, including the one tucked down Sorgrad's breeches. I rubbed at my sore wrists and wondered what chime of the night it might be. We'd let the five bells of midnight come and go before we'd set out for Barazon's house. It had to be getting on for dawn. How long had they been trying to beat some answers out of Sorgrad? When was it going to be my turn?

With what felt like sickening promptness the lock to the cellar turned with a deliberate clunk. The dozing guard sprang from his stool as the door opened to reveal a pair of broad shoulders in a

227

watchman's leather coat. There were two of them, carrying Sorgrad between them. He looked as badly beaten as 'Gren. The drunk fell silent for a moment then resumed his meaningless litany in a low mumble.

'Open up.' The one carrying Sorgrad's feet nodded at the cell where 'Gren still lay motionless.

The guard from the stool fished at his belt for a ring of keys and unlocked the metal door. They threw Sorgrad inside and he landed on the stained palliasse with the dull thump of a sack of turnips hitting a barn floor.

'And her.' The guard jerked his head at me.

I stepped back as the watchman with the keys unlocked the door. Waiting on the threshold, he reached inside but I was too far away.

He looked at me patiently. 'Come on, love, don't make it worse than it already is.'

I took a hesitant pace forward and he gripped me around the upper arm, not cruelly but firmly all the same. The two men waiting to escort me to whatever fate awaited me watched. One was impassive, the other openly anticipatory, greedy eyes on my breeched legs, lingering on my chest before he turned to lead the way up the stairs.

'Up you go,' ordered the impassive one.

I obeyed. There was nothing else I could do. Weary to my bones after a day and a night without sleep, it took remarkably little effort to summon the tears that Sorgrad and Halice had both advised in the brief deliberation we'd managed under cover of the drunk's riotous singing. That was without acknowledging the gnawing fear that we weren't going to find a way out this.

The watch house was dull white plaster walls in sore need of a new coat of lime wash. Candles in sconces caked in wax were adding to the soot stains already reaching up the wall to join the scorch marks on the ceiling. The wainscoting was the same brown oak as the stairs which were wide and dusty and hadn't seen a coat of polish since I'd discarded my housemaid's apron.

They took me to a room on the second floor and took up station either side of the door once they'd closed it behind us all.

The man inside wore a coat of brown velvet and sat behind a broad table stacked high with parchments and ledgers. He nodded to a single stool set in the empty expanse of a threadbare carpet in the middle of the room. 'Sit down.'

I did as I was told, an abject picture of misery.

He got up from his round backed chair and came to offer me a handkerchief. 'Dry your eyes.'

His tone made that paradoxically harder to achieve; stern but not cruel, regretful rather than wrathful. I mopped and wiped and drew a shuddering breath.

'I'm willing to believe you had little enough to do with this,' the man in velvet said calmly as he returned to his chair. 'Mountain Men like those two always have glib tongues to go with their light fingers. Forest maiden are you? Not really used to the deceits and counterfeits of the city? I'm willing to believe you were talked into what you thought was just to be simple housebreaking. I don't imagine you ever thought it would end in murder. That should be enough to save you from the gallows if we can recover Master Barazon's diamonds for him.'

'I don't know where they are,' I stammered.

The man in velvet shook his head and continued as if I hadn't spoken. 'We've searched the house and the yard. You didn't get far, any of you, so where could you have hidden them? Or was there another one of you, someone who got away before we arrived? Was it him who killed Master Cordainer? Tell us where he is and where he's got the diamonds and it'll be him on the gallows tree instead of you.'

'There wasn't anyone else,' I said slowly. 'Apart from Cordainer. It was him found us and told us about the diamonds. Find him and you'll find them.'

'We found him, didn't we? With his face smashed in and your yellow haired friend with blood on his cuffs,' said the watch commander with faint impatience.

I shook my head stubbornly. 'That can't be him.'

The watch commander rested his forearms on his table and steepled his fingers together. 'I could just about believe Cordainer got greedy for those diamonds himself, if they're as fine as everyone says. Did they look like a lord's ransom to you?'

'They weren't there.' I realised I was explaining this badly. 'When we got to the coffer, they were already gone.'

'You saw the empty box?' asked the commander.

'That's what Sorgrad told me.' I heard the hard note of defiance in my words and wondered if I should start crying again.

'Who could have had the gems in his pocket all along and been lying to your face,' commented the commander. 'While that brother of his found Cordainer had repented of some folly or loose words to a tavern whore. He told the other servants he was leaving the shrine dedication early just to make sure the house was secure.'

'Who roused the Watch?' I asked, trying for a sob in my voice.

'Cordainer told one of the footmen to come looking for him at the end of the prayers and to go and find a watchman if the house was still dark,' the commander explained obligingly.

I slumped on the stool and studied the toes of my boots as I thought about that. The footman can't have been too pleased. When the prayers were done was when the ale donated by local brewsters would be sold to fill the new shrine's poor chest for the first time. We'd been counting on that keeping the servants carousing long enough to let us get clean away. We'd discussed the timing with Cordainer in detail.

'I've been fair with you,' the commander said, stern now. 'Told you exactly where you stand. We'll be searching that house, the yard and the ones on each side again at first light. Tell me where your thieving friend threw those diamonds and I'll make sure it's to your credit. You need to understand, my lass, that keeping faith with those Mountain Men will just see you hanged alongside them.'

I nodded dumbly, still studying my boots. The watch commander waited for me to say something more. I swear I could hear the chains and gears grating inside the time piece on the wall, as its finger measured out my silence down the long length of its graduated scale.

'Take her back down,' he finally ordered with disgust.

I followed the guards meek and mute down to the depths below. The lecherous one unlocked the cellar door and the stolid one followed me inside. There was neither sound nor movement from Sorgrad or 'Gren. The drunk had finally fallen silent and the one noise was the slow rhythm of Halice's snores.

'You'd better go and get some sleep in a real bed,' he told the guard now dozing again on the stool with some exasperation.

As the yawning watchman departed, handing over his keys so the stolid one could return me to my cell, I found I was holding my breath. Was my luck going to take even a faint turn for the better this disastrous night?

As he locked the iron bars behind me, the stolid one turned his head to address the lecher with curt disapproval that I guessed must stem from some earlier incident. 'You can see out the night here. Come and get me when tenth chime sounds.'

The stolid one stumped off up the stairs. I unbuttoned the front of my jerkin and tugged at the laces of my shirt before turning round to press myself against the iron bars. 'Please, you have to believe me, I don't know where those diamonds are,' I hissed at the guard with wide eyed desperation. 'Please, I never meant to be any part of this. You've got to get me out of here. I'll do anything.' The neck of my shirt just revealed the creamy flesh that the sun never saw. 'Please. You've got a kind face.' I managed to summon a few tears to turn my eyes to glistening emeralds.

His greedy eyes fastened on the as yet concealed delights beneath my shirt. 'Now then, lass, you heard what the captain said.'

'But I don't have anything to tell him,' I lowered my voice, glancing back into my cell with apprehension for a moment. Halice snored on. 'I only went along with them because it sounded a better way of filling my purse than lifting my heels. I only want to get back to my people.' I ran a distracted hand through my tousled auburn hair.

'I might be able to put in a word for you.' The lecherous guard licked his lips and rubbed a grimy hand over his stubbly chin. 'If you make it worth my while.'

'Please, I'll do anything,' I repeated, trying to look like the kind of half-wit who'd believe a lowly turnkey could have any influence on her fate.

He rose from his stool, adjusting his breeches as he did so, eyes fixed on my breasts as I pressed against the bars. 'Kneel down then.'

'No, what if she wakes,' I threw a terrified glance in the direction of Halice's palliasse.

Lust had her claws deep in him now and he fumbled for the keys as he hurried over. I took a pace back as he unlocked the door, hands at the neck of my shirt to keep all his attention on me.

As the iron bars swung open, he reached for me and Halice grabbed him by the collar, dragging him into the cell, her other hand clamped mercilessly over his mouth. She smiled, finally abandoning the feigned snoring. 'I thought he was never going to take the bait.'

'I thought I was going to have to strip naked for him,' I agreed.

He struggled in Halice's grip as she twisted his collar tight around his neck. A button pinged away to be lost in the scraps of straw littering the flagstones. His struggles didn't last long, his face suffused with red, outrage vanishing behind screwed tight eyelids, tears mingling with the sweat from his forehead.

Halice held his limp body up against her own, one hand still over his mouth. 'Get his coat off, quick.'

I struggled to pull it free, tugging the heavy leather down over his shoulders and arms. 'He isn't dead, is he?' We were in enough trouble over the body we weren't responsible for. We'd definitely hang if there was another one added to our tally.

'No. Rip his sleeves off.'

As I did so, releasing a rank sourness, Halice seized the grimy linen and gagged the watchman. He was already beginning to stir as we laid him down on the palliasse, using the other sleeve from his shirt to bind his wrists behind his back.

'Come on.' 'Gren rattled the bars of his cell door impatiently.

'Tie his bootlaces together.' Halice shrugged on the watchman's leather coat and the leather protested as it stretched across her shoulders. She pulled the keys free from the lock and went to release Sorgrad and 'Gren as I did so.

As I left the cell, I realised the drunk was awake and watching us, eyes bright in an unkempt tangle of grey beard and hair. He grinned, showing me stained and rotten teeth. 'Didn't see a thing, my girl, nor hear nothing neither.'

'Livak.' Sorgrad was already at the top of the steps. 'They've been locking this from the outside. You'll have to open it.' When I opened my mouth to demur, he held up his hands. The watchmen must have stamped on his fingers to leave them so bruised and swollen.

'They took my picks.' I looked at him aghast.

'Use the loop from the keys,' Sorgrad ordered tersely. 'It's a piss poor lock.'

I untwisted the thick wire that bound the keys together with shaking fingers. With our second turn of good fortune that night, Sorgrad was right. It was a crude and clumsy lock easily tripped.

Halice licked finger and thumb and snuffed the candle in its sconce by the door. 'Ready.'

'What if there's someone out there?' I couldn't help but ask.

'Then we'll be hanging on the nevergreen tree before sunset.' 'Gren shrugged.

It was hard to tell, given the bruises staining his face but I fancied there was a hint of uncertainty in his bloodshot eyes. Perversely that put new heart into me.

'We've just got to chance it, my lass,' Sorgrad said calmly. 'Remember what I told you?'

I nodded briefly. It had sounded like madness then and it felt like madness now.

'Let's get out of here.' We moved to let Halice open the door and did our best to hide behind her, the skirts of the watchman's coat adding to her bulk. The corridor beyond the cellar stairs was empty and Halice hurried to snuff the candle burning out here.

Wordlessly, she halted at the bottom of the stairs, so the rest of us could slip up with her at the rear, hopefully no more than a watchman come in from the streets to any casual glance from below. She took the stairs two at a time, footfalls still soft all the same. Sorgrad and 'Gren were hurrying on ahead, pinching out candles as they went. Every bone, every muscle must have been screaming with pain after the beatings they'd taken. Still, better this agony than the slow choking death of the hangman's noose.

We left the floor with the commander's office behind us without incident but the runes rolled against us on the next floor. A door opened and a watchman dressed only in his shirt appeared, rubbing his eyes and frowning at the unexpected gloom. 'Who put the candles out?'

'Run!' growled Sorgrad.

We did, heedless of the noise. We took the next flight of stairs and the next. The slam of doors and confused exclamations drowned out the sound of our boots on the floorboards. We ran up the final flight of stairs and faced a blank wooden door. Halice kicked it open, barely breaking step. Just as Sorgrad had predicted, there was a garret running the length of the building. The pale light that presaged dawn spilled through cramped dormer windows. Halice stripped off the watchman's coat and draping it over her two fists, punched out the glass in the closest.

'Gren scrambled out with the thick leather protecting him from the bottommost shards.

He leaned back in and held out a hand. 'Let's be away from here.' He grinned, his teeth filmed with blood.

I climbed out onto stone slates, treacherous with moss and blinked in the pallid light. The commotion below was rising as watchmen reached for boots and breeches before starting the chase. We'd been counting on them being unwilling to chance a fight with their shirt tails flapping around naked thighs. The watchmen dressed to stop us were wrong footed and all the way down in the empty street below, their shouts echoing from building to building. I didn't look at them.

Halice followed Sorgrad out of the window, her head bumping his thigh. 'Gren was already on the ridge of the roof, running lightly along to the next building. Sorgrad had been right; these houses were built hard up against one another. I followed 'Gren, stepping lightly up onto the next roof.

Sorgrad was hard on my heels. 'Quick as you can,' he said coolly. 'Before someone down there thinks to find a crossbow.' With dawn building, he looked even worse than he had in the cellar's candle light.

'They're out,' called Halice, and I chanced a glance over my shoulder to see three watchmen cautiously emerging from the window we'd smashed, hands and feet clinging to the slope of the roof.

Turning to look straight ahead, I concentrated on running, on keeping my footing on the rough slates, on not looking down, on not thinking what the fall would do to me. End my troubles, that's what it would do. I wasn't ready to settle for that, not yet.

The shouts in the street rose to a frustrated screech. We were outstripping our hesitant pursuers. A long building boasting angular chimneys stacked in fours and sixes offered some concealment and we took a brief pause.

'Down?' Halice wondered.

Sorgrad scanned the mismatched eaves and gables ahead. 'See there, that house with the wing running down to the back. We can get down onto that outhouse roof and then on that wall.'

Halice nodded. 'Keep low, so they don't see us from the street.'

We slid down the far slope of the roof on hands and knees, pressed close to the slates. I began to breathe easier. There was no sound of any watchmen tackling the tangle of alleys and blind entries running along the back of these merchants' marts and warehouses as yet. Crouching, running bent double, hands steadying ourselves as we went, we made it without mishap to the building Sorgrad had spotted. We dropped down onto the outhouse roof without any cry of surprise from an early rising housemaid to set the Watch's dogs on our trail. It was a nerve-wracking jump to the narrow, sloping coping of the wall. We made it and down to the alley below. The others were panting and trembling just as much as I was.

'Time –' Sorgrad paused to catch his breath. 'To leave town. I know where we can get horses on the Kadras road.'

'We'll have to get to the river. Swim for it.' Halice turned to face the unseen river. She always had an unerring sense of direction.

'I can't swim!' I protested.

'You'll float,' Sorgrad assured me. 'I'll do the rest.'

'Gren smiled widely at me, setting the split in his lip oozing again. He licked it. 'So, going to say you told us so?'

'No, because I didn't.' Relief and anger were a heady mix, loosening my tongue like fine wine. 'I cursed well should have,' I said in no uncertain terms as we ran. 'It's a solid gold certainty I will next time, before I let you drag me into something like that.'

'Good girl,' 'Gren approved.

I didn't have the breath to answer him. We ran through the empty streets. Men delivering coal and kindling shouted questions after us. A baker walking slowly home after a night making the city's morning bread stopped to look at us, face appalled at 'Grad and 'Gren's injuries. The Watch would easily be able to map our course later that day if they so chose. That was no matter. We would be long gone. We climbed ivy covered walls and trampled through vegetable plots, cutting across the gardens that backed onto the ancient and lofty wall that held the river back from the city. As soon as we found one with a gate to the bank and no sentry in sight on the wall walk above, Halice and Sorgrad broke it down with swift, measured violence.

Out on the broad grassy swathe, laundresses setting great swags of linen to dry on the elder bushes watched, astonished as we plunged into the wide river with its gravelly shoals and willow crowned islets. Sorgrad was right, I did float, just about, as he dragged me across the stretches too deep for me to wade. I scrambled out half drowned on the far side, coughing and spluttering like an unwanted kitten thrown into a stream.

We found the horses where Sorgrad said. We didn't steal them, leaving Sorgrad's silver and emerald brooch pinned to a halter hanging from the stable door. We'd made enough enemies in Selerima without adding to them.

'Where do you suppose Cordainer's got to?' I wondered when we felt far enough from the city to slow and let the horses choose their own pace. I was riding pillion behind 'Gren.

He shrugged, adding venomously. 'Wherever it is, it can't be far enough away.'

'We need to get a letter to Charoleia as soon as we can,' commented Sorgrad coldly. 'She'll be out for his blood just as much as us.'

'He'll pay us back, sooner or later,' agreed Halice ominously. 'And we'll repay him with interest.'

'Sooner or later,' I echoed.

I've always been a fan of crime and mystery fiction. When I was looking for a new angle on epic fantasy, I thought about private eyes like Kate Brannigan, Kinsey Milhone and V.I. Warshawski. I wondered how an independent female making her way through life on her own, not defined by her relationships with men, would fare in a high-fantasy world. My first novel, The Thief's Gamble, was the result, published in 1999.

From time to time in The Tales of Einarinn, Livak or one of her friends refers to a grudge they hold against someone called Cordainer. A while after the end of that first series, I wrote the story of what happened. And yes, from time to time, I amuse myself by imagining what Livak is up to these days, so many years later. Perhaps I'll write those stories some day.

About the Author

Juliet E McKenna is a British fantasy author living in the Cotswolds, UK. Loving history, myth and other worlds since she first learned to read, she has written fifteen epic fantasy novels so far. Her debut, *The Thief's Gamble*, began The Tales of Einarinn in 1999, followed by The Aldabreshin Compass sequence, The Chronicles of the Lescari Revolution, and The Hadrumal Crisis trilogy. *The Green Man's Heir* was her first modern fantasy inspired by British folklore in 2018. *The Green Man's Quarry* in 2023 was the sixth title in this ongoing series and won the BSFA Award for Best Novel. The seventh book, *The Green Man's War*, appeared in late 2024.

Her 2023 novel *The Cleaving* is a female-centred retelling of the story of King Arthur, while her shorter fiction includes forays into dark fantasy, steampunk and science fiction. She promotes SF&Fantasy by reviewing, by blogging on book trade issues, attending conventions and teaching creative writing. She has served as a judge for the James White Award, the Aeon Award, the Arthur C Clarke Award and the World Fantasy Awards. In 2015 she received the British Fantasy Society's Karl Edward Wagner Award. As J M Alvey, she has written historical murder mysteries set in ancient Greece.

For more, visit: www.julietemckenna.com

ALSO FROM NEWCON PRESS
Polestars

Human Resources – Fiona Moore

Fiona Moore's work has been shortlisted for BSFA Awards and a World Fantasy Award. Her stories have appeared in *Clarkesworld*, *Asimov's*, *Interzone* and elsewhere, and have been selected for six editions of *Best of British SF*. "A collection of intelligent, thoughtful, disturbing but ultimately optimistic speculative stories" – *Oghenechovwe Donald Ekpeki*

Back Through the Flaming Door – Liz Williams

A new Fallow Sisters story; a new Inspector Chen story set in Singapore Three; a new tale set on the Matriarchal Mars of *Winterstrike* and *Phosphorus*; a new story from the world of *The Ghost Sister* and *Bloodmind*. All this and more in Liz Williams' stunning new collection. Stories that will enchant, dazzle, and delight, blurring genre boundaries and defying preconception.

Drive or Be Driven – Aliya Whiteley

The much anticipated new collection from a critically acclaimed author who has been shortlisted for multiple awards and is writing at the top of her powers.

"There are no misfires here; readers will think they've hit the standout story of the collection, only to turn the page and find another contender. It's a marvel." – *Publishers Weekly*

Elephants in Bloom – Cécile Cristofari

Debut collection from a French author who has been making a name for herself with regular contributions to *Interzone* and elsewhere. Providing a fresh perspective on things, Cécile's fiction reflects her love of the natural world and concern for its future. Contains her finest previously published stories and a number of brand new tales that appear for the first time.

Our Savage Heart – Justina Robson

The first collection in twelve years from one of the UK's most respected and inventive writers of science fiction and fantasy. A dozen short stories and novelettes, 100,000 words of high quality fiction. A collection that gathers together the author's finest stories from the past decade.

www.newconpress.co.uk